The Art of Rivers

A Coastal Hearts Novel

Janet W. Ferguson

This book is a work of fiction and any resemblance to persons, living or dead, or places, events or locales is purely coincidental. The characters are the product of the author's imagination and used fictitiously.

Southern Sun Press LLC

Southern
Sun Press
ISBN-10: 0-9992485-0-2
ISBN-13: 978-0-9992485-0-8

Acknowledgments

My thanks go out to:

The Lord who can heal all our infirmities and our hearts.

My husband, Bruce, for supporting me and for taking me to St. Simons on vacation where this story began in my mind.

Marti Jeffers for information on living in St. Simons.

Raleigh Dunham for answering countless questions about St. Simons and even sending pictures.

Jodi Jackson, Adina Welker, Amy Rylander, Bill Meredith, Rebecca Latson, and Gayle Reaves who offered information on art or art therapy.

Audrey Vaughn who works with a hospital and answered questions about the opioid epidemic.

Jada Blissard who has a heart and a passion for lifting souls from addiction.

For those of you who shared with me privately how addiction has affected you or your family.

For those of you who work with people in addiction and those involved in the Opioid Summit here in Mississippi and elsewhere.

My fabulous ACFW critique partners and my street team.

Editor Robin Patchen, mentor author Misty Beller, and cover artist Carpe Librum Book Design.

When you pass through the rivers, they will not sweep over you...

Foreword

In 2017, the year I started this novel, drug overdoses killed over 70,000 people in the United States. More people in our country died that year from this epidemic than those who were killed by guns, car crashes, or HIV/AIDS. Addiction isn't the plight of any one demographic. Drug addiction and alcoholism are devastating our children, parents, sisters, brothers, cousins, and neighbors. If your life hasn't been touched by this issue, count yourself blessed.

Addiction is a cunning and dangerous enemy, stealing the lives of medical professionals, teachers, law enforcement officers— any career you could name, along with teenagers and the homeless. There aren't enough jails or enough funds to incarcerate all these members of our communities. We have to find ways to rehabilitate. In my county, the sheriff's department is trying innovative ways to help the prisoners who struggle with addiction. Our local lawmakers are grappling with the issue. I don't have the answers.

There is heartbreak for those who love addicts or alcoholics and are at a loss as to what to do. Al-Anon is a wonderful support group for families who find themselves in this position. I interviewed dear people who battle addiction and those who try to pull people from its deadly grip. Twelve step programs like AA, NA, and Celebrate Recovery can help. If you are struggling with addiction, if you know somebody who is, or if you feel moved by this issue, please be in prayer for addicts, for their loved ones, for the community of people God has raised to support them, and for lawmakers as they contend with the issues. God's life-changing power is real. He is the One who offers true freedom.

Not everyone gets a happy ending to their addiction story in real life. If that's your family's reality, if you've lost someone, I'm so sorry for your heartbreak. Know that you are not alone, and our Heavenly Father can bring healing.

There is power, hope, and peace in Him,

Janet W. Ferguson

Chapter 1

Love, like art, took on different forms with each creator. Rivers Sullivan quickened her pace to a skip, her ruffled skirt bouncing in the muggy Memphis breeze. People rushed down the city sidewalks, and cars raced by, but her thoughts rolled with wonder over the joy in her life. Her eyes captured the way the sun lowered on the western horizon, creating long shadows, the way wispy clouds layered below the indigo sky. She couldn't seem to stop herself from mixing colors and feelings in her mind, making pictures from all she saw.

Sometimes love blurred, the shades and thin lines smudging like the dark blues and greens and purples of a bruise. Undefined. Her mother's love had been that way—before the accident.

Other times, love's colors shone clear and crisp like a beacon in the darkness, bright and steadfast. Her father's love had always been strong and true, a light leading her home. Both her earthly father and her heavenly Father's love had held her on course.

Then there was Jordan. His love burst with yellows and reds, excitement and delight, exploded with gentle blues of sincerity and commitment, a feeling she'd never expected to find. Jordan had been a lifeline thrown to a lonely girl drowning in a sea of men with no conviction.

But today, love was paperwork, lovely black-and-white paperwork that would soon bond her to the man she'd never imagined existed. A man strong in his faith, his sobriety, and his willingness to wait.

And the wait wouldn't last much longer. Her face heated with the thought. Ten days. Just wearing the sparkling engagement ring still made her finger tingle after two months. She glanced at her hand, which was dotted with paint. She'd missed a few spots.

But her breath stalled at the sight of the ring.

Oh no. The diamond was missing.

She spun, retraced her steps along the sidewalk back to her Volkswagen bug, unlocked the doors, and ran her hands across the stained seats and carpet. Her head knocked the steering wheel, but she ignored the bump. In the back of the car, she lifted the canvases and paint containers lining every inch of space. *Please let it be here.*

Her fingers stretched under the seats, searching for something—anything solid. "Come on. I can't have lost it already." Maybe the stone had fallen out in the museum while she was at work. She'd never find it there.

Then her index finger rolled across a small, hard lump. She pinched the pebble-like matter and pulled it out from under the seat. "Let it be. Let it be."

The diamond emerged in her fingers. Her neck and shoulders relaxed. "Thank you, Lord."

After removing the ring, she placed both pieces into the front glove box for safekeeping. His grandmother's ring had fit perfectly, but she and Jordan hadn't thought to check the prongs to make sure the setting was still secure. At least she'd found the diamond. She breathed a sigh and stood up straight. A jeweler would fix the ring. Nothing could steal the joy she felt today.

"Hello?" Jordan's voice warmed her ear, his breath tickling her cheek. His hands rested on her shoulders, and he leaned closer. "You're not changing your mind about me, are you?"

Rivers whirled, her heart racing. His voice did that same thing in her chest every single time. She slipped her arms around his neck. This gorgeous man standing in front of her had to be kidding. "Never. You're my heart."

She gazed into those astounding rich brown eyes, which flawlessly matched his short dark hair. How did such perfection exist? As an artist, she'd studied colors and textures all her life, and she'd never seen such faultless coordination. Not to mention the cute angle of his nose, the dimples pressed in the center of his cheeks, and the contoured lips, which left a small shadow above his chin. She brushed a kiss across his mouth, sending butterflies to flight inside her. Still. After six months and a whirlwind courtship, she could barely wait to be Jordan's wife.

"Whew. You had me worried when I saw you go back to your ugly green excuse for a vehicle."

"Hey, don't knock the Stink Bug. She's a good car, sort of. Except for the smell. And the smallness. And the age." A smile lifted her lips. "Were you spying on me again?"

"Always. That's how we met, remember?"

"I'll never forget." That day at the museum when he'd followed her to the studio still made her smile.

Jordan's gaze wandered to her lips. "We should go in before I forget why we came."

"Right. We need the marriage license to be official. I almost lost the setting from the ring you gave me. I was locking it up until I can get it repaired."

"As long as you don't lose me." His hands dropped to catch her fingers. "I'll take care of it. You will be my lawful wife. I ran all over town to finalize adding you to my deeds, my car title, my bank account, and my will."

"Don't talk about wills. That's depressing. Let's go be happy."

Jordan bowed and kissed her right palm. "After you."

She offered a curtsy. "My Prince Charming. I knew it the first time I saw you."

Inside the courthouse, her blue nail polish glinted as Rivers signed her name across the marriage license. Her fairy tale would be a reality soon. She giggled and danced a circle around her fiancé. "Your turn, sir."

Jordan grinned and tweaked her chin. "I *do* love how you move. And that cute skirt you're wearing. And your blue eyes. And your crazy blond hair. And your lips." His gaze roamed her face.

Not even the presence of the clerk could still the effect this man had on her. She took a deep breath and belted out, "I love you. I love you. I—"

"Oh, man." Jordan pressed one finger over her mouth and laughed. "Not the singing. You'll have every stray alley cat in Memphis gathering outside."

The woman behind the counter cleared her throat and chuckled. "I'm still here."

"Right. Paperwork." Grinning, Jordan stepped to the laminate counter to sign his name. *Jordan Alexander Barlow III.*

And she would be Mrs. Jordan Alexander Barlow. How sweet was that?

Once they'd finished, she followed him out of the downtown Memphis government office and onto the sidewalk. The fierce heatwave that had shrouded the city for a week swarmed them. Late September meant the beginning of fall in some parts of the world, but not here. At least they'd waited until the end of the workday instead of the blistering lunch hour to get the license.

4

The Art of Rivers

Near the car, Jordan's hand slipped to the small of her back and nudged her around to face him. "Picnic in the park? I picked up your favorite barbeque and sweet tea, and put a new sketch pad in my car."

What were the odds that she would find a man who loved her enough to know all her favorites and give them to her every chance he got? "I don't deserve to be so happy." His smoldering gaze did all kinds of crazy things to her brain. Breathing deeply beside his ear, she whispered, "Yes, we'd best move along."

"Right. Wait here, and I'll get everything." His shaky exhale made her smile. At least he felt the same. Jordan unlocked the passenger door of his Mercedes and gathered their picnic basket, sketch pad, and a new pack of her favorite pencils.

He'd thought of everything. "Thank you." She tucked the pad under one arm and the pencils into her handbag, leaving the food for him to carry.

Hand in hand, they walked toward the Mississippi. She'd painted the mighty river hundreds of times, from hundreds of viewpoints, during hundreds of sunrises and sunsets, but none moved her like the portrait she would present Jordan on their wedding day. She'd drawn him standing there, watching her work in the early morning, golden light frolicking on his coffee-colored curls and glittering in the deep pools and currents of his gaze.

"Tell me where we're going on our honeymoon. Please." Rivers squeezed his hand, made puppy-dog eyes, and batted her lashes. "I don't know what clothes to bring."

Mischief danced in his gaze. "Just bring yourself. Nothing else required." His voice held a smile.

Heat seared her cheeks and churned up a laugh. "You. Come here." She stopped, draped an arm around his neck, and

5

planted another kiss on his lips. All her life, she'd prayed and waited for this man. She hung there for a moment, staring. Could she ask the other question again without upsetting the perfect moment? "Did you call Jay?"

A sigh worked its way through Jordan's lips. "Tonight. I'm calling him tonight. I got his number from my step-uncle."

"Really? You're asking him to the wedding?"

His gaze dropped as he shook his head. "I can't do that to Mom and Dad."

"I would never want to upset your mom and dad. Brooklyn has been so wonderful to help plan the wedding."

"But you're right. I need to let him know I've forgiven him, leave the past in the past. Start a new kind of relationship with him." His chin rested on her forehead. "You make me a better man."

His stomach rumbled, and she pulled away.

"Or a hungry man." She smiled up at him.

"I worked through lunch again so maybe the office will leave us alone during our honeymoon."

"They'd better. Vast River Architecture cannot have you that week. You're all mine." They passed under a cluster of trees and shrubs, and movement caught her attention. "Did you see that?"

"What?" Jordan glanced back and forth.

A shiver crept across her shoulders. Homeless people and addicts tottered around downtown areas in most cities, and Memphis was no exception. Despite the fact that she'd been in this spot often, she stopped and scanned the scene again. Something in her spirit warned of danger. "There's someone behind those bushes. Maybe in a hoodie…"

Jordan took a step and craned his neck. "I don't see—"

An explosion like fireworks popped and rung in her ears.

Another blast, this with impact, hard and swift as a kick in the chest. A red-hot burning sensation pierced her shoulder and back. Time slowed, and a scream ripped from her throat.

Jordan dropped to his knees clutching his chest. Red spread around his fingers, contrasting sharply against his pale blue shirt.

Hot liquid poured all around her, and her vision tunneled white. A fountain of blood. But she had to get to him. "Jordan..." She stumbled forward and fell to her knees beside him, clutched his face. Spots danced in front of her eyes as the throbbing in her shoulder pulsed. Then darkness dragged her into its abyss.

Chapter 2

St. Simons Island, Georgia.

Rivers gripped the steering wheel tighter. For a brief moment, the beach views, the moss-covered trees, the beauty of this seaside town almost drowned the pain still screaming in her heart, tormenting her mind, stealing her sleep.

Almost. But black pain gathered in a huge glob on the palette of her life. Black like her insides. Void of color. Void of life. Void of capacity to feel joy.

Jordan should be at her side. He should be leading her around the town, telling stories of his childhood. The good ones, anyway. He should *not* be six feet under a slab in a Memphis cemetery. A memory flashed before her eyes—so much red—unearthing fresh anger, pushing the bile up her throat. One hand went to the indention in her left shoulder. Her blood ran cold and pounded in her ears. The exit wound was much larger. Too bad the shooter hadn't hit his mark and finished her.

She'd been robbed of so much more than a piece of flesh. Her heart had certainly been torn from her chest. And for what? Money to buy OxyContin or a shot of heroin? Meth? Jordan would've given his wallet, his watch…any material possession if asked for it.

The Ms. Snarky GPS signaled for her to turn. She'd nicknamed the voice Cruella, and she'd tried to obey the harsh tyrant. The seven times she'd gotten lost already on this trip had been enough, thanks to the inability to focus on anything, even the irritating voice giving directions.

The Stink Bug was doing well to make it this far. Taking the Mercedes she'd inherited would've been safer for this eleven-hour drive…okay, thirteen counting the wrong turns. But the one time she'd driven the luxury vehicle, everything in the car smelled of Jordan. She'd parked it in his drive and hadn't moved the thing since.

The roads narrowed before her. Vehicles and bright green trees crowded the streets in front of most of the houses. Jordan had always called his grandmother's place a cottage, but that had come from a man who'd known wealth his entire life, not a teacher's daughter with a disabled mother. The tints, ages, and styles of the beach homes varied wildly, as older ones had been torn down and replaced over the years.

At the end of the road that led toward the shoreline, the rude computer voice suggested that she'd reached her destination. Rivers scanned the place where the home should be. Overgrown hedges acted as a natural barrier in the front yard. No view of the cottage, no driveway yet, but the house was on a corner lot. She turned left, and there it stood.

Her pulse pounded as she slowed the car. The place looked just as she'd imagined. White cottage with a wraparound porch. Red brick chimney. Gray awnings. White picket fence around the back yard. A tattered American flag waved in the Atlantic breeze. She pulled into the short gravel drive—or maybe it was shell-lined—and parked. The fact that she'd inherited the summer home from the man who'd never become her husband shocked and overwhelmed her with fresh grief. Her parched throat dried as if it had filled with sand. She had to get out of the car, but how could she?

I don't want this, Lord. I want to forget.

9

This house taunted her. Reminded her of all she'd lost. The quicker she sold everything, the better. She could get back to her clients. Her life before. If only Jordan's family had been willing to help. But they'd had their own loss that still plagued them in this town, the accident that had torn their family apart. And she couldn't ask her father. He had enough on his plate taking care of Mom. Bringing her mother would only make the task more complicated. Add too many obstacles, too many questions and frustrations. More negative emotions when she couldn't handle the ones she'd already been dealt.

It's You and me, Lord.

The heat besieged her now that she'd cut the engine, and sweat beaded on her forehead. Groaning, she opened the door and forced her feet to the ground, the mix of white rocks and shells crunching.

One moment at a time. Her pastor's words. And she knew this concept from the counseling she did for others through art therapy. Part of healing was facing the trauma. Facing the grief.

God, help me get through this moment.

She made a path to the passenger door of her car and yanked it open. She threw her duffle over her shoulder and grabbed the pad and pencils Jordan had given her that last day. That horrific day. She stared at the tablet as though answers were locked somewhere inside the blank pages. How had it come away unscathed? That not even a drop of blood had splattered the cover seemed to be a miracle.

But not the miracle she'd begged for.

Hugging it close, she shut the door and trudged toward the front porch. The key was under a flower pot, according to the caretaker, some step-uncle of Jordan's. Kind of careless, but what did it matter? The glass French doors provided little protection, and no one in Jordan's family came here anymore.

The cottage's only visitors were the folks from the cleaning and landscape services.

Up the three stairs onto the wooden planks, she stepped, then stopped. The dead plant in the terra cotta container looked about like she felt. Lifeless and withered. She bent and lifted the pot. The key lay there. She stared at the dull silver finish and imagined the pain the simple piece of metal would unlock. A wind chime tinkled from somewhere nearby, its sound melancholy and haunting.

It had taken her a year to muster the courage to make this trip. Going inside was required. Emptying the place and readying the house for sale had to be done. No one in the family had come back after Jordan's grandmother died. And as much as she wanted to forget, Rivers refused to let a stranger toss away Jordan's past.

She picked up the key, its weight much heavier than the flimsy nickel should be.

With shaking hands, she inserted it and turned. Now the knob. Already the view through the glass wrenched her heart. Pictures and paintings lined the tongue-and-groove walls tinted a whitish gray. Likely photos of Jordan and his sister, before...

Blocking out her churning thoughts, Rivers burst through and stepped inside. She tossed her bag on a nearby bench but kept her sketch pad and pencils tucked under her arm. On the opposite wall, an antique side table held five photo frames. The first one she focused on jarred her, speared through her core.

Jordan, a young, smiling teen, his sister Savannah on his back. Both tanned, they dripped saltwater where they stood at the end of a boardwalk, sand covering their bare feet and calves.

Her breathing halted, imprisoned inside her chest. She couldn't look at more. She had to get out of here.

11

Help me, Lord.

The chimes drifted into her thoughts again. Maybe she could draw. Outside. The beach might be the best place. With cautious steps, she glanced around, searching for where a beach towel or chair might be stored.

A set of blinders would be nice. How could she stay here with so many gut-wrenching photos? She'd have to box them up. A narrow hall opened from the living area, and a single door on the left looked to be a closet. Lips pinched and fearful of what she'd find, she cracked the door. A linen closet. Good. No pictures. A small sigh worked its way past her lips. Stacks of sheets lined the top shelf, then blankets on the next, and, on the bottom, beach towels. Beneath that shelf lay three folding sand chairs.

She snagged a red, oversized Coca-Cola towel and a fuchsia chair then made a beeline back out the door.

Chapter 3

The pungent scent of tobacco and marijuana clung to the potential client's clothes, clung to the man's disheveled brown hair, and now it clung to Cooper, as well. Occupational hazard for a substance abuse counselor. That and a few other hazards, but the rewards were eternal.

Sitting across from Cooper in the worn wingback chair, the young man's glassy blue eyes had been immediately convicting. The thirty-something-year-old had been using within the last few hours. The guy still wasn't broken, despite losing his job and his vehicle. He wasn't at rock bottom. Yet. Blame still spewed from the client's lips. How people had let him down. How his parents had written him off back in college. How losing his job hadn't been his fault. How he could get clean on his own.

"Look at me, Blake." Cooper moved to the edge of his chair and made eye contact. "I know you've been hurt by people you care about. You've been disappointed in life. I've been in your place. But how much further do you want to sink before you reach out for the life preserver I'm throwing you?"

Blake didn't answer. There was a girlfriend in the picture, and Blake didn't want to lose her. Which was a real possibility since he'd have to stay away from her during and after recovery if she was still using. If he'd stay today.

Please open his ears and his heart, God.

"God loves you, Blake. He wants a better life for you than this. God can perform miracles. He can bring the dead to life,

13

and that includes people like us. He can bring new life. You can do this with His help."

For a moment, something like hope flickered across Blake's expression, but then his gaze fell. He shook his head. "I can't leave Star. She needs me. Someone will hurt a pretty girl like Star if I abandon her."

The moment was gone. Blake would leave and go back to Star and find his next fix. Their next fix.

"If you change your mind, I'm here. I could get Star placed, too, you know. We could probably get her a bed next door. You could both start over. If you care for her, get help."

Chin lifted, Blake stood. "We'll be fine. I can take care of me and Star." With that, he lumbered out and back onto the street.

At least Blake had come through the door this time. That was a start. For a week, the guy had walked past the sober living house and the studio, often pausing, glancing toward the entrance, the security camera catching the wistful expression hidden under the dirty baseball cap. Each time, Blake had continued on his way. Until today.

Maybe next time he'd stay and get help. Before it was too late. Heroin or meth or whatever Blake was on were formidable enemies without the Lord in the battle.

Cooper's head bowed. "God, please bring Blake and Star to You, somehow. Block their paths to destruction. Lead them, restore them, and usher them into Your kingdom."

His appointments finished and the gallery covered, Cooper left for his turn on voluntary patrol. At the marina, he turned his Jeep into the lot in front of the boat slips. He shook his head to clear the image burned into his mind, but Blake's face stayed with him, churned his gut. Those hollow eyes pierced him like a bullet to the chest. Every single time. Seeing himself in their faces, their chaos, their messed-up lives.

Remembering Savannah. Gone way too soon because of him.

Stop. Take every thought captive.

He parked in his usual spot, the Atlantic glistening beyond the faded boards of the dock. Before exiting, he let his eyelids shut, tried to block out the vision of Blake in some alley or back room, buying whatever he could find to numb the pain of old injuries, both external and internal.

Another silent prayer lifted toward the throne. Cooper asked the Holy Spirit to speak the prayer for Blake and all of the others in the Re-Claimed ministry. Many times, no words formed, just a plea, that groaning in his spirit.

Only You know how to heal them, God.

If he let the disappointment burrow in too deep, the emotions would become toxic. He'd been there, done that. He couldn't take away their loneliness or pain…couldn't fix their lives or the lies they believed. Each person, including himself, was responsible for his own choices. And his own disasters. With God's help, people could find restoration, but they had to be willing. Underneath the addiction, they had to come to terms with whatever haunted their past, accept God's love and grace, forgive those who'd wronged them, and find their worth in the One True Healer.

Warm sunshine poured through his window, and drowsiness tugged on him. He should sleep more at night.

If only he could. Another hardship he had in common with his therapy clients. He understood insomnia all too well.

His breathing slowed, the scent of that residual smoke still tickling his nose. He'd sit here a few moments more. The tides weren't coming in yet.

Drowsy, he let his eyes close. Sleep crept in.

The taste of cheap beer on his tongue, Cooper swallowed the long, white tablet. The dry pill stuck at the back of his throat. He grabbed for his can in the boat's cup holder and took a swig. Flat and warm. He tossed the can on the floor beside the captain's seat. He'd pop open another in a minute, but he needed to drag Savannah back into the boat. He may've had a few, but from the way the sun hung in the sky, he knew the tide would be coming in soon. St. Simons had fierce tides that rose rapidly. A few more minutes, and they'd make the quick trek back toward Nanna's house. He'd have to find a place to ditch the pile of beer cans.

He let his eyes shut behind his sunglasses as numbness and euphoria crept up his arms and legs, tickled its way across his chin and lips and ears. His breathing slowed. The patronizing voices nagging him quieted. He could barely hear them now as they repeated, "Why do you talk funny? You throw like a girl. Why can't you be more like Jordan? Why would you want to major in art? You'll never amount to much. So much potential wasted."

But then another thought forced through his fog. Savannah! Oh God, help him, where was Savannah? Stumbling to his feet, he charged toward the side of the boat where he'd last seen her. Something white bobbed in the distance, so he threw his leg over the side and jumped in. He held his breath and plunged below the pounding surf over and over. Salt water clouded and stung his eyes. His lungs burned for oxygen, and his exhausted muscles ached to give up against the dark currents. Until everything went black.

Cooper gasped. "Savannah!" He shook his head and stared out his Jeep's windshield.

The nightmare again.

His sweet, vibrant cousin was gone. Always would be.

And it was his fault.

The tide had begun its assault toward the beach. The sandbars would be covered soon. Another victim could be lost to the deadly pull out to sea. He burst from the vehicle and

16

sprinted toward his boat.

~~~

Rivers closed her sketch pad. She'd made at least five drawings now. More than she'd done in months. One captured the light rays piercing the swirly clouds in the late afternoon sky. Others featured the foam cresting on clear water near the shore, the majestic blue heron she'd dubbed Henrietta, who'd swooped down and posed nearby, and the tiny white crab she'd named Chloe, which now retreated to its burrow on the beach.

If only she could bury herself in the sand like that. Pretend the past year never happened. What if she'd never met Jordan? If she'd never dragged him out by the river, he'd still be alive.

Another crustacean rushed toward her...a big one, this time, with good sized pinchers. Too close for comfort. "Shoo, Big Boy! Get!" She pushed up from her beach chair, sidestepping the charging creature. "Go." Rivers clapped her hands, and the critter moved on and disappeared into a hole.

Thirst hit her when she stood, and she stared at the blasted cottage maybe fifty yards away, sitting quaint and white and pretty in the sun as if nothing bad had ever happened. As if life went on as usual. No tragedy. No death.

Her stomach rumbled. When had she eaten last? She often forgot to eat these days, a habit her father chided her over, but she didn't want to go back in there yet. The place had haunted her the few moments she'd been inside. The torment of that picture and so many more still waited.

A single tear rolled down her cheek, and she brushed it away. How she had any liquid left to cry, she couldn't fathom. She needed happy thoughts to replace the bad. Something— anything—positive. Her mind reached for the summer stories Jordan had told her, the ones that brought his warm brown eyes to life. There'd been a tale of crabbing at night with a

17

flashlight and bucket under the stars, and someone's toe getting pinched. Flying colorful kites in fierce winds to see how high they could soar. Catching waves on his boogie board under a cloudless sky. That tiny dent in his pinkie finger where he'd broken it hitching a boat. He'd laughed when he'd explained the freak accident, though it had been painful.

Would she ever truly laugh again?

She turned back to take a step toward the shoreline. Bright blues and greens shimmered, colliding with the beige sand that was marred with wavy indentions from the receding tide.

A sandbar jutted far into the Atlantic waves. It called to her like a siren song to come and draw, to pour her agony into her art. Her feet continued through a small, cool tidal pool and onto the grainy ridge above the water. What would it feel like to walk as far as she could on this little peninsula? Another tear rolled down her cheek. She let it plummet to become one with the ocean's salty water, like the sea of tears she'd cried since Jordan's death.

What would it feel like to just keep walking into the abyss? To let waves crash over her head, to let the currents fill her lungs, to let the water stop her heart from hurting so?

No. The thief comes only to steal and kill and destroy; I have come that they may have life, and have it to the full.

That verse again. She held in a groan. How many times had she wished she'd died that day with Jordan? But the bullet had only ripped through her shoulder. The idiot who'd shot them could have aimed better. He'd missed her heart by four inches. With the bullet, at least.

Her parents, counselor, and pastor all told her she'd survived for a reason. What reason? To drown in misery? To be the cover model for those trendy new *don't do drugs or you'll damage someone's life* billboards?

The Art of Rivers

Tamping down the despair, she plopped onto the wet sand, unfolded the sketch pad, and let her thoughts stop, allowing her hands to do what they knew.

Her pencil followed what her mind saw against the horizon. Shiny cresting waves, low-hanging white clouds looming closer, gulls fighting the currents of wind in some sort of melodious discord. Several minutes later, she stood to stretch her legs but continued drawing, imagining the palette of colors she could use on a canvas. The shades of cobalt and silver and emerald. If only she could paint like she used to...

The encroaching tide lapped in small circles around her feet where there had been packed sand a few minutes before. She glanced down for a moment. Maybe she should head back. A squawking pelican pulled her gaze to the azure skies with pink tinging the wispy strands in the west. The bird soared below a plane, which cut a milky whitish trail above her. She'd draw a few more minutes. It wasn't like she had anyone to get back to.

The murdering mugger had seen to that. Anger coursed through her once again.

Even the desire to create had been taken from her most days. The colors came out muddled and black. How could she draw beauty when the darkness of grief shadowed her soul?

But the new sketch pad Jordan had given her had made it through the terror without as much as a smudge. Jordan's words written inside the cover were burned into her mind, heart, and soul.

The beauty you paint comes from the pure light within you, for within you, I see the true Light of the World. Thank you for introducing me and everyone in your delightful, whimsical path to that Light. Keep shining bright for Him!

Love always,
Jordan

Sometimes she felt the person she'd been before had died that September day. The light was gone. Had been buried under six feet of river sludge. The person who'd been left behind was no more than a bitter and broken shell.

But she would paint again. For him. And for Him. Today was the time to start. A churning in her spirit wouldn't seem to leave her alone. An urge nagged her to create anew. Her hand continued its journey on the page, shading and texturing.

A wave smacked her calves, splashing rivulets of water across her waist, and she turned back to face the shore. A river of raging ocean seemed to block her path now.

A deep ravine of fear carved into her chest.

Maybe she didn't want to die after all. Raising her drawings up high above her head, she swallowed hard.

Think, Rivers.

How was she going to get back?

~~~

Almost back to the dock after his volunteer patrol, he spotted something. Flapping or waving? He squinted through the glare beaming off the waves. Not a something. A silhouette, *a someone?*

She was stuck on a sandbar as the tide quickly rose.

His pulse zoomed into high gear. A girl or woman stood waving her arms. She was tall and incredibly thin with a long neck almost like a heron, but with a shock of short, light-blond hair topping her head. Cooper pushed up the gas, accelerating the boat toward the stranded bird-woman, likely a crazy tourist. A heron would have more sense.

The boat bounced hard over the waves until he neared and cut the motor. "I'm coming to help," he called over the ocean

20

breeze.

The girl turned and waved more furiously. When he neared, she yelled, "Thank the Lord. Take my sketch pad." She stretched to push a tablet of paper toward him.

Yep, he'd found a really disturbed tourist this time, trying to save a pad of paper instead of her own life. "Let that go, and I'll tell you when to grab hold."

"No. Take this. Keep it dry." Her eyes, twin pools of blue, stared at him as if he were the idiot. "I cannot lose it. You don't understand!"

Was she drunk or high? He dropped his anchor over the other side of the deck, checked the straps of his life vest in case he had to dive in. The girl might be in need of some sort of treatment. She was thin enough, and she had that wild, desperate look on her face. Cooper held in a groan. His job seemed to follow him wherever he went.

~~~

Dark eyes and black, careless hair to match, her rescuer stared at her as if she were insane. Maybe she was. A current pulled her, launching her deeper into the rising tide. She could barely stand. Salty water splashed into her eyes and mouth. "Take this pad now! It's getting wet!" She stretched her hand as high as she could, dog-paddling with the other to stay erect.

The man finally grabbed the tablet from her. Once both arms were free, she tried to swim toward the boat ladder, but a swell slapped her in the face. A moment later, strong hands grabbed her, pushed a red floating device under her, and pulled her toward the vessel.

"Just relax. But help me kick if you can." He stayed close, guiding them along a rope tied to the hull.

At the ladder, he pushed her forward. "You go first. I'm right here. Let me know if you're too tired to climb, and I'll

21

give you a shove from behind."

The last thing she wanted was this stranger shoving her behind. "I got it." She began her ascent, one waterlogged step at a time. "And I hope you put my sketchbook someplace dry." The last sentence, she mumbled, since she probably should be thankful he'd come by at all.

"What?" The voice behind her sounded incredulous.

On board, she spied the pad lying on the passenger seat intact. "I said thanks for putting my sketchbook someplace dry." She stood there dripping while he vaulted onboard.

"That is not what you said." His brows furrowed under dripping strands of black hair.

Rivers took in the angle of his nose, observed the contoured lips leaving a small shadow above the scruff on his chin. There was something familiar and almost mesmerizing about his bone structure.

"Are you even listening?" The man snapped his fingers in front of her. "Can I call someone to help you? Have you taken something? Are you drunk?"

"What? No. I don't drink, and I haven't"—she made air quotes—"taken something."

His chin jutted forward. "Then what in the world were you doing out there? Trying to get yourself killed? The tide comes in with a vengeance, and you can be under water in no time."

Had she been trying to…? No. She just hadn't been paying attention. "I've never been here, and I was drawing. Now I know."

The furrows between his brows softened, and he breathed a heavy sigh. "Now you know. The difference in the water levels can be from six to nine feet, maybe the most extreme on the entire Eastern Seaboard. Be careful. People have lost their lives on these sandbars."

A wistfulness filled his expression until he made a sudden turn, reeled in the rope he'd used to save her, then another. An anchor landed in the boat with a clank.

"You might not be so lucky next time." His tone was sharp. "Where do you want me to take you?"

"To that beach right in front of us." Where else would she be going? Certainly not anywhere with him.

"I can't get the boat close enough to let you out on the beach. Your precious pad might get wet."

Her sketchbook. Rivers looked down and surveyed the water dripping from every square inch of her body. "Well, I… I don't know. I'm staying there. My car's there. How can I get back?"

His dark brown eyes widened, the irises appearing almost as black as the pupils. "Exactly where are you staying?"

"It's none of your business *exactly* where I'm staying." Her hands flailed as she gestured. "Just near this section of beach is all you need to know." She'd met her share of creepers. No way she would announce the address of the house she'd be sleeping in. By herself.

Dimples pressed in the center of his cheeks when he shook his head and sort of smiled— not a real smile, but one that said he was frustrated. "I'm sorry. I'm not trying to stalk you. It's just…someone I used to know had a cottage near that area. You caught me off guard." Emotion seemed to twist his tongue for those final words. He cleared his throat and went to the driver's seat. A second later, he tossed a ragged towel her way. "I can take you to the boat dock and drive you home or wait while you get an Uber or another ride."

The motor hummed to life, and she took a seat on the back bench. The farther away, the better. The boat leapt forward, and she took in his tall and lean silhouette against the dimming sky. Last year, she'd learned too late to trust her instincts. Too late to save Jordan. She'd do better this time. And something about this man—her rescuer—wasn't safe at all.

Chapter 4

Pay for a ride with a stranger or accept a ride with the stranger driving this boat? Rivers debated her options until they reached the dock. The guy hadn't spoken, except to announce they were nearing his slip. The Atlantic breeze caressed her face, and the blue sky melted to a palette of pinks and purples. The outing would've been almost enjoyable if the circumstances were different. Pelicans flew in formation against a heavy moon suspended on the horizon, and her fingers itched to draw again, maybe even paint. Except she hadn't finished a canvas since...

"You ready to get out?" A hand extended toward her, and she stared at the man offering to help her off the boat.

The wind had swept up his black hair in the front, revealing more of his dark brows and tanned forehead. Like a sculpture, his features had been shaped into a pleasing form. The angles and contours nicely matched, but gloom shrouded the edges of his eyes and mouth. She knew how sadness lined the face, had seen her share of sadness mark the children she'd counseled. Twinges of compassion and curiosity stirred in her chest. What tragedy had this man seen?

"Um, miss? Are you sure you're okay? Do you need a doctor?" His brows met above the dark eyes. "I'm Cooper, by the way. I should've introduced myself before. It's just seeing you out there with the tide..." His somber gaze drifted to another place. Maybe another time.

"Sorry. I'm Rivers." She took the hand. No wonder he'd

thought she was on something. She was sitting there like a dumb statue, acting like a freak. His grip was strong but gentle, and his nearness almost soothing as she stepped onto the pier. Perhaps she'd been mistaken about him earlier. He seemed more damaged than dangerous.

"Your paper survive unscathed?" One side of his mouth pulled into a slight smirk.

Her fingers stroked the tablet, assessing it for moisture. Not even damp. Another survival story. "I know this doesn't make sense to you."

"You can explain on the way to wherever I'm dropping you off. I've been told that I'm a good listener." He retrieved a phone from his pocket and offered it to her. "Unless you'd rather call another ride."

Maybe he wasn't a bad guy. He *had* rescued her, and her own cell was still in the cottage. "You can drive me."

"I can, huh?" An edge of *gee-thanks* sarcasm rumbled his low voice, but the tone seemed more amused than harsh.

"If you don't mind, I mean." Her gaze traveled over his face again, searching the proportion and shapes, the slant of his nose, the slightest dimples in his cheeks, the square of his jaw, his Adam's apple. Something burned in her chest, traveled down her right shoulder like an ember of a forgotten fire fanning to life. She pressed her fingers into the scar there, thankful she hadn't changed into her bathing suit. If no one ever saw the ugly reminder, she didn't have to contend with their probing stares and answer their inevitable questions.

"I don't mind." His fingers raked across the scruff shadowing his chin. "Is there something on me?"

Staring. She'd been staring. "I'm an artist, and sometimes I get lost in my own mind, taking a mental picture."

"Are you going to draw me in your pad?" Mischief

brightened his solemn eyes for a split second as he nodded toward her sketchbook.

"Who knows?" She shrugged. "I try to go where the Spirit leads."

"What spirit?" His gaze stabbed into hers, penetrating and earnest.

"The Holy Spirit. I try my best to listen, anyway." Or at least she used to. Her days as a volunteer worship artist seemed to be over. Or as any kind of painter for that matter. Some sketches here and there, but the colors had dried up in her mind when she lifted her brush, had turned into a hard lump of browns and blacks as she tried to block out the monstrous blood red of her nightmares.

A siren wailed in the distance, and he stepped toward the parking lot. "I'm into art myself." He clicked the key fob. "The tan Jeep is mine."

She followed while he rounded the vehicle to the passenger side.

After opening her door, he made a grand gesture. "My chariot. Sorry about the smell. Got rained in a few times when I left the top off."

Sucking in a breath, she sat, and a small smile fought its way out. "Almost as bad as my Volkswagen Beetle, but not quite. Apparently the first owner left the windows down on it too."

"Man, that's the worst. At least the Jeep airs out."

"Yeah, I bought the car in the winter, and the dealership must've put some really fresh deodorizer in there to mask the sour. Once the Memphis spring came, the Stink Bug reared its stanky head."

A chuckle spilled from his lips. "Stink Bug. I like it." He clucked his tongue. "So we both like art and smelly cars. A lot in common."

Was he hitting on her? Her smile faded into the black abyss. She wasn't going to flirt with another man or let him flirt with her. Not with Jordan only gone a year. Not when she could still barely eat or sleep. Not when she couldn't even manage in her regular position at work.

Not with *this guy,* and probably not ever.

The motor rumbled to life, and he backed out of the parking place. They zipped onto the street. The guy—Cooper—drove fast. Cooper... Cooper... Had he said his last name? She hadn't given hers. Her abs tightened. Here she was in a car with a stranger, miles away from anyone she knew. No phone. Nothing. Hadn't she learned anything about this dangerous world?

Wind whipped through the open windows and top. At least she could jump out if she had to. Drop and roll, right? Then what? How would she even know where she was? Dusk quickly transformed into night, and her sense of direction was basically non-existent. "Where are you going?"

"Back toward the beach you were on. Didn't you say you were staying near that section, or you have the Stink Bug parked there?" At a stop sign, he glanced her way. "Right?"

Oh. Made sense. He knew that stretch of beach. "Right."

"Did you say you were from Memphis?"

"Yeah." More ammo if he was actually a serial killer. *Hi, I'm Rivers, all alone, family hours away, and I'm unfamiliar with this town.* Didn't some psychos act normal and helpful at first?

Silence claimed the rest of the ride. Cooper-possible-serial-killer seemed to be lost in thought. Troubled even. Not the typical MO for psychopathic behavior.

The overgrown shrubs came into the focus of his headlights, and he slowed.

28

Finally something slightly familiar. "Turn here." Rivers pointed to the street where the driveway connected.

He complied and stopped, his high beams landing on her Volkswagen. So much for him not knowing where she would be spending the night. His eyes narrowed. "You're staying there? That house? That cottage?"

"This is my car." She wouldn't answer specifically. After all, he could think she was a guest.

"Are you sure this is the right address?" His gaze bounced from her to the cottage and back. Now he was getting really weird.

"I'm sure this is where I want to get out." After quickly unlatching the seatbelt, she opened the door and exited. He hadn't put the Jeep into park, but no need. He could leave.

"Bye, thanks." She waved him off, though he still stared, mouth gaping. Had he known Jordan's family? Maybe that was it. The place had been empty for five years, and now she was parked in the drive. No way was she explaining, though.

"Thanks, Cooper. I got it from here."

Her dismissal seemed to give him the hint he needed. He blinked hard and then focused on her. "Yeah. No problem. Stay off the sandbars." The darkness in his eyes deepened, if that were possible, like thunder clouds against a night sky. "They're really dangerous."

"Got it." She waited as he drove away, but those eyes stayed with her while she collected her things from the beach, while she climbed the stairs onto the porch and reentered the cottage. Now that she'd almost drowned, maybe she'd have the motivation to do what she came for. She just needed to clean out this place and give the word to Jordan's step-uncle, Shane Turner, to put it on the market. Then she could leave and move on with life.

As if.

A sob slipped from her chest, a sound that seemed to come from someone else. The memories closed in, and she braced herself for a fresh wave of grief.

Lord, hold me tight. Give me strength.

She hugged herself, eyes closed, for one more moment. After breathing deeply then releasing the air in a long whoosh, she opened her eyes, popped on the lights, and surveyed the room. Really took in the room.

Tongue and groove walls, transoms over the doors, antique tables and cabinets, and chandeliers. Photos or paintings hung every few inches, even on the back of the doors. Pottery, of all sorts, adorned every shelf or furniture top. A nearby chest was topped with a dozen colorful ceramic fish beside four clay plates with children's handprints pressed into them and painted yellow.

Rivers took a step closer and lifted the plate that had Jordan's name written on it with a sharpie. She ran her fingers over the indentions where his young fingers had once squished into the mud. Those fingers had been very much alive. Had he giggled? She pictured his dimpled smile, and her eyes burned. That black hole of sorrow reopened, engulfing her like a grave. *Why? Why? Why was she alone?*

Grief clamped around her ribs and squeezed. *Not again, Lord.* Another deep breath.

She placed the child's creation back on the chest and stared at the other three. Savannah, Brooklyn, and Pearl were the names noted there. Jordan's sister, his mother, and his aunt.

No Jay.

Jordan's cousin's banishment had been complete. Her stomach started that familiar gnawing. She'd always wanted Jordan to forgive and reconnect with Jay, let that part of his life be healed. Why had she even cared? It was none of her business. Especially now.

Suddenly exhausted, she pivoted, grabbed her bag, and walked down the hall. The drive, the memories, getting stuck on the sandbar, had been more than enough for one day. In the first bedroom she came to, Rivers slipped into a clean T-shirt then plopped down on the white comforter covering one of two twin beds. Tomorrow, she could start again. Whether she wanted to or not.

~~~

The girl, or rather the woman, Rivers, was from Memphis and staying in the cottage. Had the estate sold the cottage? Or could she be…? He pictured the strange woman riding on his boat, how the evening sun ignited in her pale hair, creating a sort of halo effect. How her pupils contracted in the light, which allowed him to study the fine textures of blue surrounding them.

All night, Cooper had tossed and turned, fighting the urge to do an internet search. He stayed offline for good reason. He also found himself fighting the urge to use something to dull the memories drowning him. The yearning hadn't been this strong in a couple of years. Sure, sometimes the smell of beer or smoke, even a song, would stir up the memory. Stress or anxiety could incite thoughts about how a couple of pills could make everything fade away into the numbing high. The triggers were so disturbing. He felt like a dog trained to salivate at the sound of a bell. The longing rarely raised its ugly head anymore, but when it did, he tried to use that feeling to remind himself what his clients went through on a daily basis.

Groggy from lack of sleep, he'd barely gotten dressed and downstairs to the gallery in time to open the doors by nine. With the light rain, customers filtered in, those snowbirds unable to take their strolls on the sand. The morning brought a couple of sales, which was helpful since Shane acted as if they might not make the budget this month. Stormy days always helped. And tonight, he'd stay up and finish another beachy abstract. Vacation homeowners here couldn't seem to get enough of them.

Between the customers and the two workers from Re-Claimed, the coffee pot near the front of the showroom had been drained, so he started another while they had a quiet moment. The intoxicating aroma gave him a boost, despite the fact that he'd given up caffeine along with any other addictive chemicals. Most addicts didn't go that far, allowing coffee and nicotine to be sanity savers. He didn't judge. Those were legal, accepted, and not as mind-altering as the other substances they battled. For himself, he wanted to stay free of any habit-forming substances. He'd been a slave long enough.

A few feet from where he stood, the bell on the door clanked, and he called a greeting over his shoulder. "Good morning. If I can help you, please ask."

No sound came of the door closing behind him, no sound of feet entering, no sound of a person followed his welcome. Cooper pivoted away from the counter where he'd been wiping stray spills of water and coffee to see who'd opened the gallery entrance.

It was her.

Rivers.

"What are you doing?" the woman gasped. "Here? What are you doing here?"

"I-I-I work. Here. I work here." Words stuttered and twisted on his tongue. Something about her undid him. Next his lisp would come back.

"Why?" Her cobalt eyes rounded and shone in the track

lighting. They reminded him of those swirly blue marbles he'd played with as a kid when he'd spent summers here with Jordan and Savannah.

"They pay me to manage the gallery." He tried to lift his lips into a pleasant expression and took cautious steps closer to her. "Like a job."

"Who is they?"

This had to be her. It was the only thing that made sense. First the cottage, and now here at the gallery. "Shane Turner, the man who manages the esta—property."

How horribly he was failing in this conversation. Her expression twisted as if he'd been the one who shot her. Somehow he always managed to wound his family.

"Oh." Her long thin fingers ran through her bangs, causing a few light strands to stand on end. "Is anyone else here?"

"Two volunteers from Re-Claimed are working. They're in the back right now setting up."

"I meant Shane Turner." Her blue gaze snapped up to him. "Re-Claimed? What kind of place is that?" Her voice became shrill like those small whistles in Cracker Jack boxes.

The bell on the door signaled another arrival, and a gray-haired couple entered.

"Hey, folks. Come in and look around." Cooper placed a hand on her shoulder and neared her ear. "Let me give you a tour, and I'll explain." At least he'd try. She was likely as tolerant as the rest of his family.

~~~

She hadn't meant to freak out, but Cooper didn't have to touch her like that. He seemed to feel the need to hush her, to calm her. If he hadn't been speaking in riddles, she wouldn't have overreacted.

But seeing him here, of all places. His dark hair about as

careless as it had been the day before. Though he wore khakis with an untucked pale blue button-down and looked at home in this place… Did he know she'd come here? *And Re-Claimed?* It better not be what she was imagining. This was her art gallery. Had been for a year, and yet, she knew nothing about it. She hadn't wanted to, hadn't wanted it to be hers, hadn't wanted to be here. Not without Jordan.

The estate—the term Cooper had almost said but stopped himself—was her responsibility, at least for the time being, so she'd better find out what in crazy-town was going on.

Cooper guided her toward the back of the spacious open room, speaking softly, hand resting on the small of her back. Why wasn't she recoiling? She didn't know this man, but somehow he calmed the raging sea of grief roiling inside. What was he saying?

She turned to focus on his soft words and moving lips. The lips captured her attention, but not the way she'd intended. Her breath hitched. He was a bit of a masterpiece in his own haphazard way.

Pay attention, Rivers.

"Local artists consign, but we need the extra income from the projects the clients at Re-Claimed donate. Some of them have real talent. I donate my own pieces, as well, to cover part of my rent."

"Rent?" This just kept getting more bizarre. What mad world had she stepped into?

His gaze fell to the thin gray carpet covering the floor, and his hand left her back to fumble through his dark locks. "I live in the loft above the gallery. It's only one room, a bathroom, a kitchenette, but it's convenient for running the gallery and working with Re-Claimed down the street."

He lived here, and there was that term again. Re-Claimed.

Please let the place be a facility for mental illness or eating disorders...maybe an odd term for a rehabilitation center for physical injuries. "What kind of place are you referring to?"

"Two sober living houses for those with substance and alcohol addiction. One for men, the other for women." The dark gaze returned to meet hers and delved there, searching, waiting for a reaction.

Rivers swallowed back the words she wanted to spew out. How her mother's binge drinking had stolen her childhood after the car wreck. How at thirteen she'd had to give up dance and every other after-school activity to be a parent to her mother. How the children in her art therapy sessions had often been neglected or abused by their drug-addicted parents. How the carelessness of an addict had cost Jordan's sister her life and had torn apart his family. How a probable addict's bullet had torn through her shoulder and ripped through Jordan's heart.

"Rivers? Are you okay?" The hand touched her again, but this time she did recoil.

"This"—she waved around the room—"is not okay." She pivoted and stomped out of the gallery. She'd find Shane Turner and get to the bottom of the situation. There was no way Jordan's step-uncle, Shane, had told Jordan's mother and aunt about what was going on in St. Simons. Brooklyn and Pearl would've warned her.

Chapter 5

Still steaming, Rivers wound around the island until she found the real estate office where Shane worked. After passing the same storage facility three times, Cruella-GPS-lady had finally guided her in.

Shane had said he'd meet her at the gallery this morning, but apparently some other client took priority. Or maybe he was a chicken. He had to have known she'd be livid about his abuse of trust. Jordan's grandmother had left everything to Jordan when she'd died. The family paid Shane good money to take care of the property. It was a wonder no one had been throwing a keg party in the cottage when she'd arrived.

Stopping right behind a red Audi, hopeful that she was blocking Shane in, she parked and stomped out of her car. Well, stomped as much as she could in her stupid flip-flops. The shoes slapped against the soles of her feet as she traversed the sidewalk toward the tan stucco building. She climbed two slight concrete steps between fluted white columns and let herself into the office building, the volcano bubbling in her chest ready to blow.

The reception desk was deserted, empty, and dusty, as though no one had worked there in weeks. Weird. Could he not afford an assistant? Or at the very least, a cleaning service? The building was small, so maybe this was a one-man show. Lights filtered down the short hall, but she lost some of her zeal to barge in and throw a fit. Instead, her scalp crawled as if she had head lice like one of her little clients. "Hello, Shane?

Are you here?"

The clatter of a door opening sent a skip through her heart. She didn't really know this guy after all. "Hello. It's Rivers. From Memphis."

"Oh, hey." The man's voice was deep. "Sorry. Be right there."

A chill scampered down her spine, and she eyed the front door, tempted to bolt. She could've called to bless him out. But since when had she become so skittish?

Oh, right. Since she'd been shot. Fight or flight was a normal post-traumatic response to the unknown. She could handle this. She was a grown-up. Had been since she'd been forced to become one at thirteen.

A second later, footfalls thudded on the carpeted floors, and a man appeared. He had dark auburn hair, stunning blue eyes, and some sort of designer button-down shirt in a weird shade of purple. Not quite lavender but not mauve either.

"You made it. That's a long drive from Memphis." He grinned and extended his hand.

She couldn't imagine Jordan or her father choosing that color shirt. His smile remained unwavering while his hand waited for hers, and it was becoming awkward. She'd shake his hand, but she was still going to give him a talking to. When she took it, his grip was soft, and he held on.

"I'm so sorry for all you've been through. Jordan was one of the good guys."

Hearing him speak Jordan's name ripped at the scab over her heart that never seemed to heal. She slid her hand from his and steered her thoughts back to why she was here. Jordan's parents had taken her in and treated her like one of their own. His mother, Brooklyn, had often claimed to love her like a daughter. Brooklyn and her sister, Pearl, had taken her shopping for her wedding dress, helped plan the ceremony and reception, picked out flowers and the food—all the things Rivers had wished her own mother could help with, but Mom no longer had the skills. Rivers had looked forward to being a part of Jordan's family. That would never happen now.

Her throat tightened. Nothing could change the past, but she needed to get to the bottom of this gallery situation. After the accident with Jay and Savannah, she sure didn't think allowing addicts to run the place was what Pearl or Brooklyn had in mind.

"Why are you allowing that Cooper guy to use the gallery for his rehab? Good grief, the residents even work there. I don't think Brooklyn or Pearl know about any of this. They couldn't. Not after what happened to Savannah."

Shane's smile wilted. "They don't know, but they never came back. When Jordan's grandmother died, they hired me to take care of the cottage and do what I felt best with the gallery. They didn't want to hear anything about it, and I felt sorry for Jay when he got out of rehab. He was alone, deserted by every member of his family, homeless and jobless."

He paused and stared at her as if what he was saying made sense. "So I let him run the gallery as payment for renting the loft. I didn't see any harm in him using the back studio for art therapy. No one else was painting there after his grandmother passed away." His mouth twisted. "I mean, Jay is an artist, so he knows his stuff—"

"Jay? You mean Cooper...?" A heavy wave of adrenalin swept through Rivers like a levee breaking after a flood. The onslaught heated her face and stole her breath.

Cooper had looked, and felt, almost familiar. Suspicion rolled through her mind. Could he be—?

Shane's eyes widened, and his throat made a gasp, as if he'd just choked on a giant gumball.

The truth blasted through her. It all made sense now. Or it made no sense, rather. "Jay is Cooper. Cooper is Jordan's cousin." Pearl's son. *James Cooper Knight.* Now she remembered only the family used the nickname Jay for Jordan's cousin.

Steam wrestled with shock for a stranglehold in her buzzing mind. Why hadn't she realized the truth right away? She pinned Shane with a hard stare. "You're letting him live and work there? With addicts?"

"Look." Shane took a step toward her, but she backed away. He planted his feet and gestured, palms up. "I know this is…unexpected, but the main thing is that you can sell the gallery. I have a buyer. You can get rid of it if you just look over the offer and sign on the bottom line. The future owner wants to tear the building down and build a Shrimp World franchise. You know with the restaurant, playground, and gift shop? It'll be like the gallery was never even there. Like Jay was never there."

He shuffled through some papers on the dusty counter. "I have a buyer for the cottage too. If you accept the offers, you can forget St. Simons and everything about this place. I'll hire someone to clean out both properties. Let me get the contracts ready. You could leave tomorrow and get on with your life."

Forgetting would be good. Less agonizing. Her thoughts rambled to the cottage, the pictures of Jordan and his family, the little handprints in clay where once flesh and blood had pressed. The familiar ball of sadness twisted in her midsection, the clammy drape of death weighed down her shoulders. Forgetting would not be possible no matter how much she wished for it. Her intellectual side knew she wouldn't have a chance at healing without putting in the required work.

"No," she whispered. "I need to process." She pressed her

fist to her forehead. "You should've warned me, though."

A vision of Cooper from the night before revisited. The brokenness she'd sensed, the worry about her drowning in the surf, the way he gawked when he'd let her out at the cottage. No wonder.

For a split second, she felt a twinge of sympathy for the guy. She'd wanted Jordan to forgive Jay—Cooper. But that was before...

The sound of the mugger's bullet echoed in her mind. The red spewed from Jordan's chest and her own.

She'd wanted to forgive Cooper, but that was before some addict had shot her and Jordan like targets on a video game.

Not so much anymore.

~~~

"You have reached your destination." The electronic voice came through the Stink Bug's speakers as Rivers put the car in park and gripped the steering wheel. Dizziness made it hard to think, and a heaviness weighed down her limbs.

Finally back in the cottage driveway, she couldn't stop the tears streaming down her cheeks. Good grief. Why was it so hard to find her way? Frustration was chewing her up and spitting her out like a rotten fish. She turned off the engine and pushed open the car door. The leaves of the ghostly oaks dripping with moss rustled as a cool wind kicked up.

"Rivers, are you okay?" A soft masculine voice met her ears.

Still in the driver's seat, she turned to see who was near. Dark eyes met hers—expressive, caring—and shells crunched under Cooper's deck shoes when he walked closer.

Fire exploded in her belly. What was *he* doing here? Cooper or Jay or whatever he was going by now... And why did he have to look so compassionate?

40

"I'm fine." Even though the thought of walking into the house exhausted her.

The breeze licked her damp cheeks, reminding her she'd been crying. She ran her fingers across her face to try to clear the evidence.

"I don't think you're fine." Cooper leaned one arm against the door of her VW. "I'm really sorry. I hadn't put all the puzzle pieces together until after you left. Now that I have, I can see why you were upset." His voice exuded sympathy.

"Puzzle pieces?" What did he have to work out? She'd been the one kept in the dark.

"You were engaged to my cousin." More soft words.

"Yes. And I don't think anyone in the family, other than Shane, knows about this cozy little setup you've had going, do they?"

Gaze falling to the ground, he gave a slow shake of his head. "I don't know."

"You don't know? I think Jordan would've mentioned it." Pain overflowed the banks of her heart and spilled out. "Before some drug addict shot him, I think I would've heard about you living in Jordan's gallery and letting *those people* work there."

"I'm sorry. Really." Liquid pooled against his dark lower lashes. "I guess I wanted to think my family was okay with it, and that someday they might forgive me. But I haven't seen any of them for five years." Emotion pressed his lips together as he paused. "I'll find a place to move. Shane keeps the books, but I can show you what I do for the gallery so you or whoever you hire will know how to manage it."

The way he held himself, the regret that slumped his shoulders, those lines near his eyes that hinted at great sorrow, all of it formed a picture in her mind. A young man completely alone after a tragedy. His own fault, but still, she knew how

41

harsh a blow a sudden death dealt.

Her anger receded. Jordan's family hadn't kept up with the property or Cooper. Jordan had said as much. They'd left the tragedy in St. Simons and never looked back, as if they could pretend none of it ever happened. She'd wanted Jordan to deal with the loss, had told him not doing so was unhealthy.

Now she understood how hard her appeal had been.

A drop of liquid rolled to her chin, and she realized she was weeping. Again.

Suddenly self-conscious, she glanced in the rearview mirror. No mascara under her eyes because she hadn't remembered to pack makeup for the trip, but her hair… One piece in the middle stuck straight up. "Oh man, I look like a Teletubby." She pushed her fingers through the wayward strand.

A slight chuckle came from Cooper. "I haven't heard that term in a long time." He sniffed. "What's that smell?"

She pinned him with a sarcastic stare. "The Stink Bug, remember?"

"I won't forget now." He crinkled his nose, and his lashes mashed closed. Dark, long lashes most women would pay to have. They looked masculine on Cooper, though. When they opened, he held out one hand. "Walk on the beach?"

Really?

Dear Lord, help me.

What should she do? Part of her wanted to hear what he had to say. She hadn't expected him to be so kind. Hadn't expected to suddenly feel so needy.

~~~

Cooper waited with his hand out while she deliberated. Offering to walk on the beach with her had just slipped out. Why would she ever want to be anywhere other than a

42

thousand miles away from him?

But something about those cobalt eyes—tears sliding from them down her high cheekbones... And her mouth...

He couldn't even go there, but an overpowering urge to kiss away those tears ached within him. Other than his coworkers and his clients, solitude had been his only close companion since the accident. He'd been around broken men and women on a daily basis, but none had embedded into his heart like this woman.

Rivers.

And in only twenty-four hours. There was something—

"Okay." Soft fingers slid into his, stalling his breathing and ability to think. Her slim form stood and stepped toward him. A sniffle followed. "Lead the way. I seem to stay lost in St. Simons."

"You've been lost?"

"In so many ways," she mumbled.

"Don't you have GPS?" Guiding her with slow steps down the street toward the shore, he stared at her, acutely aware of her hand still in his. Was he supposed to let go now that she'd exited the car? She hadn't let go yet. Her walk was almost a stagger, and she looked so frail and thin.

"She's mean."

"Who's mean?"

"Cruella. She's always like 'Turn around when possible,' or 'Get back to the route.' If I knew the route, I would obviously get back to it."

He couldn't stop the laugh. "Sounds like someone's directionally challenged."

"Cruella's just messing up all the time. Not saying something until it's too late, or telling me too early so I turn too soon."

"I better not let go of you." He lifted her hand and smiled. "You might never be found again." And he'd be blamed, of course.

An adorable wave of pink flushed her face. "We're just crossing the street."

"But if we walk down the beach, do you know where to come back through to get to the cottage?" Because letting go of Rivers was the last thing he wanted to do. The longer he held onto her, the more right it felt to keep her hand protected in his.

Her chin lifted, and she rolled her eyes. "No clue." They neared the water's edge and waves lapped at their shoes. "Which way, leader?"

"I'm not much of a leader." He'd not been called that by anyone outside of the treatment program. "Jordan was always one, though."

Her grip tightened.

Why would he say something so stupid? Some days he wished he still had his lisp. Maybe she wouldn't have understood his idiotic words. And it wasn't like he ever talked to anyone about his family. He slid a glance to check her reaction.

"He was." Her head bobbed. "Tell me about your life with him. And coming here." She made a sweeping gesture with her free hand.

Clouds thickened overhead, and a wind kicked up, as if the ghosts of the past waited to see if he would paint them in a good light. How could he do anything but brag on Jordan? Everyone else in his family had.

"Jordan excelled in everything. Sports, academics. He was good with people of all types. I can't think of one person who didn't admire Jordan. I did."

"Not a surprise." Head tilted, Rivers stared out toward the gray horizon. "I've seen his awards from school and sports. Did you play together on any teams?"

A bitter scoff escaped. "Not hardly. I was born premature, was small and stayed sick a lot as a child. Something about an immature immune system. And I had a terrible lisp, went to speech therapy, and I sure didn't talk to kids my age if I didn't have to. My big growth spurt didn't arrive until I was, like, seventeen, and by that time..." Cooper shrugged off the memories of the teasing and the isolation. "Jordan tried to include me." Not that it helped. "He did what he could."

"I'm sorry." Her gaze roamed his face now, tender and sincere. "I've treated children who've gone through similar situations. It's hard, especially when comparing yourself to a successful sibling, or a cousin in your case."

"Treated?"

"Art therapy. That's my main profession. I also worked in a gallery, taught a few private art lessons, and painted for worship services."

She was a therapist, too? He let that sink in. "That's a lot of jobs for one person."

"Paid off my student loans. Living at home after college helped too. Well, I had moved some of my things into the new house we were going..." Her hand left his, cool air replacing it.

Head leaning forward, she covered her eyes. She swayed as though she might fall, and Cooper caught her around the waist. Her weight was even less than he'd guessed, her loose shirt concealing the fact that she was skin and bones.

"Have you eaten at all?"

"I don't think I remembered to do that." Her voice came out breathy and weak.

"Can I help you back to the cottage? Order pizza delivery?"

"I don't know."

"You've got to take care of yourself, Rivers." Did she have a death wish? Yesterday the sandbar, and not eating today. How long had she been starving herself?

"Okay." She clung to his neck, the scent of lavender disturbing his sanity. What fresh torture was this? He turned them toward the cottage and clomped through the sand, assisting her as best he could. At least they hadn't walked far. Once he reached the porch, he helped her sit on the top step and pulled out his phone. "What kind of pizza do you like?"

"I don't care."

That much was obvious. She didn't care what happened to her anymore. The local pizza parlor's number was programmed into his phone, and he pressed the contact.

Three rings later, a man answered, "Mario's."

"Hey, Devon. It's Coop. You making it?"

"Staying clean."

"Good deal. I need my standard order times two. Different address." Cooper reeled off the house number he hadn't spoken in five years.

"Really? There?"

"Long story. Can you make it quick? I've got a pretty woman fainting here."

"For you, no. For a pretty woman, I'll be right over."

"Thanks." Cooper cut the connection. If only he could support Rivers in some way. Maybe she wasn't an addict, but she was definitely fragile.

Chapter 6

How embarrassing that Cooper had been forced to practically carry her to the porch steps of the cottage. Rivers shoved her third slice of the Canadian bacon and pineapple toward her mouth. Oddly, he had chosen her favorite pizza toppings. Hunger had roared to life once the aroma of pizza hit her nose. Goodness, she was ravenous.

"Um, you might want to breathe between bites." Cooper nudged her elbow.

Still chewing, she rolled her eyes but couldn't help a muffled laugh. Once she swallowed, she pinned him with a look. "You're the one who was worried about me eating, and now you're making fun of me." Something Jordan might have done. She buried that thought away.

"Yeah, well…you're not going to purge or something after all this, are you? I mean—"

"What? No. Gross. I hate throwing up."

His dark brows furrowed. "But, seriously, if you have an eating disorder, I know someone local you can talk to."

"I do not have an eating disorder. Thank you." But she had lost twenty-five pounds this past year. Pounds she hadn't needed to lose. "After…" She hated saying the words shooting and murder and tragedy, hated thinking the thoughts. Her ridiculous bottom lip quivered every stinking time. "After I was released from the hospital, my appetite disappeared. I forget to eat. I'm not trying to lose weight or anything."

"Grief will do that." His expression softened. "Can I see

your phone?"

She took another bite while she deliberated the odd request. He did the same, seeming not to mind the wait.

"My phone's on the console in my car."

A long sigh came from Cooper, and he wiped his fingers on the small napkin that rested on his leg. "I guess I'll brave the Stink Bug then." He stood and strode to the VW as if she'd given him permission.

"What are you doing?"

He ignored her question, and a minute later, he sat at her side once again. "Whew, I survived. Now, do you want to punch the code in or give it to me?"

"You seem to be making yourself at home with my things, so 567326." Give a possible addict access to everything. *Smart.* But maybe being alone in this town and dealing with all this mess was robbing her of sanity. Or maybe Cooper just seemed...kind.

Once he'd cleared the home screen, he opened the clock settings and fiddled with the alarm times, then added a contact. What was he doing?

"Here." He offered the cell to her. "We serve three meals a day at Re-Claimed. I set an alarm for thirty minutes before lunch and dinner. My number's in there if you get lost." He shrugged. "Or make your own meal. Just don't ignore the reminder. You have to eat. You have to take care of you."

That was a tad thoughtful—something she might've suggested to an older client in therapy—but that didn't mean she wanted to eat with a bunch of people in recovery. "What's your position with *that place*?"

"The sober living houses?" One brow lifted suggesting a hint of sarcasm.

"You know that's what I meant."

"Well, at *those places,* I admit clients, counsel them in groups and one-on-one, and in the evenings, I offer art therapy for the men."

"What qualifies you to do all that?"

"Degree. Florida State."

"Hmm." Florida did have an accredited program. A good program actually.

"Oh, crud." He scrambled to his feet and took off toward his Jeep. "I have to go."

She blinked, and he was in his vehicle, in reverse, and gone.

"Okay." That was officially weird.

"High tide, you know," a female voice chirped.

Rivers turned toward the side yard where a woman with salt-and-pepper hair stood. Sort of stood, anyway. She was bent forward, leaning on a metal cane.

"He's one of a crew that takes turns going out at high tide. All that guilt they laid on him." The woman's hazel eyes sparkled above a pair of reading glasses that rested on her sloped nose. "That girl wasn't any saint, but the women in that family wouldn't hear the truth."

"I'm sorry. What?"

"Little Jaybird. That's the nickname Jordy gave him one summer." The woman flapped her free arm toward the street. "Such a sweet child and so talented in the arts. His mother, Pearl, never gave him credit. She just wanted the perfect son like Brooklyn's Jordy. They all doted on that one. Even Stella. And I told Stella she was old enough to know better." The woman clucked her tongue. "A grandmother shouldn't play favorites."

Little Jordy? Brooklyn was Jordan's mother's name. "You're talking about Cooper and Jordan's family?"

"Poor souls. One tragedy after another." Nodding, she

took careful steps forward. "I'm Priscilla Kelly, and I'm younger than I look." A wide smile lifted her cheeks.

Rivers took in the whole picture of the woman before her. Though arthritis twisted her fingers, her face did appear to belong to a woman near Mom's age, maybe a little older, in her early sixties.

"I'm Rivers."

"You bought the cottage?" Priscilla asked.

That ball of hurt twisted in her chest. Bitterness coated her tongue. "Inherited it from my fiancé," Rivers managed.

"Oh, honey, I'm so sorry." Priscilla had finally made it close enough to reach out and touch Rivers. "You were the sweet girl engaged to Jordy."

All Rivers could offer this lady was a single nod. The quiver in her lip was joined by blinding, burning tears.

"I know what it's like to lose someone. My husband passed away, but we had over thirty years together. And our son." A sheen covered Priscilla's eyes too. "It wasn't fair what happened to you."

Exactly what Rivers had wrestled with—what she had banged on the doors of heaven with—for twelve months. If onlys. If only they'd had more time. If only they could have at least gotten to become man and wife. If only they'd had children.

And often…if only she'd died with Jordan.

"Come have tea with me, honey. I'm your next-door neighbor." Priscilla's hand returned to give a comforting pat. "And you need a friend."

Having a friend here did sound nice. "Okay."

Rivers set the pizza box just inside the door and followed the woman's slow steps down the sidewalk to the small house behind what was now hers. Having not really paid attention

50

since arriving, she studied Priscilla's gray stucco ranch. This design also looked left behind from another era, certainly not one of the new builds. The period was unclear, but the metal roof looked new. Was that tin or painted copper?

Priscilla rambled apologies about the yard not being kept up as well as it used to be and the house being dusty. At the door, she turned the knob with an awkward grasp that looked painful. "I should've asked if you're allergic to animals."

"I love dogs and cats." The door opened, and something scurried out from under a side table, running straight toward them. Its beady eyes weren't that of a cat, and its tail belonged to a rodent. "Don't move! A nutria rat's gotten into your house. I'll chase it out."

"No, wait, dear." Priscilla chuckled. "That's Phoenix, my opossum. He's tame, and don't worry, I have a permit as a Glynn County wildlife rehabilitator." Her gaze dropped, and her smile fell away. "My husband was a vet, so people brought us injured animals. I sold the practice when he passed, but a couple of years ago, someone brought this fellow to me. I couldn't say no." The animal stood near their feet.

"I think I could've said no." Rivers took a step back, but the thing kept coming at her.

A second later, soft fur brushed against her ankle. Rivers froze. It made sort of a clicking sound and stood on its hind legs. Small paws with what looked like fingers extended, and the teeth... A shiver shook her shoulders. "How? Why would you still have that?"

Priscilla struggled to bend down and pet the animal. "Opossums are marsupials. One of the only kind in the U.S. He's a sweet boy rescued as a tiny thing from a forest fire. That's how I came up with Phoenix." Her gaze lifted, and she smiled. "Clever, right?"

The name maybe, but keeping the animal in the house? "Sure."

"You'll love him once you give him a chance." Priscilla winked. "Like little Jaybird. How did you two meet anyway? He hasn't been to the cottage since the accident."

For good reason. "The gallery." And the sandbar incident, but she didn't feel like bringing that up. "I'm cleaning out to sell. Or at least I plan to. I'm having trouble getting started."

"It's hard, I know. Give yourself time. You don't want to make big decisions in a rush."

Fatigue weighed on Rivers, her eyelids suddenly heavy. So much to take in. So many decisions. So many sleepless nights. "Can I take a raincheck on the tea? I'm more exhausted than I realized. Maybe I'll try to rest."

"Of course, honey. I'm here whenever you need me." She grinned and lifted one hand. "I'm not much of a weight lifter anymore, but I can come over and find a way to help. I'll even leave Phoenix at home if I have to."

Help would be nice, even just someone being there while Rivers plowed through the past.

"I would love your company." *And yes, leave the weird pet behind.* "We'll talk soon." She managed to lift her lips into a small smile before turning back toward the door.

"Oh, Rivers, wait."

She glanced back. "Yes, ma'am?"

"There's an outdoor storage closet off the back porch. You might find more answers there."

"Answers?"

"The past has light and shadows we don't see without looking from a different perspective."

Chapter 7

The patio door opened with the squeak of old wood and humidity. Rivers blinked back the sleep still blurring her eyes. She'd only drifted off for thirty minutes, but her dream had felt like it stretched much longer.

Water, colors, and tides had swirled and pulled her out to sea. She floated aimlessly until suddenly she was home in Memphis beside the majestic river, its brown, muddy currents flowing strong like they did after a spring storm. The Southern sun warmed her skin, and her paintbrush dabbled blue across the sky of a new canvas. She glanced from the river to her picture, but the colors dripped and changed. The river streaked red, and so did her painting. As crimson as blood, flooding over the banks, rolling and sopping and gushing everywhere.

She'd awoken with a gasp for air. A lot of good it did to try to rest. Now she paced the house, debating where to start working. Priscilla's mention of the outside storage niggled for first place.

Plastic bins of various sizes lined the shelves from floor to ceiling inside the small outdoor closet. Her gut sank like a stone in a pond.

Another overwhelming task. How long would it take to clean this out?

"One thing at a time," she whispered and picked a box. This would do for now. She turned to close the door, but a yellow keyring caught her attention. The words Reliable Storage were printed on the tag.

Well, shoot. Did that mean Jordan's grandmother had another whole storage unit filled with painful memories? Leaning her load against the doorframe, she freed one hand to grab and pocket the key.

Later. She'd deal with it later.

Once she navigated inside the house with her load, she laid the container on the antique walnut dining table. Her stomach fluttered as she opened the lid. What new agony lurked inside, waiting to be aired out?

Photos. All turned face down.

Her hands trembled as her fingers hovered over the top layer. Might as well pick a large one. She flipped over an eight-by-ten. A young boy's face greeted her, maybe eight years old, lips downturned for a school photo. The hair was lighter, but there was no mistaking Cooper's haunting dark eyes. The sadness that shone there pricked at the walls of her heart. He looked like so many of her little clients. She shuffled through the stack finding more of Cooper. One picture in particular pinched at her chest. A Vacation Bible School foam frame with hearts surrounding it, along with the words Jesus Loves Me. Cooper's hair poked up in the back like Alfalfa. A purple bruise underlined his right eye. Had he been in a fight?

If someone had helped him back then, would things have turned out differently?

The past didn't matter now. He'd grown up. Savannah had died because of his addiction and neglect. The damage was done.

So these storage boxes were where Cooper had been banished. She flipped over photo after photo of him. Different ages, different seasons, the same sad eyes. Once she flipped through them all, she replaced the lid and attempted to expel the pitiful images of him that seemed branded into her mind now. What should she do with them? Would he want them back?

She retrieved another container, a large one, and began again. This one held a child's artwork from preschool drawings to preteen sketches. Even at a young age, talent glimmered through. Once he could write, he'd signed his pieces Coop. He'd had an eye for color, composition, texture.

Box after box, she filtered through drawings and paintings he'd composed and art awards he'd won in high school and college. Hours passed, and a crick formed in her neck. She'd quit after just one more search. How had all Cooper's things ended up in this closet? Had his mother sent them here?

The next container's photos were older, some even black-and-white. Many were ancient family photos. There were photos of Jordan's and Cooper's mothers as children, Brooklyn and Pearl standing next to a black-haired man with dark eyes reminiscent of Cooper's, only they lacked the soulfulness. The terse line of the man's mouth was hard, along with the furrow between his brows. At the bottom of the container, a large brown envelope held letters and a journal, the paper old and yellowed.

Should she read them? The letters had been addressed to Stella, Jordan's grandmother, and the journal had to be hers as well. Something about opening them felt intrusive.

But, Stella had left them for some reason. She could have thrown them out a long time ago. Rivers ran her fingers over the cracking cover of the diary. Or was it simply a planner, with appointments written in it?

An obnoxious alarm clanged, interrupting her deliberations. She stood and scanned the boxes. Where had she left her phone, and why was it ringing at this time of day? Or rather evening? Daylight dwindled outside the cottage windows.

After circling the room twice, she spotted the blasted thing and shut it off. Five-thirty?

Why in the world?

Her stomach rumbled in the quiet room. Oh, right. Cooper had set it for dinner. He was correct in saying that she needed to eat, but she didn't have to eat with him and his...clients.

She stared at her phone. Where should she go? Maybe a grocery store? That way she'd have food so when the crazy reminder went off later, she could make a sandwich. Jordan had told her about great barbeque and seafood in St. Simons.

He should be here to eat with her. The bitterness bubbled up again and churned around her insides like a whirlpool sucking her into mire.

Go see.

The impression hit almost audibly. Go see what?

But she knew in her spirit what that nudge meant.

And something about the pictures of that sad little boy pricked at her heart. How did therapists go about helping those lost in addiction? People like her mother. And Cooper.

She had to see for herself what was going on with the gallery and the place Cooper had called Re-Claimed.

~~~

"While there's a lull, let's set up for the evening therapy before dinner. It's almost closing time." Cooper waved the two workers toward the studio in back. By let's, he mostly meant they would do it, and they knew it, knew what to do.

They went to ready the easels and blank canvases, pulled out palettes and paint. These guys would be graduating in only a few weeks. They'd stuck it out and done the work to stay clean a full year. Davis hoped to remain connected in a paying position at Re-Claimed as an alum. He felt called to counsel others. His way of spouting out the truth was rough, but his style worked with some of the more difficult cases. He'd already started classes online which might help temper his approach. Angelo had applied for a position with a ministry to the homeless in Atlanta. He had a heart for those people others avoided. He should be hearing any day if he'd been accepted.

Thank you, God.

Cooper released a long sigh. It had been a hard and holy journey for both of them, but they'd made it to sobriety. Certainly not all of Re-Claimed's clients did. In his line of work, he'd seen recovery, but he'd seen heartbreaking losses too.

There were no good statistics, since people often came and went from programs without staying in contact, but for every person who turned his life around, another was lost back to his addiction.

Blake came to mind. The guy hadn't returned. Cooper tamped down that thought. He couldn't reach everyone, and if he dwelled on the losses, he'd get bogged down in negativity.

The bell over the door jingled, announcing an arrival. Cooper headed to the front of the gallery. Maybe they'd make one last sale today. If they sold a large painting, the gallery should make budget another month.

He blinked, not believing his eyes. But there she was. All cleaned up, wearing faded skinny jeans, boots, and an emerald-colored tunic, as if she'd walked out of a J.Crew ad.

He glanced at the clock on the wall. Yep. Almost dinner time. The alarm must've gone off, and she'd taken him up on the offer.

"Hey." He closed the distance between them.

"Hey." Her forehead took a tentative lift. "I came here because I didn't know where the dinner is served. And I didn't feel like getting lost." She shrugged. "Or eating by myself."

"I wouldn't either." But sometimes he longed for the quiet, true introvert that he was. "Perfect timing. We were about to close. The guys are setting up for therapy." He motioned for her to follow him to the back. Good thing he'd already locked up the cash so they could leave now before she changed her mind.

Once he reached the door to the studio, he pushed it open and waited for her to pass through.

"Hey, Coop, tell Angelo my art don't stink." Davis turned, and the short, stocky man's eyes widened when he saw Rivers. "Well, aren't you hot as a two-dollar pistol?"

Angelo's head pivoted with astounding speed. "Shut up, Davis. You'll scare the nice lady. She doesn't know you from Adam's house cat." A smile lit up his amber eyes. "Welcome. I'm Angelo, and my obnoxious coworker is Davis. He has filter issues, but he's okay, so please excuse his lack of couth."

"I'm Rivers," she squeaked out.

Cooper sucked in a breath. He should've warned everyone to be on their best behavior, but he hadn't expected her to actually come. "She's our guest for dinner. Y'all about done?"

"Sure are, and I'm starving." When was Davis not starving?

"Finish up, and come straight over. I want to introduce Rivers to Gabriella and Kevin before things get too busy."

~~~

And he'd left her gallery in the hands of addicts.

So far, not so good.

Shadows from the overhanging oaks and the haunting sway of the moss swallowed most of the moonlight. Rivers followed Cooper down the dark sidewalk toward a towering square home. From what she could tell, the exterior of the large house was covered with weathered wooden paneling. Light escaped from the downstairs window panes. A breeze kicked up, stirring the humid air and sliding down her neck, teasing her hair.

Up the front porch, she stayed close to Cooper, anxiety poking needles into her stomach. What would this be like? Why had God nudged her to come here?

"It's spaghetti night." Cooper gave a casual smile before opening the door. "You mind Italian again?"

"Anything is fine. Thanks." Already the aroma of garlic reached her nose, and her stomach growled.

"I didn't get a chance to let everyone know who you are, so some might assume…" He paused, searching for the right word. "At first, they might—"

"Assume I'm a new intake?" She got it. "No worries."

"The guys live in this house, the girls live in the one next door. My friends Gabriella and Kevin live with the clients, Kevin here and obviously Gabriella next door, as sort of house parents. They're a brother and sister with a passion for the lost." He turned the knob and waited for her to enter first. "The lost of all kinds."

What did that mean? Rivers swallowed with a dry throat and stepped onto scuffed teakwood floors. A black chandelier hung high above her head in the foyer. The walls had been freshly painted a soothing pale blue. From eye level upward, canvases covered nearly every inch of space.

Cooper's hand rested on the small of her back, and he pointed with his head. "Art therapy. We get a lot of donations to our collection. Some are sold at the gallery. Others that don't sell—would never sell—" He shrugged and raised his brows. "Deck the halls."

Rivers took in the colors and shapes and different skill levels. "It's a nice idea."

"Hey, hey, Coop. Who's your guest?" A vibrant, deep

female voice came from a side hall.

Rivers turned to find two smiling faces greeting her. They had to be the brother and sister, their facial structure looked so similar. Their copper skin and matching light brown eyes shone below short dark hair. Both were tall. The woman had to stand over six feet, and she made a beeline to Rivers, hand extended.

"I'm Gabriella." Her strong fingers clasped tight. "And you look hungry. I hope you're staying for supper. It's spaghetti night."

"I heard." Rivers found herself smiling at Gabriella. The woman had an earnestness that drew Rivers in right away. "I plan to eat with y'all."

"I wanted Rivers to learn more about our ministry from you two." Cooper made a broad sweep with his hand. "About what we do here. She's the owner of the gallery."

Kevin's head snapped toward him, his forehead contorting. "What?"

Cooper waved him off. "I'll explain later."

"I'll show her around." Hooking arms with Rivers, Gabriella led her down a narrow hall. "You guys, go take care of business," she called over her shoulder.

Gabriella took Rivers into a room that probably once had been a large living area but now looked to serve as a chapel of sorts.

They stopped and Gabriella leveled a heartfelt gaze on Rivers. "I'll share my story if you'll share yours."

Chapter 8

The last thing Rivers wanted to do was share her story. Every nerve in her body recoiled, and Gabriella seemed to sense her apprehension.

"How about, I'll share mine. You wait until you're ready." The tall, muscular woman gave her arm a light pat. "This ministry—we call it Re-Claimed—started when Kevin and I were in a deep place of grief. A place we never wanted to be. A place we never would have chosen for ourselves…yet, God called us to it." Gabriella used her free hand to swipe a tear that clung to her lashes. "Sorry, I cry every single time. Let's sit." She pointed to a couple of folding chairs.

Rivers complied without speaking. There was nothing to say. She understood all too well the kind of place Gabriella had found herself.

"My baby brother and I played basketball all of our lives. Won scholarships to Georgia." She let out a chuckle. "Couldn't get rid of that pest—Kevin—always wanting to meet my friends." She sucked in a deep breath. "He fell hard for my roommate Tamara. I didn't mind that much, really. They made a good couple." Her head shook, and her gaze drifted. "One winter, we got one of those unusual Georgia snows. A deep one too. We all went out, like college students do, found a hill, and had some makeshift sleds. Tamara smacked into a pine tree. The vertebra in her neck were injured. That's when everything went south."

A pause hung between them like dense morning fog, as if

Gabriella were waiting for a response.

Rivers shifted in the metal chair. "I'm sorry." Did she have to say more? She knew how quickly one moment in time could change everything—could start a waking nightmare. Her mother's accident. Jordan.

"Surgery followed." Gabriella began again. "Excruciating pain. Oxy and other meds were prescribed. The Tamara we knew and loved changed into a completely different person. She'd never been a partier, but once they started her on those drugs, she'd do or say anything to get more." A long sigh followed as she collected herself. "We tried to get her help, but when Tam couldn't get the Oxy, she switched to heroin. Cheaper and easier to get." Massaging long fingers over her forehead, Gabriella groaned. "Only a year after her surgery, her body was found in a drug house. Fentanyl had been laced into the heroin."

"I'm sorry." Rivers grasped for something more to say. "Fentanyl?"

"A synthetic, even stronger than heroin. Deadly." Abruptly, Gabriella stood and whooshed out a breath. "That's enough sadness. Let's go stir up some hope. That's why we started this mission. I became a nurse, and Kevin's a licensed therapist. Not all of the residents make it, but some do."

Following her lead, Rivers rose. One thing still gnawed at her worse than her empty belly. "But how did Cooper become part of your ministry?"

"Coop?" Gabriella leveled a wide-eyed gaze her way. "You don't know?"

"I haven't known him long."

"Okay." Gabriella gave a slow nod. "He won't mind me saying, because he's open about it. He was our first intake. Our first success story."

~ ~ ~

How long was Gabriella going to drag Rivers around? No telling what she was saying, or even worse, asking the poor girl.

Cooper checked his watch for the fifth time. There was a good reason why he and Kevin had dubbed Gabriella with the nickname Gabby.

The residents had the places set, the food arranged, and were prepared to take seats around the dining tables. The first year in this house, Kevin had remodelers move the center wall over a few feet so all evening meals could be served under this roof. Breakfast and lunch, the ladies and men were separate, but one family-style meal a day allowed Kev and Gabby to have time together.

"And now that you've seen this side of the center, let's eat." The rich, deep tone of Gabriella's voice flowed into the room, smooth and joyful as usual.

Cooper searched for a view of Rivers. Yep. From the off-kilter press of her lips and the way her eyes darted from person to person, assessing them like a scared rabbit, ready to bolt at the first whiff of danger, he knew she was freaking out inside. Inviting her had been another of his stupid ideas.

Idiotic move number five-zillion-one.

He had to rescue her. Scrambling to her side, Cooper placed a protective hand on her back. "You making it okay?"

One of her slender shoulders lifted. "I'm still standing."

"Attention, brothers and sisters of Re-Claimed." Davis clanged a spoon against a water glass and spoke in another ridiculous attempt to sound like a reverend. He took his leadership role a little bit over the top. Or a lot over the top. "The time has come for you to claim a seat, and I will bless this humble but scrumptious ethnic meal of spaghetti and meatballs we are about to eat. Often wrongly attributed to the

63

country of Italy, by the way, when its meatball and pasta origins are American."

Something about Davis's stupid speech made Cooper laugh.

Everyone sat, but Davis stayed on his feet and continued. "I hope you all had a blessed day at work and that you found something to be thankful for. You know, when you offer up praise, you pour heaping coals on the enemy."

He motioned dramatically. "Don't ever be fooled. You are in a legitimate war. Satan prowls like a lion hoping to devour you. Satan will keep coming. He wants to scare you, to discourage you, to rob you of hope." His voice rose in volume and strength. "But don't you quit." He raised his fist. "Resist the enemy. Your God is a Mighty Warrior. He has won the victory already. Draw near to God. Quote the scripture in Jesus' name, and cry out to heaven for help."

He pointed to each person. "Lean on each other. Get on the J train, and let your freak flag fly—instead of staying in your train wreck. Be honest, people."

Taking a deep breath, he sat. "Now, bow your heads." Before they'd all complied, he continued, "Oh, Lord, thank You for Your bountiful blessings and this food and this place and the people who contributed money so we can be here, and for Gabby and Kev and Coop for working so very hard for us. I mean really hard. And for those who prepared the meal. Amen." Clapping his hands, Davis made a silly grin, similar to a donkey in a petting zoo begging for a carrot. "Did I ever tell y'all about how the seven worst years of my life were in high school?"

"That joke was old the first time you told it." Kevin rolled his eyes. "Let's eat." He lifted a bowl of noodles and held it toward Rivers. "Cooper has a guest, and everyone needs to stay on their best behavior." One side of his mouth quirked up. "Make that better than your best behavior."

All eyes turned to Rivers, and she shrank in her chair, the tendons in her neck visibly tightening.

Cooper took the bowl. "Want me to scoop some out for you? Say when." He dropped clumps of pasta onto the plate. Someone hadn't known to add a bit of sauce or olive oil to keep the noodles from sticking together. This meal might not look so appetizing after all.

"Save some for the rest of us." Davis again. "Although she does look like she needs a little meat on her bones. You…" He pressed his lips together, apparently realizing he needed to shut down whatever he was about to say. Maybe he'd learn.

The sauce came their way, and Rivers took it, so Cooper threw a pile of pasta on his own plate.

"You know, I don't get it." Davis was on a roll tonight. "Why do the ladies wear short hair or all that long, boring straight hair? I wish the eighties would come back. I'd love seeing some eighties hair. I mean some big, long hair all teased up high. Rapunzel, Rapunzel, tease up your golden locks."

"Aren't you a party pants tonight?" Gabriella laughed. "You gonna sport a mullet then?"

"I could pull it off." Davis quirked a brow.

"I have some chemically dependent hair." A newer resident named Britt chimed in. "Not sure I could tease it, spray it, and keep bleaching it this blond without it all falling out."

"I could pull off some big hair back in my day." Their oldest female resident, a meth addict, spoke up. She was the most recent intake but seemed to have settled well into the group so far. "No color here. I'm a natural redhead."

"That's a big ole baloney sandwich right there," Davis

spouted, and everyone laughed. Maybe even a snicker came from Rivers.

"Hey, hush your mouth. I have to cover a little gray now that I'm a woman of maturity." Her chin lifted in mock defiance.

The volleys continued around the table, good-natured teasing, thank the Lord. Because, some nights—okay, a lot of nights—supper wasn't this peaceful.

~~~

These people weren't so terrible, but she knew firsthand the havoc they could wreak in a person's life. Rivers plucked up the last meatball on her plate with her fork and shoved it in her mouth. She had been hungry. Maybe even making-up-for-lost-pounds-hungry, because this was the best marinara she'd ever tasted, though she'd almost choked on a clump of noodles. Still...she was ready to leave. Emotionally spent.

She turned to find Cooper watching her. He'd stayed close once Gabriella brought her to the dining room. Been protective. For that, she was thankful. Her thoughts drifted, and for a moment she imagined what he would have been like when he'd first become a client here. Alone. Addicted. Everyone in his family hating him. His own fault, of course, but still. A tiny part of her heart pricked at the image it formed in her mind.

"You okay?" he asked.

"Tired."

"I was wrong to invite you here so soon. I could've taken you out to the Barbeque Shack or out for seafood."

"You aren't responsible for me. Or my meals." Although he seemed to have rescued her a couple of times already. "I think I'll take off. Gabriella can show me the other house later in the week."

"Right. You should rest."

Her brows raised. "Are you going to start telling me when to go to bed now? Set another alarm?"

Light flickered across his dark brown eyes as a smile crinkled the edges of his temples. "If necessary." He stood and pulled back his chair. "I'll show you out."

"No." Her answer came out too firm, but she didn't need him to baby her. "Finish your dinner."

He ran his fingers through his hair and seemed at a loss for what to say. "Okay. See ya." A momentary contorted twist of his lips hinted that she'd hurt his feelings.

She didn't owe him anything, though. Already she'd gone out of her way to understand what was going on and why. Wrenching away any guilt, she stood and circled her chair. "Thank you all for a delicious meal, but I have to leave."

"What?" Davis practically shouted. "You haven't had any peach cobbler yet. I spent all day slaving in the kitchen and that's the thanks I get?"

"Be quiet, Davis." Gabriella waved him off. "Boy, you make coffee nervous." She turned her focus toward Rivers. "Thank you for coming, and I hope we see you again. You're welcome any time."

"Right. Thanks." Rivers made her exit before anyone else could try to talk her into staying. The people here brought to mind the kids she'd worked with in the past. She often wondered how they'd turn out as adults. So many of them had endured trauma. Some were bound to deal with addiction, despite receiving therapy. A screaming reality bludgeoned her. What about those children who live through ordeals of suffering or abuse and never have anyone help them sort through and process those emotions?

Outside, the moon struggled to glow through a thin veil of

clouds. Still pondering, she made her way down the porch steps and along the sidewalk, back toward the gallery.

In the darkness, she shivered, but not from the chill. Someone was here. Her heart kicked up a notch. A shadowy figure approached from behind an oak, a slow and unsteady march.

Every fiber of her being froze. She couldn't move, couldn't breathe. Her mind buzzed and fogged. She was in Memphis again. The blood. The searing pain.

The hulking form stepped into the pale light spilling from the windows.

Heart thudding, Rivers blinked to clear her head.

A man...carrying a woman.

"Need help," he murmured.

He clumsily plodded closer. "Hurt," he slurred.

No gun pointed at her. She was in St. Simons, not Memphis.

Someone was hurt.

They needed help.

Reeling herself back to the present, she forced air into her rigid chest and took slow steps closer. Close enough to touch the young woman, a pretty girl in her twenties, light brown hair falling across her face. The girl's skin was cold and clammy. Was she breathing at all?

"What's happened?"

"Needs help."

Clearly the man was too far out of it to give a good answer. "What's her name?"

"Star Youngblood."

Rivers patted the girl's face. "Star, can you hear me?" Was she alive?

The guy staggered. A ring of dried saliva circled his lips.

His eyes alternated between closing and bugging open wide. They looked unseeing though, unable to focus. Had this man hurt her?

"You have to come inside Re-Claimed."

His eyes blinked and then stared forward.

"Come inside now."

She nudged him toward the house. If she ran ahead to get Cooper, would the man follow, or would he leave? She could run faster than he could, and the woman needed help. Rivers took off and hoped the man wouldn't disappear. She jogged down the sidewalk and flung open the door.

"Cooper!" She sprinted into the dining room and slid to a stop. All eyes turned to her.

"Cooper, help!" she screamed. "There's a man out here. Hurry."

Cooper jumped up so fast his chair clattered over. He was at her side, his hand slipped in the crook of her arm. "Are you okay? Did he hurt you?"

"I'm fine." She pointed out the door. "They need help."

The man stepped under the porch light. "Something happened. Needs help."

That's when she noticed the blood.

Chapter 9

"Come this way. Lay her down on the couch." Despite his racing heart, Cooper fought to keep his tone calm as he steered the couple toward the living room. The girl didn't look good. "Kevin, call 911. Gabriella, can you make sure Rivers is okay?" He glanced over his shoulder at Rivers once more. Her complexion had drained to the color of cold ashes.

Blake had finally come back, but not the way Cooper had hoped. Blood dripped from the woman who he assumed to be Star. She was young and pretty, the way Blake had described, but apparently taking care of her hadn't gone well. Kind of hard to take care of someone else when he couldn't take care of himself.

They reached the couch, and Blake gently laid his girlfriend there.

"Is this Star? What happened to her?" Cooper knelt at the woman's side.

"I found her like that behind the bar." Voice quivering, Blake bent over, hands on his knees. "It's my fault. She was looking for me."

St. Simons usually didn't have this kind of violence, but maybe a dealer from over in Brunswick had brought Blake's drugs. Something went bad.

Blood oozed and formed a dark stain on Star's ripped shirt. "Star, can you hear me?"

No answer.

Footsteps joined them, and Cooper turned to find

Gabriella with Rivers close behind.

"I'll do what I can until the ambulance arrives." Gabriella nudged his shoulder. "Get me some clean towels and the first aid kit, Coop."

"Got it," Kevin called from the doorway, where the other residents huddled, faces and eyes straining to get a glimpse of the drama.

Gabriella bent over the girl and carefully rolled back the bottom of her shirt to reveal the injury. A small tear in the skin just below the ribcage was all they could see, but blood trickled from the gash. This wasn't the first time Cooper had thanked the Lord that Gabriella was a nurse.

"I'm hoping that's not too deep. We'll need sterile non-stick gauze until the medics arrive." She looked Star over, finding bruises and scrapes. "Appears she was in a fight, but the other injuries aren't bad." Her attention turned to Blake. "Are you hurt?"

Looking down at his feet, Blake shook his head.

"What's she on?" Cooper asked. That would definitely make a difference on how medical staff could treat her.

Blake's eyes shifted back and forth as if he were debating whether to tell. Or maybe trying to remember.

Cooper stood and tried to connect his gaze with Blake's. "I know you care about her, and we want to help her. We need to know what she was using."

"Xanax, weed, alcohol." His head tilted as he slurred out the words. "That's usually it. Can't be sure."

No, they couldn't be sure. Cooper nodded. He knew from personal experience, there were points when some addicts could become garbage disposals, pretty much taking whatever they could find.

Star groaned, and Rivers knelt near her head. "Help is

71

coming," she whispered. "Just hang on." She caressed Star's forehead and cheek while Gabriella attempted to clean the area around the wound. "We're going to take care of you."

A lump formed in Cooper's throat. Rivers was obviously a natural caregiver, despite her own trauma.

Red lights flashed through the side window, and a moment later, they all stepped back to let the emergency personnel do their work.

Cooper made his way to Rivers. "Are you okay? That had to be scary finding them out there, and sometimes one trauma reopens old—"

"I'm fine." Avoiding his gaze, she looked anything but fine. She ran her fingers through her short blond hair until it almost stood straight up, and she craned her neck to see what was going on with the girl.

After checking vitals and airways, the emergency workers laid Star on a gurney and strapped her in place. Gabriella told them what she knew, which wasn't much. Kevin stood with his hand on Blake's shoulder speaking in low tones, hopefully convincing him to stay here and check in.

The gurney clicked as they raised it, and Rivers approached one of the EMTs. "I want to go with her."

"You'll have to follow us."

Nodding, Rivers trailed behind them, keys in hand.

Cooper caught her arm. "Let me drive you. The hospital's not far, but they'll take her off the island, and it's dark out." And her navigational skills seemed questionable under normal circumstances.

She paused, considered his offer, and then nodded. "Let's go."

This woman had more gumption than he'd given her credit for. With all she'd been through, he'd expected her to fall apart.

Any minute, she'd probably fall apart. Rivers rubbed her palms up and down on the legs of her jeans, adrenaline still coursing through her body. She took deep breaths in through her nose and slowly expelled them through her lips.

Ahead of Cooper's Jeep, the ambulance's red light bounced off the low-lying fog that was blurring their view of the road. Thank God he'd offered to drive. It was black outside, and they'd crossed several bridges with the murky mist making visibility rotten. If she'd lost the ambulance at a red light, Cruella-GPS would likely have sent the Stink Bug into a swamp.

And she'd never admit it to Cooper, but seeing the blood streaming from Star had reopened a vision of her own nightmare. But she'd been living with it every day since the shooting.

"It's nice of you to do this, but you don't have to." Cooper kept his eyes focused on the road.

"She doesn't have anyone else that we know of. That Blake guy can't do it." Though he couldn't see her, she shrugged as if he could. "I don't know. She almost looked like a child lying there. I have a heart for children dealing with trauma." At least she had in the past.

"I bet you're an amazing therapist with kids." He blew out a long sigh. "When she wakes up, you may not find her to be so...childlike."

"Yeah." She scoffed. "She's going to be hurting and in withdrawal. Not a great combo." Memories of her mother's early recovery surfaced. The anger and confusion that followed a traumatic brain injury left no emotion untouched. Her mother's nightmares woke Rivers and her dad off and on for years.

"You've worked with addicts?"

"Just my mother."

"Oh."

"She's not anymore." She bit her lip and debated how much to spill. What did it matter? She didn't have to worry about impressing anyone here. "After her car accident and traumatic brain injury, she couldn't drink. Couldn't even remember that she used to binge."

"Rivers, I'm sorry." They reached a stop light, and his gaze found her. "You've been through too much."

Her abs tightened. She hadn't asked for his pity. "Her situation kept me from ever drinking or taking other substances."

"Something else you and Jordan had in common."

An ache spiked in her chest. That had been one of their many commonalities. That and their faith. Their desire to wait until marriage. Their love for the arts.

She'd known the only reason her parents had married was because of their unplanned pregnancy with her. The two were polar opposites. Her mother had been an all-business, high-dollar architect by day, a drunk by night. Her father was the inner-city school teacher who championed the rights of the downtrodden and cared nothing about money. They couldn't have been more different. A few dates when they were in their mid-twenties had created Rivers.

No. She knew God had created her. He'd given her a purpose and a heart for children, like her father. And she'd never once seen her dad drink. He took responsibility for everything in their little family. He'd recommitted to his faith and had been her pillar of strength.

"Rivers?" Cooper's gentle voice wound around her memories. "I asked, what are you thinking?"

Oh. "I was thinking how great my dad is. He's had more than his share to deal with."

"What's he like?"

"He took me to a million dance practices, came to every recital with a bouquet of roses, never missed an opportunity for us to participate at church. While Mom spent late hours at *the office*." She made air quotes around the last word.

"So she wasn't really at the office?"

"Maybe, but not alone. The night of her car accident, another man from her firm was in the car with her."

"That's a harsh blow." Cooper flipped on the blinker and slowed to turn into the parking lot. Once he found an empty spot, he slipped the Jeep in and shifted the gear to park. He reached out, his hand hovering over hers, hesitant, then he covered her fingers. "But your father was there for you?"

His touch both soothed and electrified her. What madness was this?

She closeted that question for later. "Always. Well, until the accident." The disappointment of the past coiled around her chest like an old fishing line caught on hidden debris. It pulled tight and squeezed, reminding her why she'd sheltered her heart so often. She'd buried her emotions, but they seemed to always slip into her art. "We both had to take care of Mom. She had to relearn how to do everything. Speaking, walking...the bathroom. She became the child."

"And you became the adult." He gave her hand a gentle squeeze. "Do you have any good memories with her?"

Typical counselor move. Try to incite the positive. "Of course." She chuckled. "She was funny, beautiful, loved to sing and dance." She felt her lips lift into a smile. "A lot of nights we danced to eighties tunes for hours. Still do, but we have to be careful. She gets dizzy. One side of her body is weaker than the other." Rivers raised one finger. "Oh, she loved art. Like me."

A light flickered outside, reminding her why she came. "I need to go see where they have Star."

"I'll stay, too." Cooper's gaze roamed her face, unnerving her.

"You have a job, people who need you." She managed a smirk. "And my gallery to tend." Maybe that would get him to leave.

"Okay, bossy boss." A smile colored his voice. "I'll just stay until we find out how serious it is. One of us will come get you later."

"But—"

"The others will want a report." He released her hand, opened the door, and stepped out of the vehicle.

It seemed she wasn't getting rid of James Cooper Knight any time soon.

Chapter 10

No more excuses for Rivers to stay away from Cooper in the waiting room. She'd gone into the hall, called home, and spoken to both of her parents. Her father had promised they were fine. Then she'd checked in with the substitute taking care of her clients in therapy and waded through her email. She'd even texted Jordan's mom. Brooklyn was still suffering, but of course, it was no wonder. She had lost both of her children way too soon. That kind of loss had to seem like a sea of grief too wide to cross.

How did a woman anchor her faith when faced with so much pain? Rivers swallowed back tears. Before she'd lost Jordan, she'd thought she had the answers. Now she struggled to feel safe in her own skin and cling to a scrap of faith.

Brooklyn's twin sister, Pearl, had come to stay with her after Jordan's loss. It was so strange to think of Pearl as Cooper's mother, to think of Mr. Knight as Cooper's father. From the way the family had spoken of Cooper—Jay—one would think he was some sort of hoodlum. Hardly the man she'd spent the past couple of days around.

An elderly woman scraped by using an old walker for balance. The lady needed some tennis balls on the front legs so the contraption would move more smoothly. Rivers tisked. If she were in Memphis, she would find a way to get some.

But she was here.

Rivers forced her feet back toward the waiting area. At the door, she waved her hand below the sanitizer station. The cool foam squirted onto her palm, and she rubbed her hands together. A habit from when her mother had been in and out of the hospital for multiple surgeries.

A young couple milled about at the snack machines just inside the entrance, trying to choose between the unhealthy selections.

Her gaze fell to Cooper across the room. He was bent forward, elbows on knees, chin propped in his palms. His dark hair hung down and shadowed his brows. With his eyes closed, his lashes touched the olive skin below.

Her breath hitched. He was a beautiful creation.

A current of emotion rolled through her, and a picture formed in her mind. If only she had canvas, oils, and brush that would work together to capture this moment.

Crazy thoughts.

What had it been like for Cooper growing up? A late bloomer, while Jordan shone so brightly. That light probably both blinded Cooper and overshadowed everything he'd tried to do. He seemed to be a tender soul who'd ended up caught in the murky waters of life in a fallen world.

More crazy thoughts.

She blinked them away and slipped into the seat beside him.

Though she'd tried to be quiet, he shifted and opened his eyes. "Everything okay? You were gone a while."

"Just checked in with my family and my substitute at the clinic."

"Your substitute?" His voice was the usual low, gentle tone.

"My friend has been filling in." Getting much more than she'd bargained for. "She's agreed to stay one more month while I handle the properties here." It had seemed another thirty days would be more than she needed when the trip was planned. But now...

"Right. You intend to clean out and sell the properties." The corners of his lips turned down. The plan that would crush his current setup. "Someone's taking your place at work for a month?"

"Actually over a year. My friend agreed to help until I could get myself together enough to counsel the kids. She had no idea she'd still be doing it. So I have to decide whether I'll go back to work as an art therapist or if they should hire someone else permanently."

"What have you been doing since the...incident?"

Was she really ready to share so intimately with him? She stared at the bland poster framed on the far wall. "I stayed at home in bed for a good while. Dealt with paperwork that is demanded when someone dies." Bitterness coated her tongue, and that dense layer of gloomy fog lay heavy over her faith once again. Death seemed so final, despite what she'd always believed. A crimson void of emptiness where once her beloved had been so vibrant and alive.

"I'm sorry." His hand wrapped around hers, warming her chilly fingers. And maybe her heart for a brief moment.

"Eventually, I worked some. I led tours, did paperwork, checked people in at the front desk of the museum." She caught her lip between her teeth for a moment. "I just couldn't counsel others while my own emotional state was such a mess and my faith so wobbly. I couldn't paint in our church's worship gatherings anymore either. My heart seemed like it had become a swirling mass of black."

"How is your faith now?" The pad of his thumb made light circles on her knuckles, sending mini ripples straight to that achy place in her chest.

"I picture my faith floating over a deep abyss, barely hanging on by a golden strand. I mean, I believe in God, but I never saw something like that coming." She sucked in a shaky breath. "I thought my mom's accident was our cross to bear." She should stop talking, but somehow the truth wanted to spill out. "I don't know how much more God expects me to take. My heart feels absent, like I'm a deserted shell."

"He's still with you. You know that, right?" His other hand cupped hers now, too, and squeezed. He shifted to face her, his gaze fervent. "He hasn't deserted you, and He won't. This may or may not be the hardest chapter of your story, but He loves you. His plans are still good."

"That's the thing. My mind knows all the ways to heal. My church upbringing gives me all the right words. But I'm floundering when I try to get the messages into my broken heart. My spirit keeps wrestling with the ancient truths I've always believed."

"Wrestling is okay." He squeezed her fingers. "It proves you're alive."

"Yeah." But maybe the problem was she didn't want to be.

"Family of Star Youngblood?" a man's voice called into the room.

"We're her friends." Cooper gave her hand one more squeeze then stood to face the doctor, leaving cool air where his warmth had been beside her.

The doctor gave them a suspicious once-over.

"Actually, I'm Cooper Knight, a therapist from the Re-Claimed sober living house where she was brought with the injury." He nodded toward Rivers. "And this is Rivers. She's an art therapist who has agreed to sit with Star. We don't know if Star has family."

With a nod, the physician motioned for them to come into

the hallway. Once they were out of earshot of other families, he stopped. "Star was stabbed, maybe with a screwdriver. She was lucky the wound didn't go too deep. I was able to get it closed. She also has some bruising where she fought her attacker." The doctor folded his arms over his chest. "I hope she'll agree to get help once we release her."

"When will that be?" Rivers couldn't imagine the terror of being stabbed. Being shot from a distance had been horrendous enough.

"A day, maybe two, as long as there's no sign of infection."

That quickly. Hospitals didn't keep patients long anymore.

"What about pain management?" Cooper seemed to be moving into his addiction counselor role.

"We can try to avoid the opioids, if that's what you mean. We'll try Tylenol through her IV at first. See how it goes."

Rivers let her fingers run across the indention in her shoulder. The searing pain she'd endured after her surgery had been rough. This doctor had said Star's wound wasn't bad, but it would hurt while she healed. The area would need to be kept clean, and Star would need to rest.

"Are you sure you're okay staying here with her?" Cooper asked.

Would she be okay? Not necessarily. Rivers shifted her feet.

"You have so much on you already." Cooper's warm hand captured hers.

Nothing about this trip had been easy, but helping this girl was more important than her comfort.

"I want to stay."

~ ~ ~

He really had to stop touching Rivers. Cooper slid his hand away, immediately missing the contact. But something about her bravery in the midst of her own fragile situation drew him to her even more.

Like a moth to a blazing inferno or a match to TNT.

He needed to go to a meeting later. Not thinking about Rivers might be as hard as his previous addiction. Cooper pressed his palm to his forehead while the doctor gave her a few instructions for the night ahead.

Any other single woman in the world, and these emotions stirring within him might make sense. But this was Jordan's girl, for goodness' sake.

First, she'd never be interested in a guy like him, and second, even if she were, it would be another savage blow to his aunt, uncle, and his parents. They already hated him.

A month. Thirty days or less.

Rivers was leaving after that. He could white-knuckle his ridiculous attraction for that long, then sink himself deep into some heavy-duty counseling. That and look for a new place to live, hold art therapy, and sell paintings.

"Do you have a headache, Cooper?" Rivers stared at him, searched his face, her blue gaze concerned, kind.

"Something like that." Not a lie. His brain was scrambled.

"You go back. They're sending her to a room now." Her head cocked to one side. "And didn't you say something about art therapy with the guys tonight?"

He gave a slow nod. Yeah. He should go, but something about her gaze was like a whirlpool sucking him in. His feet took him about an inch from her. "Call me if you need anything. Or if you change your mind." His hands lifted, but he commanded them to stop before he touched her again. "No matter what time."

"I will." Her voice was soft, barely above a whisper.

"I... I should..." The hospital's bright overhead lights

shimmered in her flaxen hair, which hung in loose strands around her face, framing blue eyes the color of the Caribbean on a clear day. What was it he'd been saying he should do?

"You can go. Really." Her brows raised as she gave him a soft nudge on his shoulder.

His fingers threaded through the front of his hair. "Right. Going." He turned to leave, realizing as soon as he took a step that the exit was behind her, not the way she'd sent him. Of course, Rivers was the one with no sense of direction. Pivoting back, he restarted on the correct course.

"What? I'm fine."

"It's actually"—he pointed toward a red exit sign beyond her—"behind you."

A giggle slipped through her lips when she turned. "Sorry. I—"

"I know." Smiling, he passed her, hands stiff at his side.

No looking back, either, bro.

Now he was talking to himself. Even more than usual.

Half an hour later, Cooper stood in the studio in front of eleven men who were already armed with easels, brushes, and acrylic paints. Earlier in the day, he'd formulated his agenda. But with thoughts of Rivers screwing up his mind, he struggled to remember what that game plan had been.

The great thing was that the creative process allowed his clients to express their emotions, often even in the most closed-off cases. Using art to communicate what was bottled up inside somehow felt less invasive than talk therapy.

He might as well begin with an old standby. "Let's explore color with abstract paintings. Use a pencil and draw off a few sections on the canvas. Think of your addiction as a color. Picture your sobriety as another color. Where do they meet? Where does God fit into the picture? What color represents

Christ? His sacrifice? Imagine a shade for forgiveness for those who've wronged you, and another for forgiveness you receive from God for yourself, your mistakes."

A few nods answered him. The group was no doubt somber because of the earlier trauma. Most of these guys had seen violence and tragedy, so a new encounter often dredged those memories to the surface. Another reason he'd been so worried about Rivers. What would the trauma do to her?

He should say a few words of encouragement. "Tonight was hard. We've all been in those dark, dangerous places, but praise God, we've been given another chance. So have Star and Blake. Her injury isn't too serious, according to the doctor." Pacing, he said a silent prayer. *God, give me the words they need to hear.* "Don't look inside and get depressed, look up and see a powerful God. Tell every big-mouthed enemy voice whispering those old lies in your ears to get gone in Jesus' name! Say it out loud if you need to."

Some in the group spoke the command.

Cooper's passion and volume rose. "There is power in speaking His name. Sing praises, even when it makes no sense. More power. And when nothing's working, go to the Lord and say, 'Search me and see if anything is keeping me from hearing you.'"

"Amen." Kevin and Davis chimed in. The others nodded.

"Okay, that's my sermon." Cooper removed his phone from his pocket and held it up. "Y'all want a playlist while you paint?"

No one answered.

"Playlist it is." He opened one with his favorite worship bands and turned on the Bluetooth speaker.

Near the back wall, Kevin sat on the newbie couch with Blake. Frequently, first-timers preferred to watch, but in

Blake's case, it didn't really matter what he wanted. The guy probably couldn't hit the canvas with a brush if they gave him one. His heavy eyes had become almost slits but would sometimes pop open as he mumbled something that sounded like Star. Or Thar or Gar. When clients slurred, it often brought back memories of his own lisp.

Man, he'd hated the way his stupid tongue had twisted. He'd hated being called little Jaybird too. It reminded him of his lonely childhood, so he'd ditched the nickname Jordan had given him when they were kids and taken his middle name. No one had called him Jay since elementary school other than his immediate family.

"Coop, you look like the kid on the front of a Sour Warheads package." Davis laid his brush aside, walked over, and held out his arms, a goofy grin covering his face. "Does someone need a hug?"

"Don't even start with your shenanigans." Yeah, they offered hugs at times, but Davis was messing with him.

"Let's go outside and chew the fat a minute. My first layer of paint is drying, and I want this one to be my masterpiece." Davis motioned with his head toward the door.

Was Davis having issues, or would the powwow be about tonight's incident? "Kev, you all right for a few?" Cooper called.

"Not going anywhere. Take your time." Kevin's brows rose as he pointed a gaze on Blake, whose head bobbed, fighting sleep.

"All right. Let's talk." Cooper led Davis out the door onto the small porch behind the gallery. "What's happening?"

"So tonight was a little bit of scary town, right?" After pulling a pack of gum from his pocket, Davis popped a couple of pieces in his mouth.

"You shaken up?" Davis didn't look it.

"Nah, not me. But your little woman seemed to be." He blew a bubble the size of a Ping-Pong ball, then popped it. "I don't mean to get up in your grill or break man-code, but you got eyes for that Rivers girl. It's as obvious as a dead skunk on a highway, and I'm worried. Is she in recovery?"

Nice. What a gross metaphor. And the attraction was that obvious? "She's not." Cooper shot Davis a hard look. "Remember when I asked your opinion? Yeah, me neither."

"Oh, is this one of those never-miss-an-opportunity-to-keep-my-mouth-shut things?" He crossed his eyes and gave a sideways grin.

A hearty laugh tumbled out of Cooper. He'd been a tad hard on Davis. The guy was just doing what he'd been taught to do. Be honest. Ask difficult questions. "Sorry. You're on track. It's just that Rivers isn't what you think." He raked his fingers through his hair. "Between you and me—and Kev and Gabby, of course—Rivers was Jordan's fiancée. She inherited the gallery and came to sell it."

"Whoa. I did not see that one coming." His head bobbed. "Harsh news about the gallery, and you have a thing for her too. Your cousin's—"

"Shut up, dude." Cooper massaged his temples as if it would do any good. "I never said I had a thing for her."

"Didn't have to, but I'll keep that part between me and the Big Man Upstairs when I pray for your gooey-eyed self." He clucked his tongue and mumbled under his breath, "But it's as obvious as a dead sku—"

"Enough with the skunk." Cooper looked up. Please don't let it be that obvious to Rivers. He'd need to come to terms with his attraction before he messed things up big-time.

Chapter 11

There was nothing quite like the sterile anticipation of sitting in a hospital room. Rivers let her gaze travel from Star's sleeping figure to the drab walls around her laden with printed signs about patients' rights. If these walls could talk, they would likely weep from all the sadness, heartbreak, and difficulties they'd been witness to.

The aroma of coffee mingled with the scent of cleaning fluid. Maybe a nurse could direct her to the source of the fresh brew.

"Momma..." Star's moan interrupted that thought. The sheets rustled as the girl repositioned herself.

"You're going to be okay." Rivers caressed Star's forehead.

Star's eyes closed. No matter their age, it seemed everyone called for their mother when they were in pain. Even when their mother was long gone. Or unable or unwilling to care for them.

Rivers had longed for her mother's comfort this past year. The nights in the hospital healing from the shooting. And after her release, through long days filled with grief. Though Mom had done her best to understand that Jordan was gone, because of the short-term memory issues, she often forgot and asked about him.

But Dad had been there, ever faithful, ever the comforter and caregiver. Maybe Cooper's sensitive nature reminded Rivers of that. Maybe that's why she'd leaned into the compassion he'd offered.

It did nothing to explain the zinging warmth she'd experienced when he touched her, though. Or the fact that she missed his presence the moment he'd gone through that exit door.

Yep. Crazy thoughts were plaguing her here in St. Simons. It had to be this place. The situation. She couldn't feel anything for…

She couldn't even finish that thought. *Cooper was Jay.* And Jordan had been her one true love. Not that she believed in the whole Hollywood soulmates propaganda, but she could never love any man the way she'd loved Jordan.

"Who are you, and where am I?" Star's scratchy voice held more strength than Rivers had expected. "Where's Blake? Is he okay?" She lifted her arm and examined the IV. "What's in here? I need to go."

Rivers stared at her. The girl sure had woken up.

"Are you deaf or something?" Star snapped. "Can you answer me?"

"You're in the hospital. The doctor thinks you may've been stabbed. There's a gash just below your ribs, but it wasn't bad."

"Easy for you to say." Star tried to lift herself and groaned.

"Here's the remote for the bed." Rivers pointed at the buttons.

"I'm not an idiot." Star pressed the arrow, and the head of the bed rose. "Where's Blake? Did he bail on me?"

"He's at the Re-Claimed house sobering up. I offered to stay with you tonight. I'm Rivers."

"Great. What kind of name is that? And I said I need to go." Her fingers found the button to raise the bed and pressed. "Like now."

A girl named Star criticizing her name? "You need to stay here tonight."

"Ms. Do-Gooder, I mean I need to go to the bathroom." A bitter scoff pressed through her clenched teeth, and she twisted her feet to hang over the bed. "Are you here to help, or do I need to buzz a nurse?"

"At your service." She tried to sound perky.

Help me with patience, Lord.

Rivers placed her arm below Star's, careful to avoid her wound. "Let me get the IV pole." At least she had experience. Her mother had been a difficult patient. That was the reason Rivers had worked hard to be kind to her own nurses after the incident, despite feeling angry at the world.

Star showed no such inclination. "What's in my IV?" she asked as they made a slow walk across the room.

"Antibiotics and Tylenol."

"Figures. Not much of anything. When will they release me? No reason to stay if they won't treat my pain." Star pinned her with a hard look. "And they're not taking me to psych."

"They said you could leave tomorrow or the next day, depending on the wound and whether there's an infection. But you need to heal someplace safe. And clean." Rivers stopped at the restroom door. "You want me to go in with you?"

"Do. Not." Star's brown eyes hardened. Hands shaking, she grabbed the IV pole from Rivers. "I got this."

The pole's wheels scratched across the tile, and the door closed. Rivers sighed. She should've called for the nurse.

The door opened, and Star held out a hand. "I'm dizzier than I expected."

Rivers took her arm. "Lean on me. We'll get you to the chair. It's closer."

"No." The sharp tone again. "The bed. I need to sleep."

They took slow steps across the whitish floor.

Looking up, Star begged with big, sad eyes. "Please ask the

desk for something to help me sleep. It's not fair. I mean, I was stabbed." A curse word followed the plea.

"I'll buzz the nurse once you're safely in bed." But she doubted they'd supply a sleeping pill.

"They won't listen." Star scoffed. "I should call a lawyer. People should be treated with respect." More cursing.

"They're taking care of you. I've been watching."

With a quick jerk, Star yanked her arm away. "I don't know you. Blake said he'd take care of me." She reached the bed and climbed up, her face taut and pale, the pain evident. A moan slipped out as she leaned on the pillow and her eyes fluttered shut. "Buzz the nurse. I need something."

Rivers complied. The emotional whiplash Star displayed grated on her nerves. Somewhere in her purse, she had some lavender essential oil her friend had given her. She usually forgot to use the stuff, but it was supposed to be calming. Maybe she should slather the entire contents all over the both of them. She grabbed her handbag and dug around. At the bottom, she felt the small bottle and retrieved it. After pulling the top, she dotted her wrists, her neck, then rubbed some on both of her temples.

She put the lid back on, but popped it back off. A little on the back of her neck wouldn't hurt.

A quiet knock followed, and she turned, expecting the nurse.

"Hey." His voice barely above a whisper, Cooper entered. "How's it going?"

"About as expected. Why are you back already?" Did he not trust her?

Nearing, he sniffed her hair, his presence sending warmth to her cheeks. "What's that aroma? I can't quite place it."

The oils were a bit strong. She might've overdone it.

"Lavender."

His head bobbed as he studied her. "Is it working?" The tiniest smirk lifted one side of his mouth.

"Why are you here?"

The smirk was replaced by a more serious expression. "Blake's in the emergency room. We weren't sure what he'd been using, but we know now it was heroin. He needs withdrawal treatment." He shook his head. "He's in worse shape than Star, and he hasn't been stabbed."

"Oh, no." She'd heard that heroin use had become an epidemic.

"What?" Star's eyes opened. "Don't let them put him in psych." The girl sure had good ears.

"He needs help with detox." Cooper stepped closer to the bed. "If you care about him, you'll let him get cleaned up, then you can both work to get sober."

"You know nothing about us."

"I don't know you, but I know Blake came into the sober living house where I work to talk about getting clean, except he didn't want to leave you alone. I don't know you, but I've lived the throes of a heroin addiction. I know I couldn't get clean on my own and kept relapsing. I know the ministry at Re-Claimed was there for me when no one else was, and with God's help, I am five years and twenty-eight days sober."

He *still* counted the days. Rivers absorbed the sincerity in his words, the low, patient tone of his voice. How hard had each one of those days been for him? Were they still hard? She was surprised by how much she hoped and prayed he was no longer tempted by narcotics.

~~~

The lights of the hospital blared in the early morning while Cooper made his way down the maze of halls to find Rivers.

The scent of coffee stirred a hankering for caffeine, which he'd ignored, but maybe she'd like a cup. It had been a long night for both of them. Fortunately, volunteer counselors had shown up to take their place. Re-Claimed was blessed by these dear people with a heart for addicts. Not many people could handle the frustration. One woman had trained in counseling because of her sister's addiction, and the other man was a recovered alcoholic who'd retired after spending years working as a counselor. They both served as relief workers at the Re-Claimed houses.

Cooper reached the lobby, where he'd asked Rivers to meet him. It was impossible to miss her profile standing in front of the entry window, the sun gleaming through the light blond hair, which poked up all over. She was already nursing a half-empty cup of brew, so no need to offer to buy her another.

"Hey, Rivers." He joined her at the window. "Ready to go get your Stink Bug so you can rest?"

Tired blue eyes met his. "Ready." A smile played on her lips. "Not sure you're entitled to make fun of my vehicle since yours smells like a wet dog. I'd dub it the Reek Jeep."

"Touché. But it will take us away from this place." He motioned toward the automatic doors, waiting for her to exit first.

"I can't wait to smell it then." She chuckled and did some sort of little dance move with her arms and shoulders, nearly spilling her coffee.

It was absolutely adorable. Cooper's heart did a similar frolic just watching her. "What the heck was that?"

Her eyes widened, and her brows rose. "Oh wow. I did my happy dance. I haven't... That hasn't happened since..."

No stopping his arm. It wrapped around her shoulder and squeezed. "My Reek Jeep has never excited anyone so much."

He pulled her close as they walked, careful not to knock the coffee in her other hand. His gut twisted thinking about how her sentence would've ended.

Chapter 12

"Do you want to come in? I can ask Davis to bring breakfast to the gallery."

Rivers blinked at Cooper's question. She'd been lost in thought for most of the ride home, and soft praise songs had filled the silence in the Jeep. Her stomach rumbled as Cooper parked beside her VW, and she pressed her hand against her abs. Maybe he hadn't heard it.

"I'll take that as a yes?" One of Cooper's brows lifted in a sarcastic arc.

He'd heard it.

Why not? She still hadn't found the grocery store. "Sure." She glanced at the clock on her cell. Eight-thirty. "What time do you open?"

"Nine. I need to run upstairs to change." He turned off the vehicle and removed the keys. "I'll let you in while I call Davis. It won't take me long. You can look around."

"Okay." She should know more about the gallery she owned, after all. On her last visits, her brain had been in another place. Overwhelmed, shocked, angry, she hadn't taken much in.

Following Cooper along the sidewalk in the morning light, she tried not to notice the depths of the dark shade of his hair. Or the way, though tousled, it never looked an unruly mess, unlike her own chaotic mop. She'd done her best to beat down her wayward strands this morning, but her efforts hadn't accomplished much.

Suddenly self-aware, she ran her hand across the top of her head. "Cooper, do you have a baseball cap I can borrow?"

He reached the door and turned the keys in the lock, earning a jingle from the bell inside. He pivoted to pin his gaze on her, and lines crinkled the corners of his eyes. "Why? You rock the Teletubby do."

She scoffed and rolled her eyes. "Thanks for nothing." He was a little funny, though.

"My bad. I'll find a clean one."

"Clean works." She couldn't stop a small smile and averted her gaze from his penetrating stare, those dark eyes like onyx stones reflecting the sun. "I'll look around."

"Make yourself at home. It's yours." His tone wasn't bitter but carried more of a defeated edge, dredging up a smidgen of sympathy, not only for Cooper but for the others she'd met at dinner. Would closing the gallery affect their ministry?

Instead of checking his expression before he walked away, she focused on the walls, the art.

Colorful abstracts dominated the left side of the space. One large piece had a white background, but reds and yellows streamed down from the top right corner. Red had been the color of her nightmares since the shooting, but in this painting, the red tones with the yellows moved in ways that felt warm and inviting. The intensity of the colors and the sweeping waves flowing down drew her in.

"He calls that one Second Chances." Davis slipped up beside her. No mistaking Davis's playful voice. But then again, during his prayer, his tone had carried fire. "I hope I didn't spook you."

She'd been so immersed, she hadn't heard the door's jingle. Though she hadn't noticed his approach, Davis hadn't set off the jumpiness she'd been plagued with since the accident.

Maybe she was getting back to normal. She read the printed card below the painting. *Second Chances by J. C. Knight.* James Cooper Knight.

Rivers pulled her gaze from the painting to make eye contact with Davis. "Cooper did this?"

"His paintings are popular." Davis's head bobbed. "I put your food in the studio. Gabby had already thought of boxing it up for y'all. She's good that way."

The painting stayed in the forefront of her mind, the warm feelings that washed over her. She'd love to give that feeling to someone again. "So Cooper offers a lot of his own work?"

"Their sales pay the bills here and help with expenses at Re-Claimed. The man should wear a cape, like a superhero."

Certainly not the way he'd been described to her. "How long have you been a part of Re-Claimed?"

"Three-hundred and thirty-nine days." He nodded toward the back. "Get your food while it's hot. I can watch the front for Coop."

"How did you end up...? Sorry. That's none of my business."

"No worries." He shrugged in his carefree way. "I tell this story whenever the need calls." He glanced at a clock, which had been mounted on an easel and hung above the front counter. "We don't open for a few more minutes. I'll follow you." He scanned her form, but not in a seductive way. "You need to eat more, sister."

His straightforwardness was somehow refreshing. "Okay, okay. Got it. Gain weight. Where's the food?"

He led her through the doorway into the back studio. More canvases lined the walls—some partially finished, some not-so-great, others amazing abstracts, still life, impressionistic. Her eyes tracked up and down, taking them all in. There were even a few pop art and cartoonish works.

Being surrounded by the pieces brought a sense of home the way her Memphis gallery and studio used to. A sensation washed over her that she hadn't been able to recapture in the past year...the unmistakable urge to create.

"Here you go." Davis handed her a Styrofoam box from the counter. "You eat. I'll talk."

She sat on a stool in front of an easel with a blank canvas resting on it, the white space beckoning her.

Davis cleared his throat loudly and pointed, hinting not-so-subtly for her to put food in her mouth. She opened the box. Eggs, bacon, grits, and toast. That should hold her for a while. A plastic fork lay on top, and she scooped a bite of grits. The buttery carbs melted on her tongue. Delicious.

"Me and Angelo were in the same Army platoon. Spent time in Afghanistan. One day, we were on a routine patrol, and an IED exploded." He pressed his lips together before continuing. "Lost one of our brothers. Marcus."

"I'm sorry." A lump rose in her throat, and she struggled to swallow. "That had to be traumatic."

He gave a slow nod. "Mayhem."

"Were you injured?" She didn't see any visible scars, but she had her own concealed wounds.

"I lost hearing in one ear. A lot of burns. Could've been worse. Same with Angelo, but he had some vertebrae injured." He sucked in a deep breath. "We couldn't shake the violent images or the nagging questions. What did we miss that could've saved him? Why spare us? Why let Marcus die? He was a good man, had a wife...a baby, while we were just two single dudes living day to day."

Oh brother, she could relate to the why questions. Her own survival over Jordan's had felt wrong on so many levels.

How easy it would've been to take something to numb the pain. Only she'd seen full well how that choice damaged everyone around the person doing the numbing. "I can imagine."

"Angelo already had some issues. Came into the Army hoping to pull out of trouble." Davis swiped his fingers through his hair. "We started drinking. A lot. One thing led to another. He kept ending up in jail."

"Not you?"

"Don't ask me how, but I kept a job as a handyman at some condos. Free place to live, too, although it wasn't the nicest in town."

"What changed you?"

"I went to get Angelo out of jail—again—and there were Cooper and Kevin talking to him. I was hungover." A wry huff followed. "I mean I was hung-over. My head felt like a seed tick done sucked out all my brains and spit them back in." He planted his palm on his forehead as if remembering the pain. "They convinced me to come, but I would've done anything to get them to shut up."

Rivers couldn't help but laugh at his honesty.

"What in the world are you telling her?" Cooper's voice held both teasing and warning. He handed her a blue Atlanta Braves baseball cap. She took the offering and quickly placed it on her wayward hair.

"I cannot lie. I shared my story. Part of it, anyway." Davis presented Cooper a takeout breakfast.

"It gets worse. Stay tuned." Cooper shook his head.

Giving Cooper a playful nudge, Davis snorted. "Hey, were you not the man who said, 'Showing your scars is showing who you are'?"

"That and 'stay in your own hula hoop.'" Cooper's black

brows arched.

Rivers tried not to choke on her food, but the picture the phrase painted in her mind had her laughing.

Davis scrunched his nose. "Sounds vaguely familiar." He spoke the words in a fake hillbilly accent.

"I asked him. Me being nosey." Rivers ran a napkin across her lips, then scanned the easel in front of her. Her fingers tingled for a paintbrush. The waves, the birds, the sky she'd seen that first day, all flowed through her mind. "Would you mind if I paint?"

Cooper stared at her as if she'd offered to walk a plank and jump into shark-infested waters.

She sucked in a deep breath. "Is it against the rules? I'll pay for the canvas and supplies."

A shadow flickered across Cooper's face before he regained his composure. "You'll do no such thing. Have at it. What medium?" He stepped past her to a long table that ran the length of one wall. "We've got some of everything here, and there's a sink and paper towels in the bathroom."

She stood and joined him, perusing the blues, greens, and yellows. They cried to her to bring them to life. "I'll go with acrylics. You guys have work to do, so don't mind me."

Cooper still stood there, his mouth slightly gaping. "Aren't you exhausted?"

"Aren't you? But you're still going to work." Rivers shooed him with a flick of her hand. "I'll clean up and leave when I'm tired."

"Finish your breakfast first, young lady," Davis chided.

She nodded and took a bite, but she had to paint now, before the impulse slipped away.

~~~

Basically driven away, Cooper took his breakfast and left

the studio. The gallery opened in two minutes, and Angelo hadn't made it over yet, so Cooper shoved the food in his mouth, barely tasting the flavors. The weird thing was, not only did Rivers have to be exhausted on so many levels, but she'd claimed she hadn't been able to paint since losing Jordan. Part of him worried she needed to rest after the drama last night. Another part warned him to stay out of her life. The last thing she needed was him butting in more than he already had. Then there was that piece inside of him, which, despite his best efforts, had gone berserk and wanted to curl Rivers into his arms, against his chest, and hold her. For a really long time.

A very bad idea. Stupid, insane idea. Not an idea he could allow to flourish. He tossed the food box away and visualized tossing the ridiculous thought in the trash too.

"Wanna talk about it?" Davis punched Cooper's bicep before cranking up the praise station they played on a daily basis. "She's occupied."

"No." His tone came out sharper than he'd intended.

"Oh, cool. Let's talk about it." This former military man had never been easily intimidated, which made him a great candidate to become an addiction therapist.

"What is there to say? I explained all this last time."

"Not about the Titanic girl-crush. How is this affecting you regarding the gallery? That's a harsh blow, buddy. This place has been your baby. Your lifeline."

A dull ache began in Cooper's forehead and spread, the candid truth ricocheting between his temples. "You're right. The gallery is important to me."

"The enemy will try to get you locked down. Get you bummed. The temptation will follow."

"True that. He watches for our weak moments." He'd need to pray and work the steps because everything he'd built since becoming sober was being threatened—his home, his means to help support himself and Re-Claimed. "Thanks for saying something. I'll come to you if I get in that place. In the meantime, keep me prayed up."

"I'm covering you already, bro, but I can speak over you now if you want."

The shop should be open, but there was always time for prayer. "Bring it."

Davis placed a hand on Cooper's shoulder, and they both closed their eyes. "Father, fight for my brother, Cooper, in the heavenly realms. The battle is intense and real and present, and the thief comes to steal and destroy our sobriety. The enemy's weapons are fear and lies, so we will stand against him with Your Word and combat him with truth and love. You are the King, the Healer, the Mighty Warrior. Guard Cooper's way before and behind, above and below. Let Cooper trust You, God, with his uncertain future. You have never let him down before, and You hold him now in the palm of Your nail-scarred hand. Strengthen Cooper in the days, weeks, and months to come. Give him wisdom and peace. In Jesus, we ask and we thank You."

"Amen." Cooper's eyes and nose stung at the tender yet powerful words. "Are you sure you don't want to go into ministry instead of counseling? You do have a message for the hurting." He chuckled. "And the blunt truth."

"A traditional church would probably fire me the first week. They'd think I was weirder than a rug lizard."

"You're probably right. What's a rug lizard anyway?"

"If you don't know, I can't tell ya." His eyes twinkled. "I'm more into sneaky-stealthy strategies in introducing the Gospel to addicts and prisoners. Black ops kind of stuff."

"There is nothing stealthy about you and your mouth. Let's

get to work." Rotating toward the door, Cooper glanced over his shoulder. "Thanks, brother." And he meant it. Facing the future without the gallery would be quite a blow.

Chapter 13

The praise music streaming through the studio speakers ruptured the levee Rivers had erected around her heart. Emotions emptied out like black waters being cleared during a spring storm, a current deep and swift. The brush in her hand glided over the canvas almost as if possessed—but a good possession. The Holy Spirit seemed to whisper quiet words of comfort to her throbbing heart.

Blues filled the upper portion of the piece, sky and soft clouds set above a gleaming sea. Majestic white pelicans stretched their wings and soared above foamy cresting waves. Healing rays of light streamed down from a nail-scarred hand in the right corner of the canvas, sending warmth flowing over her body and soul like a soothing balm.

On the pearl-colored shoreline, the heron she'd seen at the beach that first day stood regarding the horizon, the little crab at the bird's webbed feet. She'd often painted a lion on his haunches, mane massive and red, and a lamb resting in perfect harmony at his side beside a river, but this time the colossal bird and a little crustacean would serve well her vision of peace.

A smile tickled her lips as she recalled all the times she'd begged and cajoled her father into reading *The Chronicles of Narnia.* When she'd grown old enough to read, she'd recited them back to him, imitating the funny voices he'd used.

A speck of sorrow burrowed its way into her consciousness like a tick aiming to begin a festering sore. Memories of reading to her mother after the accident sprouted, and her hand paused over the painting. All the nights Rivers had spent at Mom's bedside, hoping and praying for healing, her heart had bled, the sharp truth penetrating with the realization that her mother would never be the same.

No. She wasn't going into that rabbit hole. Her gaze fell to the nail-scarred hand.

Behold, I make all things new.

Someday her mom would be whole. And Jordan was alive in God's presence. Those facts provided some comfort.

But what about now? Her grip tightened on the brush in her hand. Did God have restoration for her heart through painting? Would she heal by working with others through art again?

Praise Him.

As if summoned, verses tumbled into her mind like a gentle rain.

They will enter Zion with singing; everlasting joy will crown their heads. Gladness and joy will overtake them, and sorrow and sighing will scurry away.

Let everything that has breath praise the Lord. Praise the Lord.

Worthy is the Lamb, who was slain, to receive power and wealth and wisdom and strength and honor and glory and praise!

As long as she still had a pulse, she'd lean close to her Savior and offer up praise. Her wobbly voice pitched to try and sing along with the tune playing from the speakers, a song about chains breaking for a sinner. She lifted her hand back to her canvas and brushed on details and highlights and shadows. Smudges of gold, white, and azure. Her gaze returned to the hand in the corner. She still hadn't been able to bring herself to place a spot of red on the painting.

Though your sins are like scarlet, they shall be as white as snow; though they are red as crimson, they shall be like wool.

Jesus had shed his blood for her—for all who chose to receive His gift. Including her mother and Cooper and the people of Re-Claimed.

The brush hovered over the palette. She could do this.

"Hey, am I interrupting?" Gabby plowed through the gallery door and into the studio. She stopped behind Rivers. "Are you finished? Because that's amazing!"

Davis leaned on the frame of the door dividing the two rooms. "I wanted to know what all that horrible racket was, but Cooper wouldn't let me come back here. He claimed it was singing of some sort. I thought it was a turkey mating call."

"Shut up." Worry slathered over Cooper's face, pinching his forehead, and he moved past both Davis and Gabby to kneel in front of Rivers. "Are you okay?" His gaze roamed her face.

With the back of her hand, Rivers wiped her cheeks. She'd not realized she'd been crying. "I'm fine. I get emotional when I paint."

"I can relate." A gentle smile lifted the corners of his mouth. "Sometimes it's like going through both a winepress and the refining fire combined when I pick up that brush and try to feel where God is leading, the work He wants to do in me. The creative effort is tough, but cleansing and freeing, and hopefully in the end, healing."

Whoa. Cooper actually understood her process—the offering of worship and emotion through art. It seemed as if this man could peer deep into her soul. More tears blurred her vision, and the little quiver in her chin annoyed her to no end. Why did it have to be him who understood? Brooklyn and the rest of Jordan's family would never approve of their friendship. And having a friend who got her was feeling pretty nice.

She offered a quick nod and averted her gaze. She'd be out

of here in a few weeks anyway.

Gabby squeezed her shoulders. "I don't want to put any pressure on you, but I could use an art therapist to work with the ladies. The sweet girl we had got married and moved to Charleston, and we haven't replaced her yet."

"I'm only in St. Simons for a month."

"That would be perfect." Gabby let go and gestured in her exaggerated fashion. "A few more weeks would give us time to find the right person."

Fear clawed at Rivers. *Am I ready to help others, Lord, while I'm still struggling?* It was one thing to consider going back to working with children, but adults? With addiction? "Can't Cooper do it?"

"Been there, done that, and it might as well have been a Sasquatch painting in front of them." Davis walked farther into the room. "Oh, those ladies watched our boy all right, but had not one clue what was on the canvas. It was as if they'd swallowed their own lips drooling over him."

Rivers allowed herself a peek at Cooper, who shook his head with a grimace. She could imagine his brooding, dark attractiveness being a bit too much for a group of recovering women.

"We don't have to flesh it out right now." Cooper gave her knee a squeeze, then shot a warning look toward Gabby. "We can all pray about the decision first."

"Yeah, well"—Davis snorted—"just throwing this out there if you take the challenge, leave off the joyful noise or hand out earplugs. Maybe give everyone their own cool supersonic headset to mask your turkey-screeching. I mean singing."

Rivers intended a huff, though what escaped her mouth sounded like a snicker. She'd heard her own voice, and it was pretty sad.

Cooper snapped toward Davis and pinned him with a hard stare. "Dude. Seriously."

"I know." Like a scorned puppy, Davis's head lowered. "Dead man walking away now."

"I'm taking off too." Gabby followed. "Let me know what you decide, Rivers."

Rivers couldn't help but have warm feelings for this whole crew and the way they interacted—admonishing, joking, encouraging.

~~~

Step one. Admit he was powerless over his new addiction. *God, help me.*

Cooper pried his gaze from Rivers, stood, and forced his attention onto the picture she'd painted. The landscape in front of him did zilch to cure him of his Rivers fascination, which was quickly evolving into a reckless obsession. The work mesmerized him, swallowed him like the big fish that ate Jonah, but in such a way that he didn't want to be spit out just yet. He knew full well the brain chemistry associated with viewing beauty on or off a canvas, how the dopamine released, triggering feelings of warmth and pleasure. And his dopamine was exploding like Mount Vesuvius over Pompeii.

The color, the shapes, the composition—the sheer power of the piece woke places deep inside him—barred off places that had been chained shut. Because he and the ocean had an immense love-hate relationship. The beach held sweet memories of his childhood, a place where he could escape the inevitable bullying he'd endured because of his speech impediment. But the Atlantic had stolen and buried Savannah and then shredded his family.

On this canvas, Rivers had taken in the beauty of the

Atlantic, and her artistic and spiritual voice in the scene swept his breath away. As if a veil had torn away from a blind man's eyes, he could see the ocean anew, Christ's hand above all, his scars forgiving Cooper's failure. There came an almost physical nudge in his soul that this particular message—this painting— was meant specifically for him, and it was not just a message from the earthly fingers that had held the brush.

"I asked, do you like it?" Rivers spoke barely above a whisper.

"The way this speaks and communicates to me...my soul..." His throat clogged with emotion, so he swept his hand in a broad gesture toward the painting. "You have an incredible gift. I don't know how to convey how remarkable."

Rapid blinking accompanied a blush. "Thanks. This is the first time I've gotten caught up in the Spirit the way I used to before..."

Before she lost Jordan. His mind finished for her. She never seemed able to speak it. "I'm glad something here unlocked the creativity for you." Could her heart be unlocked somehow, too?

He needed to squash that line of thinking like a mosquito. A pesky mosquito carrying West Nile or something more deadly.

"I have one more touch on this piece before finishing, and then I'll go to the cottage. More cleaning out." Thoughtful, her chin tilted. She gazed at him, melting him into a puddle inside. "Would you be able to deliver dinner tonight? I have some things I want to give you."

"Yes." *God, help me.* Although he craved being with her, the idea of reentering the cottage with its memories spiked like a nail in his temple and revived the headache that had been forming earlier.

She turned and dipped her brush in a tiny glob of red paint, then ever so slowly dabbled a spot on the nail-scarred hand. Expelling a long breath in a whoosh, she stood and threw the brush into a jar of water. "I'll clean up now and go."

"Okay." That was weird. "I'll let you know when I head your way." Davis was going to have a field day with this new development. Steeling himself, Cooper returned to the front of the gallery and tried to strike a nonchalant pose beside Davis and Angelo.

"Doesn't take a genius squad to see that mini-typhoon you're being sucked into." Davis shot him a hard look.

"More like the storm of the century."

Chapter 14

Once she'd rested and then cleaned out a closet, Rivers eyed the old brown envelope on the table. She'd been avoiding the emotional landmines that possibly waited in their yellowed pages, but something told her she should wade on in. As if the past held a key to a locked door.

With hesitant fingers, she opened the letters addressed to Brooklyn and Pearl's mother.

Dear Stella,

You and your wealthy daddy don't understand the way I came up. It was hard times, most nights nothing but cornbread for supper and a beating with a belt. Sleeping with the cold wind blowing through the cracks in our shotgun house.

I work hard every day and in the evenings, too, keeping you and the girls well fed and dressed nice. So, I have some drinks at the club. You knew that when we met. Why do you keep hounding me? Drinking helps me relax before a performance.

It's not like you've never had a sip of wine. Stop being a baby.

Come back to Savannah and act like a wife.

Frank

~~~

Stella,

You wanted to get married. You decided we'd have kids even though you knew I played the clubs at night. Now, you have the twins—women have children every day. It's not like you're in a shack in the country. Don't play the martyr.

Frank

~~~

Dear Stella,

I heard our sweet Pearl was in the hospital. I didn't realize how sick she was. Can you please forgive me? I promise I'll help. I'll stop drinking. I can stop for you and the girls. This time will be different, I promise.

Love always,

Frank

~~~

Stella,

You keep telling me I have a problem, but I'm nothing like my daddy. It's not my fault that blond came onto me. I didn't go after her, and things weren't what they looked like. Yes, she kissed me, but that was all.

You always blame me. You're always looking for something to be angry about. It's no wonder I have to drink. You push me too hard.

Frank

~~~

Dear Stella,

I'm sorry about last night. I didn't even have that many drinks after the show, so they must have made them strong. You know Vick and his sense of humor. I promise I'll change. I don't care what that policeman said. I never meant to hurt you or the girls. It was an accident, and maybe Pearl and Brooklyn got in the crossfire.

You know me. You know I'd never deliberately injure a child. I pray they're not hurt too badly. This is the last time, I promise. Just let me come home. You'll see.

Love always,

Frank

~~~

Rivers tossed the correspondence back onto the envelope they'd been stored in for so many years. Under the letters sat a news clipping about a one-car accident on a Thanksgiving Day.

Frank and the woman with him had died after crashing into a tree. Maybe the blond, maybe another woman, but obviously not Stella. The death certificate indicated that the wreck hadn't been long after that last envelope was posted. He hadn't kept his promise.

The one-sided correspondence painted a vivid, bleak window into Stella's life. The scenes Rivers imagined twisted her insides. And she hadn't even opened Stella's journal yet. What nightmares had been recorded there? No wonder Pearl and Brooklyn separated themselves from Cooper. The twins had already endured having a parent who'd broken their trust, who'd physically abused them. Then they'd endured such a great loss due to a son. One they'd raised with good husbands at their sides. One they'd taught right from wrong.

Rivers understood what Stella had gone through. A familiar ache grasped her chest.

She'd get back to the matter at hand, before she got sucked down too deep. Turning her attention back to the piles of old scarves, purses, and costume jewelry, she searched the cabinets for a container or bag to store them in. No luck. Those items could be let go. The letters and the journal she'd give to Cooper. Maybe reading them would help him understand his mother, aunt, and grandmother better—why they'd shut him out after the accident.

They also might break his heart further. Guilt might push him over some precipice, causing him to start using again.

She squirmed at how much the idea of Cooper landing back in the clutches of addiction bothered her. The heaviness of it was like a boulder mashing against her chest.

The cool wind through the open windows cleared the cottage of some of that musty closed-off staleness houses got when they sat empty and unused. A lot like this morning's art session had freed something inside of her stale soul.

She sucked in a deep breath of the salty air. The birdsongs and sounds of nature invigorated her. God's creation had that effect.

She'd have to ask Cooper or Gabby where the best place to donate was. The Stink Bug couldn't carry much, so maybe a charity that picked up. Of course, Cooper deserved to have first dibs on the bigger items she discarded. He might need them, especially when she sold the gallery. Or, *duh*...They might need used furniture and castoffs at Re-Claimed.

Oh, some smaller things would be perfect for art therapy. Her adrenalin pulsed as creative ideas came alive in her mind. The fabric, buttons, feathers, paint, yarn, and seashells would make a great mixed media project. Maybe the costume jewelry too. Not everyone enjoyed painting on a canvas. In fact, that process intimidated some children. These ladies weren't that young, but sometimes a person got locked into the age when a past trauma occurred.

She froze. Was she really going to try to help *those* people?

The atmosphere shifted in the room. Darkness seemed to stalk her thoughts as if to consume them. She imagined herself exposed and fragile in front of a group of recovering addicts—the raw issues and the devastation that went along with addiction.

Stop. Rivers rose to her feet. Grappling with the dilemma required prayer, not wallowing. Maybe it was time for some music. Her lips lifted when she felt that almost physical tap on her heart. And, yes, dancing.

She grabbed her phone and cranked up a tune, setting the music to shuffle. Her feet moved to the first song, a slow one, full of praise.

Great choice, God. The Lover of Her Soul knew she needed

to stretch after sitting on the floor for so long, sorting through the past.

After a few pliés and lunges, she broke into twirls and spins and kicks like a child. Her voice strained to join the worship song. When that tune ended, another faster one began. Bouncing around the room, she belted out the words to the theme song from Trolls. "Can't Stop the Feeling." Dance. That was what she needed. To shake off all the negativity clawing at her.

~~~

He should've stopped watching her ten minutes ago because the food was getting cold. But Rivers hadn't answered the doorbell, and Cooper couldn't break his gaze from the window—and her dancing inside.

Would she want him to interrupt?

Yeah, because standing here spying on her is not creepy at all.

As it was, he already couldn't take his mind off this woman. The rescue at the beach. Her caring for Star. The intense painting at the gallery. The horrible-joyful-mournful singing this morning. And again now, her voice was blasting through the open windows. But add in this dancing...this beautiful, strange, passionate dancing.

His whole body shuddered with emotion. The mix of ballet and modern dance. It was crazy, stirring, her form willowy and flexible. Rivers had told him her father had taken her to dance lessons until her mother's accident. Too bad she hadn't been able to pursue that dream, because she had talent. But what did he know other than he couldn't take his eyes off her?

Well, one other thing he knew...he'd love to sketch her. If he could somehow capture the kinesthetic control and fluidity of her movements. The arc of her muscles. And curve of her lips.

Stop. Don't go there.

Her voice hit a squeaky high note at that moment, and a small laugh escaped his lips. Man, she sang badly. And loud.

The music changed to a new song, a love ballad, and she suddenly plummeted out of sight. A guttural sob shredded his trance.

"No. Why? Why?" Rivers wailed.

She must've hurt herself. Heart pounding, Cooper's fingers found the door knob, and he barreled inside.

She knelt with her face in her hands.

He dropped the meals and sank to his knees beside her. "What happened?"

Her watery blue gaze lifted to meet his, and her torso shook. "This was what we were going to dance to. Our first dance as man and wife at the wed—" Her head plunged, and the weeping began again.

His whole being grieved along with her over the loss of her fiancé. Jordan had been like a brother to him before Savannah's death. Cooper's arms strained with the desire to pull her to his chest. To comfort her, even though he had no right.

Chapter 15

Rivers leaned into Cooper's chest. The move felt like betrayal to Jordan, but she could no more pull herself away than she could erase her past.

His arms wrapped around her, the hold feeling so different from Jordan's. Cooper was lankier, leaner, but she fit nicely in the crook of his shoulder.

"I'm sorry," Cooper whispered next to her ear. "I would trade places with Jordan if I could."

She glanced up at his face between the cracks of her soaked eyelashes.

"I didn't mean…" His head dropped, and his dark hair shadowed his brows. "I mean, he should be here with you, and I should be the one in a grave. I deserve it, but he didn't."

The song echoed on through the cottage living room, Ed Sheeran crooning about falling in love and starting a family. Why hadn't she deleted it already? Crying exhausted her, and she sunk closer, deeper against Cooper's chest and the curve of his shoulder. She should say something. Part of her thought he might be right—Jordan did deserve to be here more than Cooper. Her human nature craved having somewhere to pour her pent-up blame, someone on whom to spew her anger.

But another part whispered that no one was righteous. There was only One who hadn't fallen short. But for God's grace, all would be lost.

Sniffling, she found her voice. "It's not your fault. We live in a broken world, but someday everything will be made right."

Though her head knew the truth, often her heart lagged behind. But even after the short time she'd known Cooper, she'd discovered worthwhile qualities in him, no matter how she tried not to.

And he still held her. The blasted song finally switched, and the beat of her breaking heart slowed. She was suddenly aware of the thump of his heart pulsing in his chest. She forced herself to inch away.

"Sorry. I still fall apart sometimes." Rivers cleared her throat against the tightness there. "A little thing can trigger it—a commercial for a show we binge-watched or the scent of his shampoo. A friend and I went to eat sushi, and a memory of Jordan trying to use chopsticks just about strangled me."

A soft chuckle came from Cooper. "Yeah, he was never a fan of sushi, and for a talented architect, chopsticks were his kryptonite. He must've really loved you to try."

"What? He didn't like sushi?"

"He used to hate it. He'd gotten a stomach virus after eating crab one time, and something about sushi reminded him of being sick." He shrugged. "Maybe he got over it. What do I know?"

"He could have, but he never seemed overly enthusiastic, now that I think back." She couldn't help smiling at the realization that he'd gone only to make her happy. Learning more about Jordan through Cooper's perspective, though painful, might be part of her healing journey. Her eyes met his dark gaze for a moment. It might be too dangerous a journey, though.

"Speaking of food." He stood and picked up a brown paper sack then offered her his hand. "Let's eat. We could grab the lantern in my Jeep and take it over to the beach."

Fresh sea air sounded like a good idea. "Sure. I'll get a towel to sit on. Or two." One seemed way too intimate. After retrieving two blue-striped beach towels from the closet and stuffing them into a tote, she ignored the letters on the table and the pile of items to donate to charity and joined him on the porch. Those heavy subjects would wait until after dinner.

"Ready?" He offered his arm, probably remembering how she'd almost fainted from hunger last time.

She slipped her hand into the crook of his elbow, trying not to think about how nice it felt there. Arguing she didn't need help might make them both feel awkward.

More awkward.

A gentle breeze swept over them as a few frogs and cicadas began the evening chorus. Not as loud as the nightly cacophony near the Mississippi River in Memphis, but still a comforting sound of home. Pink streaks contoured the sky in the west, and more music met them as they made the short walk down the street to the boardwalk.

The water lapped much closer to the boardwalk than the day she'd been out. "Tide's in again, I guess."

"Yep." Cooper kept his gaze straight ahead, scanning the horizon.

"Did you go out on your boat today?"

"No time, but I have a few friends who can take turns with the patrol."

"Are y'all like the Coast Guard or something?"

"Just volunteers wanting to save others the grief we've gone through."

Her mind flashed back to the spot along the river where she'd lost Jordan. A shiver crossed her shoulders at the thought of going back there on patrol to save others.

A crab scampered as she placed her foot on the sand, its bulging eyes staring at them. "Oh! Digger, you scared me!" The creature's sideways walk gained a chuckle, though.

"Digger? Do you know him personally, or do you name everything?" Cooper's mouth quirked into a sideways smile.

The crustacean scooped a bit of sand from a hole in disgust, tossed it her way, and then disappeared.

"He looks like the one I saw shoveling sand the other day."

"And you can tell that one from the thousands of others?"

"Maybe. There was Chloe the crab. She looked sweet but feisty. Big Boy was, well, big, and..." As if summoned, movement caught her eye near a pile of broken bamboo-looking sticks, and two larger crabs emerged. They danced around each other before skittering toward the water.

"See now, there's Fred and Ginger." She couldn't stop a smile at their funny movements. Until she looked past them down the beach. Her stomach took another plunge, and her feet stopped.

~~~

Cooper checked her expression then followed her gaze toward the small gathering to the south. A wedding.

Of course, that'd be his luck. Try to distract Rivers from the wedding song, only to lead her to an actual wedding.

Nice job, Coop, as usual. The bride and groom saying vows at sunset, a beautiful sight under different circumstances. A sight he tried to not think about too often, either, since he'd pretty much determined to avoid romantic relationships. Too complicated. He'd had no problem steering clear of women.

Wide blue eyes stared up at him.

No problem until now, that was. And being with Rivers was more than complicated. His emerging feelings were convoluted on a catastrophic level, considering his family discord.

Cooper gave her arm a tender squeeze. "You want to go

119

back? It might be too windy out here to eat." Though the mild breeze felt great.

Rivers shook her head, her eyes becoming even more luminous in the low light. "I have to keep going. There's not much other choice, is there?"

Much other choice? Please, Lord, don't let her give up on life. He carried enough guilt to last a lifetime, and losing her, too, would be unfathomable. "There are plenty of other places we can go right now." However, avoiding difficult situations for extended periods of time could be detrimental to her emotional health.

"Let's sit here." She released his arm, spread two towels, then plopped down on one, her posture sagging.

"If you're sure." He joined her and lifted the takeout boxes from a sack plus two bottles of water, placing one of each in front of her, the others before him. "Some cold but tasty boiled shrimp with the usual potatoes, corn, and onions, but Gabby believes in the power of healing foods, so she's boiled cauliflower, broccoli, mushrooms and even Brussels sprouts."

"Brussels sprouts? She is into whole foods all the way."

"You don't have to eat them. It took me a while to get used to the taste." He picked one up with his fingers, since he'd forgotten to put forks in the bag. Thankfully, Gabby had piled a stack of napkins and even a few finger wipes. "They have a kick, so be careful."

He popped one in his mouth, and his eyes immediately teared up. At least the spices distracted him from the weird little balls. It tasted like eating a whole head of cabbage at once, but they were supposedly super healthy.

Rivers followed his lead, earning a muffled cough. She grabbed the water bottle, and her eyelashes fluttered as she worked to swallow. "Whoa, those are hot."

"Sorry. I guess I'm used to it. The vegetables catch more of the heat than the shrimp, so maybe stick with them." He offered his water bottle. "You can have mine, if you need it."

She waved him off and picked up a shrimp. "I'll ration my supply." After peeling a good pile of the crustaceans, she ate one after another. "Good stuff," she managed between bites.

"Glad to see you eating like a ravenous shark over there."

"Always the critic."

A pang of guilt struck through him, but when he studied her face, her lips quirked into a smile. A smile that pretty much undid him. She could ask him for most anything at this moment, and he'd probably hand it over. All his worldly possessions...his kidney...the gallery. He should give her the keys and walk away now. Like this very second. He hadn't taken a vacation since he'd gotten sober, other than a few mission trips, and he'd had several friends invite him to visit their summer homes. His leaving would surely make things easier for her, wouldn't it?

"Let's ask if we can crash the wedding." Her voice and strange request slammed into his deliberations.

"What?" Why would she want to plunge deeper into her pain?

"You heard me." Her shrimp cleared from the box—man, she was a fast eater—she closed it and stood. "They're starting the reception music. Let's ask if we can dance with them."

"Won't that...?" Make things worse? Remind her of Jordan and the wedding that never happened? He wanted to question her but couldn't finish, because she'd held out her hand to him and pinned him with her blue gaze.

Fumbling to close his food and stand, he obeyed her summons and took her hand. The last of the sun's rays had disappeared, and stars had overtaken the responsibility for lighting the shore. That and the waiting bamboo torches down the beach. After ditching the rest of their meal in the trash, rolling the towels into her bag, and turning on the lantern, they walked arm in arm toward the party. And, considering his track record, they were aiming toward the place of their possible destruction.

Chapter 16

"It's not really crashing a wedding when you ask." Cooper couldn't seem to stop smiling at the grinning blond dancing before him. "And do you really like this song?"

Rivers giggled and kept her feet moving to the beat. "'Play That Funky Music?' Yeah. My mom loved these old dance songs."

"I don't know about your taste in music. I heard that Justin Timberlake tune you had cranked up earlier."

One fist went to her hip. "Hey, are you having fun or what?"

"I am." Too much. Rivers had almost immediately found the mother of the bride and asked if they could dance along. The woman offered them a cup of punch and begged them to fix a plate, explaining they'd had a lower turnout due to one of their cousins delivering a baby earlier than expected. They'd taken her up on the punch and a piece of cake, but Rivers had dragged him to the dance area as soon as he'd swallowed the last sugary chunk of icing.

Thirty minutes later, they still danced—an activity that wasn't his forte nor in his comfort zone, but he couldn't seem to say no. No matter the song. At least the young couple's friends mostly requested fast dance tunes.

Was this similar to what her wedding to his cousin would've been like in Memphis? Under the stars, maybe on the rooftop of a fancy hotel overlooking the Mississippi River? If Brooklyn had any say—and he was sure she did—the venue would've been top-of-the-line for her only living child.

That old guilt and pain kicked up in Cooper's torso. If only he'd been sober that day with Savannah, maybe he could've saved her. If only he'd stopped her from drinking so much. He'd known she was binging, but he didn't feel he had the right to say anything given his own addiction.

"What's wrong?" Rivers leaned her head close to his ear, her soft fingers traced a line on his forearm. "You stopped moving, and the music's still going."

Looking at his feet as if they belonged to someone else— maybe they did now—he shook his head. "Sorry. Lost in thought. I do that."

"I do that too." Her head lingered close. "Creatives. We have a lot in common."

Too much in common maybe, but worlds apart. He forced his feet to move again from side to side, but then the song abruptly ended.

"Better late than never." She shrugged with a teasing grimace.

A slow song took its place. Her feet finally halted their graceful steps, and her eyes darted to the skies. Her lips silently moved.

Was this another of her and Jordan's songs? "Are you okay?"

A small smile lifted her lips, and she held both arms toward him in an uneasy offering. "Shall we?"

An overwhelming and reckless current of emotion pulsed in his chest, but he took her invitation and inched close. So close, her lavender scent and her nearness flooded his senses. His heart had been on lockdown for years, and for good reason. Yet, this woman seemed to be unbolting those shackles with a glance. A touch.

This was such a mistake. Another mistake in a long line of blunders.

Lord, help me.

~~~

This might be a mistake, but something deep within Rivers spoke otherwise. Though she'd argued with God in a quickly-spoken prayer, the nudging toward Cooper was something fierce. He was Jordan's cousin—the hated and abandoned black sheep of the family she'd been about to marry into. Why would God lead her to him?

Maybe he simply needed to know he was forgiven. Not only by God, but also by Jordan. Relieving the guilt laid on Cooper might allow him to move forward without feeling he had to pay penance for the rest of his life. He'd been alone and guilt-ridden long enough. That must be why she was here. She needed to help him move on.

And maybe she needed to do a deeper search of her own heart for places where bitterness had taken up residence.

Cooper's arms held her loosely and cautiously, so she moved closer. Inclining her head near his ear, she gathered her courage to release the cleansing words. "Jordan was going to call you. He'd forgiven you. Completely. He missed you. If not for his parents, he would've invited you to the wedding. We even talked about you that last day."

For an instant, his muscles flinched. His eyes found hers—wide and expressive and hopeful dark eyes, as if searching out the truth of her words.

She gave a slight nod to affirm it all.

Relief seemed to wash over his features like a cooling waterfall on a humid Memphis day.

She rested her head on his shoulder. Speaking freedom felt right, but even so, it was emotionally difficult dredging up *that day.*

As if he understood how hard the revelation had been, his embrace enveloped her. He held her close, an offering to absorb her pain and to give his strength. Like a tourniquet to her bleeding, gushing ache for Jordan, Cooper held her tight. And somehow a warm peace filled her, the grief transforming from a debilitating tidal wave to a bittersweet stream.

Oh, that this peace would last. Not that she ever wanted to forget Jordan, but being able to breathe and eat and live with a new normal would be okay.

Guilt stabbed at her for wanting to go on living when Jordan couldn't.

I am the resurrection and the life. He who believes in Me, though he may die, he shall live. And whoever lives and believes in Me shall never die. Do you believe this?

The words Jesus had spoken to his friend Martha in the book of John had been read at the funeral. She even had the first two sentences printed on the cover of the program they'd given out. The verses came to her often, challenging her to trust in her Savior. Jordan wasn't here on this earth, but he had been a believer, so he wasn't really dead and gone. That was the crux of her faith, and she had to remember and believe.

"Now you've stopped moving." Cooper tipped her chin. "Is all this too much? I'm worried about you."

Her gaze pulled to study him. His beautifully sculptured face lingered near, those dark eyes and that black hair framed by the night sky lighted only by the twinkling stars of the Milky Way. Then her gaze fell to his contoured lips and held there as if some giant magnet drew her.

"Rivers, throw me a bone or scrap or something. I need to know what's going on in here." His fingers grazed her forehead, only increasing the magnetic force pulling her toward him.

There was no way she could believe the yearning that was going on in her mind, much less tell him.

Because right now, all she wanted was to kiss this man. Cooper. She wanted to kiss away his years of isolation from his family, his years of being picked on as a child, his years of disappointment for always being considered less than Jordan, his years of emotional pain mixed with the chemical processes and the fallen world that had led him toward the excruciating path of addiction.

But not only did she want to kiss those hurts away, she wanted to kiss the man who'd rescued her, who'd fed her, who'd made her laugh. The compassionate man who spent his days trying to reach the lost and hurting. The man whose art moved her so.

But this inclination—no, this formidable craving—had to be wrong. Her emotions had to be muddied with everything going on.

Cooper was her fiancé's cousin. It would be wrong to fall for him. Wouldn't it?

~~~

He had to do something before he ruined everything. As usual. But the longing to kiss Rivers was drowning him.

His fingers traced her jaw, hoping she'd say something— anything—to keep him from crossing a line that could never be redrawn.

He'd suffered through intense cravings and beaten them. He needed to take his thoughts captive.

Only God could restore his sanity.

Help. The one word he'd often prayed when nothing else would come.

The music ended, and in the moment of quiet, the tinkling

of his phone reached his buzzing brain.

"I have to…" He dropped his hand to his pocket. "This might be Re-Claimed."

The spell broken, Rivers stepped back, blinking and shaking her head. "Of course."

Cradling the phone, he caught the breath he'd been holding and answered, not even checking to see who it was. "Hello."

"Hey, Coop, sorry to bother you." Gabby's voice sounded somber. "It's just our volunteer scheduled to stay with Star cancelled, and I can't find anyone else free. I'm in a real bind because I don't want to leave her alone. She'll probably bolt."

"You're right about that." He named a few female sober companions he knew, but Gabby indicated she'd already tried all of them.

"Do you think Rivers…?" Gabby trailed off. "No. It's too much to impose on her again. Forget I mentioned her."

"She's here. You can ask." At least Gabby asking her might further break the spell that had come over him. He offered Rivers the phone. "It's Gabby."

She grabbed it faster than she'd gone for the water bottle after the spicy Brussels sprout. "Hello." Her brows furrowed as she listened. "I'll do it." Her answer had come way too quickly.

Had she needed an escape as badly as he had?

No. Surely, he'd imagined the connection between them. His crazy feelings had to be one-sided, and he needed to keep this madness to himself.

Chapter 17

As Rivers made her way back to the cottage, she fought the urge assailing her. The urge to run and hide. To bury her heart away forever, because she never wanted to dishonor Jordan or hurt his family.

Shame crept over her. How fickle must her heart be to want to kiss another man only a year after she'd lost Jordan? Another man who was James Cooper Knight.

"No need to run." Cooper touched her shoulder. "God's got this under control. You can trust His timing."

Her lungs stopped working, and her frantic, clumsy steps in the sand halted. Could this man read her mind? She gaped at him.

"Gabriella just left Star, and we can only do what we can do. I don't want you to hurt yourself in a mad rush to get to the hospital."

Here she was tripping over herself to escape, but maybe he'd not felt the same pull she'd felt toward him. The noose around her chest loosened. "Right. I'll be careful." Careful with her heart. And her words.

Her gaze dropped to his mouth. His lips.

"Yes. Careful." His voice was barely a whisper.

Oh, she needed a new focal point. Something to fixate on like a beacon or a lighthouse to keep her on track in St. Simons. She forced her gaze skyward. The golden moon hung dense and low, likely churning up some of those deadly tides. Its glow seemed to lay open those painful hollows that grief had carved into her heart.

Just keep moving.

The voice in her head prodded her on. Stepping forward, she continued her march toward the cottage, but at a slower pace, ignoring the opposing desires wrestling within her.

At the house, she stopped on the porch steps. "I've got it from here. I'm sure you have more important work to do than babysitting me all the time."

"Nothing's more important." Shuffling his feet on the broken shells lining the driveway, he cleared his throat. "I mean I don't have anything pressing, so I could drive you over."

"No." The force of her answer shocked her, and Cooper took a step back, his dark eyes widening.

"Sorry." Rivers softened her tone. "I have to learn my way around, or I'll end up dependent and clingy." More dependent and clingy. And confused. She tried to give a nonchalant shrug to lighten the mood.

"Of course. Be safe." His shoulders collapsed a little as he turned and walked away.

His posture reminded her of a kid discarded from a neighborhood game of kickball, and her chest ached to erase that image. "I have your number. Can I call you if I get lost?"

He glanced back and offered a tender smile. "Always."

And she just kept making this puddle muddier. His presence lingered on the breeze even after his Jeep whizzed away. Oh, God help her, because her world was off balance.

She'd forgotten the reason she'd asked him over. All the things in the cottage she wanted to ask him about. Stella's letters.

Where was she even going now? The hospital. Star.

Too bad she wasn't in Memphis. She always kept a hospital bag ready in case Mom had a seizure or something requiring a sudden trip to the ER. A book, a small pillow, a sweater and socks did the trick. It always seemed cold in those places. Surely she could come up with something similar in the cottage.

After dumping the tote that held the beach towels, she glanced around the living room. A throw pillow and afghan lay on the couch, so she grabbed those and shoved them in the bag. At home, she had a hundred novels waiting to be read, but she hadn't had the wits to pack even one when she'd made the painful decision to face this place.

Her thoughts meandered to the journal on the table. That could be additional emotional torture. She'd rather stare at the hospital walls. But...she'd come here to clean out and move forward. Before she changed her mind, she snatched the journal and her keys, and then continued out to the Stink Bug, stopping only to lock the door of the cottage.

Through the darkness she drove, slowly following the slave driver Cruella's ever-rude directions. Only two wrong turns, but she'd been able to *Turn around when possible* and *Make a U-turn* fairly easily. And she'd even accomplished it without tears cried or threats spewed toward the technology supposedly guiding her.

Not many anyway.

At the hospital, Rivers found her way easily back to the hall where Star's room was located. All the time she'd spent in these kind of places with her mother helped now. She'd learned that most of the healthcare centers had a somewhat similar order.

Nurses in blue scrubs. The AC blowing. The smell of sanitizer and disinfectant mingling. All familiar. This was doable.

At the room, the television droned, and a sturdy brunette nurse stood in the doorway. "Hey, are you the friend of

Gabriella's?"

"That's me." Rivers stifled a chuckle. Friends was a relative term.

"Great. I was keeping an eye out for you." Brows raised, the nurse motioned with her head toward Star.

"I know Gabby appreciates your help."

"I don't need a babysitter," a grumpy voice called from the hospital bed. Star was awake.

The nurse plunked her hands on her ample hips. "She's actually doing well, considering. Good luck."

Pressing on a smile, Rivers nodded and entered the room. "Hi." She took a seat on the reclining chair.

"The girl with the weird name is back."

"Yep. I'm Rivers."

"Like I care," Star mumbled.

"Need anything?"

"Quiet. I need quiet."

"O-kay." Seemed like Star would turn off the television then. Rivers retrieved the blanket and the journal, settling in for a long miserable night. Perhaps a safer night than if she'd stayed on the beach with Cooper. Her mind meandered back to his profile under the stars. A place she really didn't need to return. In fact, she needed to go back to Memphis. Maybe even sooner than she'd planned.

"I'm so tired, but I can't sleep." Star flicked the remote from channel to channel and cursed. "There's never anything good on TV."

That was one thing they could agree on. Rivers turned and studied the younger woman. Dark circles plumped the skin under Star's eyes, muddling her pretty face.

Rivers had read that detoxing wasn't for sissies, that it was physically painful, along with the emotional and psychological torment. A small burst of unexpected compassion surfaced in her heart for this girl. "Sorry you can't sleep."

"I don't need your pity or your judgement. I need—"

"Quiet. Got it." Rivers opened the journal. Its contents couldn't be worse than trying to carry on a conversation with Star.

~~~

June 1957

I was fooled. Tricked. Manipulated.

No. I am the fool. I allowed it all to happen.

Meeting Frank that night at the party felt like a fairytale. The swanky way he played piano and sang had all the girls swooning, and out of everyone there, his gaze landed on me. Me, of all people. I thought I was the luckiest girl in the world when he asked to see me again.

If only I'd listened to Daddy. He said Frank was a no-account and a conman after our family money. My sister, Betty, warned me to be careful, and my dear friend, Sue, did, too.

But Frank and his dark eyes and his sweet talk were all I could see or hear. What a mistake. And poor Lars, the faithful boy-next-door who'd mooned after me my whole life, was heartbroken. I'd strung him along for so long. I can't erase the memory of the stunned expression on his face when he saw me sneaking out my window to meet Frank.

That was six months, an elopement, a disownment, and what seems like a lifetime ago. If only I could take it all back. If only I could wind back the hands of time and stay home that night. I would marry Lars and have the life Daddy planned for his youngest daughter.

But here I am, utterly alone, no idea where my husband is, weeping for what might have been while Sue and Lars marry today. All my friends and family are celebrating the happy couple, and I'm an outcast.

I am getting what I deserve for being a stubborn fool.

~~~

Janet W. Ferguson

August 1957

Mrs. Thompson, an older woman in the boarding house, is teaching me how to live on a shoestring, as she calls it. I'm learning what it means to budget here in Savannah. I save Green Stamps and buy what we need wholesale or second-hand. She's taught me to can vegetables from the farmer's market. I've shelled peas and pecans until my once-tender hands are covered with thick calloused skin. Scabs dot my arms from picking blackberries in the brambles along deserted country roads. But my cupboards won't be empty this winter. Maybe Frank will appreciate the effort, and maybe he won't have to drink so much. If only he could look at me like he did that first night.

~~~

December 1957

I'm doing my best to make this a good Christmas. Working at the jewelry store, I've been able to squirrel away enough money to put down a deposit to rent a little house if Frank would agree. Maybe if we had a place of our own, things would be different.

I made Christmas cards for each member of my family in Atlanta, though I doubt any of them will open the letters. I'm such a scandal to them all, marrying a lounge musician. Would Momma have disowned me if she'd still been alive? Would she have let me come home once I explained that my husband stayed out all night or that when he didn't, he came in drunk and belligerent? Would his threatening words or the way he grabbed and bruised my arms be reason enough for me to leave? Wouldn't that be a worse scandal—divorced at twenty years old?

~~~

January 1958

Gone. It's all gone. I know it was Frank because he went on a three day bender. My house fund took months of scraping, and in one long weekend, he blew every last penny. Again, I am a fool.

~~~

The Art of Rivers

February 1958

We were kicked out of the boarding house when Frank threw one of his drunken fits, but I managed to find us a room in town above one of the shops. I just have to clean the store every evening once they close. It's better than nothing, and maybe Frank will be less frustrated, not having to live around other people in the boarding house. He says they don't understand him. But neither do I.

~~~

The lonely voice of Jordan and Cooper's grandmother poked at Rivers and pinched her heart—the ghosts of addiction still haunting the present.

Rivers glanced up to check on Star. Glazed eyes stared at the blinking lights on the television screen. Sleep didn't seem to be on the agenda any time soon, so Rivers turned her attention back to Stella's journal, scanning the entries.

October 1958

If my belly swells any larger, I feel I will split open, but already I love you, my children. When the doctor said he felt two babies, I couldn't have been happier. You two will always have each other, and I will do anything to protect you and shelter you from the mistakes I've made. You shouldn't have to suffer because of my stupidity. I even wrote and begged Daddy for help for his grandchildren's sake. He allowed my sister to come visit me, and she finally convinced him to give me the beach cottage. Betty must've made my situation sound really pitiful because he even offered to give me a small allowance as long as I keep Frank's name off the deed. We will have a place of our own, sweet babies. Maybe your father will love you more than he loves me. Maybe having children will help Frank mature.

~~~

January 1959

The fever's still raging. My whole body aches with this flu. I haven't slept in days. The girls seem to cry nonstop. If one sleeps, the other wakes. They are always hungry, and since I took ill, my milk's not been enough. I never knew life could be this hard. Frank refuses to listen to my pleas for help. I don't know how long I can go on like this. Alone, but for my children.

~~~

After a quick knock, a nurse came in, this one rail thin and wearing glasses. "I'm Lynn. I'll be taking care of you tonight. I have some Tylenol and the antibiotic for you." She fiddled with the IV attached to Star. "Can I get you anything? Some Sprite or ice cream?"

Star groaned. "Sleep. I need something to help me sleep."

"I'm sorry, sweetie. It'll get better." The nurse's voice was kind and reassuring.

"How would you know?" Star shot back.

"You're not the only one who's been through this. I promise you can come out on the other side."

A pang of guilt rippled through Rivers. She hadn't really put much effort into trying to comfort Star, just plopped down into the pity puddle of her own situation.

The nurse exited, and Rivers set aside the journal. "I'm here if you want to talk."

"I don't need *anything* from you, Malibu Barbie." Star snapped off the TV and the lights.

Chapter 18

God is in control. Cooper drove around town, trying to calm his raging emotions. Like a juggler tossing up one too many objects, his attempts were failing. Between the thought of losing the gallery and his home and his unquenchable feelings for Rivers, he needed help.

A late-night open AA meeting was about to begin at a local community center, so he exited his Jeep and made his way across the dark parking lot. It had been a while since he'd participated with this group, since he usually preferred the Celebrate Recovery meetings near Re-Claimed, but tonight, a tiny bit of anonymity would be nice. Though most people in these groups around town knew him, at least his current clients wouldn't be here. He pushed open the door and blinked against the bright lights of the recreation room.

A group of about ten men and women sat in the circle of folding chairs. He recognized several, and the others looked familiar. The smell of coffee and cigarette-smoke-infused fabric filled the room. For the first time in a long while, his mouth watered at the thought of a cigarette. The yearning pressed against him like a heavy hand. Clearly a spiritual battle was approaching, and a bone weariness settled over him.

How many times and for how many years, Lord, must I war against my own body?

"I thought you might be here." Behind him, Davis approached. "Got permission from Kevin to use the van and come join you."

Thankful for his friend's concern, Cooper nodded and shook Davis's hand, but then his stomach sank. Yeah, it was thoughtful and perhaps an answer to prayer, but acknowledgment of what he was dealing with would be harder in front of someone who knew the whole score. And Davis sure had him figured out.

Tonight's meeting leader, a fiftyish man in a fitted, gray business suit who Cooper knew was an attorney in the community, began with the usual announcements and readings. The repetition of the twelve steps and serenity prayer calmed some of the angst churning in Cooper's heart and mind.

The floor was opened for discussion. One after another, group members shared their current struggles, most of them much worse than some silly crush, but Cooper recognized signs of a problem brewing in his mind. When a quiet moment spanned the room, he knew it was time for him to talk.

"I'm Cooper. I'm an addict."

The group answered, "Hi, Cooper."

"I've been in recovery five years, but I'm having an emotional trigger right now. The first in a long time. A person who, without meaning to, is churning up the painful past with my family." He paused, not wanting to admit the romantic feelings, but Davis's larger-than-life presence beside him spurred him to deeper soul-searching. "I'm also struggling with an emotional attraction to this person who is off-limits for me."

That probably sounded all wrong. "She's not an addict or married or anything, but the situation is too complex. I know I need to meditate on God's word, pray, and keep giving God control…the control He already has." He sucked in a deep breath. "I think I really need to paint tonight or run a marathon or something to work through all of this turmoil inside. That's all I have for now."

"I try to have a plan in place for when temptations come," the man who'd led tonight's meeting commented. "Following a plan, meeting with my sponsor, reworking the steps keeps me focused."

"Admitting triggers right away is always a step in the right direction," a woman added. She was probably late thirties with tattoos running down her arms. A gold ring pierced the right side of her nose. "People often substitute one thirst for another. I like to look at the core of what's driving the trigger and deal with that issue. I talk to my sponsor about it and give control to God."

She was right. He'd seen substitution happen time and again. Trading drugs for alcohol or food or porn. Exercise and even art. Anything done obsessively to avoid the real problem.

A few others commented, offering encouragement, and the leader gave out sobriety chips as warranted, then they all circled up and said the Lord's Prayer.

Outside, cicadas hummed in the night air, and Davis walked beside Cooper without talking. A miracle in itself. A year ago, Cooper would've never imagined the obnoxious guy who'd tagged along with Angelo to Re-Claimed would become such a good friend.

Headlights flashed as cars exited the parking lot, one by one. At the Jeep, they stopped, and Cooper gave Davis a little punch on the shoulder. "Thanks for the support, man. You're going to make a great therapist." He shrugged. "Already are, actually."

"Learned from the best." Davis tossed a punch back toward Cooper. "Wanna stop in with me at Re-Claimed and have a cup of decaf or hot water or something equally tantalizing?"

"I guess, since you'll probably just keep pestering me if I don't."

"Pestering you?" Davis's chin jutted forward. "I only asked once, and you hit like a girl, by the way."

"Didn't want to make you cry." Cooper chuckled. "I'll follow you."

"Always a stalker, aren't you?" Davis gave a thumbs up and headed over to the white van belonging to Re-Claimed.

The house was quiet when they arrived. Everyone had probably hit the sack. Between the carwash and the landscaping business the other guys worked for, they put in some long days to earn their keep. Kevin and Gabby set up a savings account for each one, so when they left, there would be enough for apartment deposits or car down payments when they needed them.

Quietly, Davis led the way to the kitchen and started a pot of decaf. "I'm going to run upstairs and grab my Bible."

"Always a good plan." Cooper shot him a smile and pocketed his keys. He stared at the dripping liquid that smelled so much better than it tasted. He'd paint tomorrow. Tonight, he'd read God's Word, pray, and go on to bed. It was doubtful he'd sleep much, but he should try, rather than stay up all night spewing emotion onto a canvas.

A minute later, Davis reappeared. An unusual dent carved hard between his brows. "Do you know any reason Angelo wouldn't be here? I mean, I peeked in the living room, and he's not there. It seems like everyone else has lights out."

The feeling of walking through cobwebs crept over Cooper. In that instant, he knew in his gut that Angelo had bailed. "Wake up Kevin. See if he wants us to look for him or let him go."

"Wow, that's jacked up." Davis's posture wilted. "He was so close to finishing."

"Yep, and he's still on the court-watch drug testing schedule for one more week. Kevin and his dad stuck their neck out getting him this chance."

"Did I hear my name?" Kevin stood in the doorway, tired eyes studying them. "What's wrong?"

"Angelo's not in our room." Davis's voice was flat. "Bed's still made, but I'm praying you know a great reason he's not there."

Kevin drew a heavy sigh. "Better change the focus of your prayers, because he said he was going to bed right after you left. You two can go looking if you feel called to it, but I'll have to report him missing since he's on probation."

"Man, I had no idea he was struggling." Davis put his hand on his head. "I wouldn't have left him tonight."

Davis's desperation jabbed at Cooper's heart. It never got any easier when one of the clients—one of their friends—had a slipup...or worse. "Don't let it shake your faith. This happens. We can go look for him. We can pray. But ultimately, when people crash and burn, they're in God's hands. He knows exactly where Angelo is right now."

Davis scoffed. "I wish God would tell me, because I feel like beating the mess outta that dude. Let's go."

"We'll take the Jeep." Cooper pulled his keys back out of his pocket. This had already been a long, hard night, but now it felt like he was steering a sinking ship. Driving around his former drug-buying stomping grounds with another guy in recovery was the last thing he should be doing, but maybe they'd find Angelo before things got worse.

Chapter 19

The heavy pounding of a car radio's bass bumped through the open windows of Cooper's Jeep. He and Davis had made their way around St. Simons, checking bars and houses where Angelo might've gone—from wealthy suppliers dressed in polos and khaki shorts and living in beach houses to disheveled dealers in trailer parks and abandoned lots. Without a vehicle, they'd hoped Angelo hadn't traveled far, but someone could've picked him up.

People knew about Cooper and what he was trying to do and for the most part stayed out of his way. They knew he'd been in their shoes. Addicts usually didn't set out to be in the circumstances they were shackled to, and many—if they were honest with themselves—held out a tiny sliver of hope that, one day, they'd be free of the substance and shame enslaving them.

With no luck finding any sign of Angelo, Cooper changed course to the neighboring port city of Brunswick, a larger metropolitan area with more opportunities to use and more ways to get lost in the shuffle. And Davis knew of a guy Angelo used to sell for.

What were the chances they'd actually find him? *Guide us, Lord.*

The dark, low-lying roads of the downtrodden neighborhood dredged up haunted memories of another life. A life Cooper had spent in a haze, numb and disoriented, trying to pretend he was someone else.

Anyone but the loser he'd always heard and believed he was.

He slowed the vehicle to a crawl. Young men walked the streets, hoodies or baseball caps over their heads. Cars were parked in yards and on the sidewalks. A lookout rode by on a bike, one hand at his waist, probably packing a gun. Danger lurked here where hope had fled, driven out by evil.

"You thinking what I'm thinking?" Davis pointed out the front windshield.

"Yep. He'll be letting them know strangers are on the way." Praise God, Cooper and Davis were no longer regulars here, but that put them in a precarious situation.

"Too bad your Jeep isn't bullet proof. You could at least get a hard-top next time though." Davis knocked on the canvas roof. "And for all that's right in the world, wash the interior down with some Febreze."

"Dude, I've done that twice."

"You know what they say about the third time." He held up one hand. "Stop here. That's the place."

Through the streetlight's beams, the blue house looked familiar. The yard was groomed, split by a sidewalk leading to the porch.

Next door stood a crumbling, faded yellow house tagged with graffiti. The broken-down chain-link fence no longer guarded it. A ripped screen had long given up covering the front porch, and weeds rose shoulder-high.

"I've been here." Cooper breathed the words in a whisper. "How are they still in business?"

"One dealer gets arrested, another takes their place. And the cops have their hands full."

"The house next door is abandoned. No one with any sense wants to live there for long." Cooper's stomach churned as the fuzzy details became clearer. "I was so desperate one night that I bought, waded through the jungle of a yard, and stumbled inside that rat trap." The memory of the euphoria sent a spike to his pulse, and a wicked yearning swept over him. "To use."

Please, God, no.

"Uh-uh," Davis grunted. "Don't go there."

God knew, he was trying not to go there, but a spiritual tug of war raged in his spirit. "It's an inexplicable dark grip that absolutely enslaves every atom of your being, squeezing the life out of you."

"Slavery and torture from the belly of hell." Davis nodded. "But now you offer others a way out of those shackles and into the light."

"Father God, bind up the powers of darkness in this place, and deliver us from evil, in the powerful name of Jesus." Cooper spoke the prayer into the dense cloud falling over him.

With an exaggerated swagger, a young man, late teens at most, in a white T and covered with tattoos, made his way toward the Jeep. Probably a runner checking out why he and Davis were on their turf. "You lost?"

"Looking for a guy named Angelo, a friend of ours."

"You the police?" His gaze shifted down the street as if expecting a raid any second.

"Nope. Just want to help Angelo."

"My memory needs some help." The kid wanted money.

"I got twenty, but I need to talk to the guy inside. See if his memory's good."

"You're asking a lot now."

"Okay, forty, when you get us in."

"What's your name?"

"Tell him Cooper. Or Coop. Looking for my friend

Angelo." He pulled two twenties from his shirt pocket so the kid could see, then pushed them back in. "What's your name?"

The kid hesitated, studying Cooper. "They call me Z. Wait here." He sauntered toward the house.

A minute later, he returned. "Park over there." Z pointed to the buckled sidewalk in front of the abandoned house.

"All right." He pulled the Jeep into the spot, then cut the ignition. "This could be the worst idea I've ever had." Cooper mumbled the words as he got out.

Chortling, Davis followed. "Nah, you've had a lot worse, and I've only known you a year."

"You sure you're not cops?" Z led them up the porch, where the pungent aroma of marijuana hit full force.

Cooper's muscles coiled at the craving that washed through him. *Take this from me, Lord.*

"I run a sober living house in St. Simons. Help people start over." Cooper leveled a compassionate gaze on the young man. "I can give you the address."

The door cracked, and a muscled man stood half behind the door, half concealed. He looked over Cooper and then Davis. "Well, look at that." He pulled the door the rest of the way and tucked a black nine millimeter in his belt. He shook one finger at Cooper, a gold and diamond pinky ring glittering in the overhead light. "Old Coop. I remember you from way back." A sneer crossed the man's face. "You look better than you used to." He glanced at Davis. "He was one messed up freaky dude. And who are you, by the way?"

"Davis. Served in the same unit with Angelo."

"Looking for someone named Angelo, huh? And y'all thought you'd just show up at Lewis's house? Am I Google?" He spewed a few profanities. "What if I just show up at your house uninvited?"

Cooper held up one hand. "Got an open door for anyone trying to get clean."

"You saying I'm dirty?"

The situation was going nowhere fast. "We're just looking for our friend. Worried about him."

"Maybe you really want to hang out. Get something to take the edge off." He ran his large fingers across his chin, his flat beige eyes mocking. "I can see it in your face, you want to, old Coop."

A cold sweat broke out on Cooper's forehead. Addiction's fangs struck at him. It was as if the devil himself were in the room taunting him, luring him.

Chapter 20

"In the name of Jesus, we are freed from this temptation. Get behind us, Satan. Amen." Davis's voice rang out loud and strong.

"What?" Lewis's head whipped toward Davis. "You're trippin'." He turned back to Cooper, eyes wide. "Is he for real?"

"He's been that way since God got a hold of him." Cooper's trance temporarily broken, he struggled to tamp down the urge to run for his life and another urge to laugh at the boldness. Only Davis—with God's help—could put that kind of fear into this man.

"We're done here." Lewis's face darkened, and his fingers fell to his gun.

"Have you seen Angelo?" Cooper pressed. They hadn't come this far to give up now.

"He ain't here. And don't come back, yo." Lewis's spine straightened, and his gaze narrowed. "I won't be so hospitable."

~~~

Searching for Angelo had been a waste of gas and time. The only thing they'd confirmed was that there were places where drugs were still being sold. That was no surprise and not something he or Davis wanted or needed to dwell on.

They'd come home unscathed, praise God, and had given Kevin the rundown, so he could alert his father. Mr. Barnes had been the sheriff for eight years. He was a fierce giant of a

---

man with an equally fierce and giant heart for the lost. The talks and prayers he'd had at the jail with Cooper after the accident had convinced him that God still loved him. And Jesus's sacrifice was powerful enough to cleanse any and all sins, no matter how many or how big. Those talks and prayers had led Cooper to Christ, and then to Kevin and Gabriella's newly founded sober living houses.

The men of Re-Claimed gathered around the coffee pot after breakfast, waiting for an update. Word had spread quickly about the previous night's escapades. Cooper prayed this letdown didn't ripple out and become a tidal wave of residents jumping ship.

Kevin clanged a spoon on his ceramic cup to get their attention. "You all heard Angelo took off. The enemy will use his actions to shake our determination, to cause fear, to tempt us to lose our courage to stay the course. But courage is only fear that has said its prayers. And we are going to pray."

"Amen," Davis interjected.

"I've heard that the Bible says, 'Do not fear,' three hundred and sixty-six times." Kevin shoved up one finger in an exaggerated wave. "That's one for every day plus leap year. Grasp onto that. James 4:7 says, 'Submit yourselves, then, to God. Resist the devil, and he will flee from you.' We will not be beaten. God is a shield before us, behind us, above and below. He is your bulletproof vest. Prayer isn't your Hail Mary pass at the last minute. Use that shield every day, all day." He motioned toward Davis.

Lifting his arms, Davis nodded. "Let's circle up."

During the prayer, each man shared his heart and concerns. When they finished, Davis sent them to their rooms to retrieve their Bibles.

With a groan, Davis refilled his coffee cup. "How about I

get a little me-time, like shut in a closet eating Reese's Peanut Butter Cups?"

Chuckling, Cooper reeled in his unsteady emotions. "You deserve a break, bro. Right after church."

The suddenness of his triggers still rattled Cooper. He'd slept on the couch here, just because he didn't fully trust himself alone in the loft. A fact that frustrated him to no end. Going to worship was what he needed.

Before the currents swept him out again.

~~~

"Good morning, ladies." Gabby waltzed into the hospital room, a huge grin lighting her face. She wore a purple dress and black pumps. The nurses and techs had already come, gone, and were preparing release papers for Star. People were sure up early today.

Though drained from lack of sleep, Rivers managed to conjure a smile. "Don't you look nice? Where ya headed?"

"I came to pick up Star and invite you to church."

It was Sunday? Rivers stared at the phone in her lap for confirmation.

A moan came from Star. "I agreed to go to the sober living house, but you aren't planning to drag me to church today, are you?"

"Not today. I have someone who can stay with you at the house, but you should be well enough soon." Gabby leaned over and caressed Star's forehead.

"Church isn't really for me." Star's lips pinched.

"You are a daughter of the King, reclaimed and dearly loved. You are exactly who the church is for, same as me."

"You're too much." Though Star shook her head, her countenance wasn't nearly as harsh when she looked at Gabby as when her gaze turned to Rivers.

"Got a lot of love in here." Gabby patted a hand over her heart. "And I'm not selling it, I'm giving it away. Everything for my King." She lifted a gym bag. "Got you some clothes to wear home."

"Home?" Star mumbled something under her breath and took the offering. "I need someone to get my stuff from where we were staying then. My IDs are in my backpack."

"My brother, Kevin, will handle that today."

Rivers stood, eager to escape the room where she was clearly not wanted. "I guess I'll head out."

"I know you're tired, but the late service at the Island Church starts at eleven, and that's the one Re-Claimed residents attend."

She normally didn't miss church in Memphis, but lying on a real bed for a while sounded especially enticing right now.

"You have time for a nap, and I bet Coop could pick you up if you're afraid you might get lost."

He must've told Gabby about the directional impairment. What else had he told his friends?

Star observed the interchange with narrow eyes, as if judging every move Rivers made. Almost like a pair of siblings she'd counseled, each dying to find the other doing something wrong. What was with that? The girl really had it out for her.

Rivers pinched the bridge of her nose and then wiped the sleepiness from her eyes. "If you send me the address, I'll find it and meet you there." The less she relied on Cooper, the better.

~~~

Back at the cottage, Rivers threw herself onto the bed. She had two hours to rest, change, and find the church, but the journal she'd placed on the night stand captured her attention. Stella had occupied her thoughts and dreams all night. Rivers

150

reached for the book.

March 1959

I've been home from the hospital for a week. I'm finally able to hold Brooklyn and Pearl. The pneumonia almost killed me, but I guess God thought my sweet girls still needed their momma. Betty has been taking care of all of us. At last, Frank came home. He's sober. I don't know how this miracle occurred, but I'm so thankful. The girls adore him, and he them. He's a completely different person when he's not drinking. If I had to almost die to get to this point, then it was worth it. I just pray things stay this way.

~~~

The journal entries went on but were sparse. Having twins likely kept Stella busy, but she'd recounted their milestones— their first teeth, crawling, walking, their first words both being "Daddy." She recorded a few bad storms blowing in on the Atlantic and some sunny days playing with the children. Normal days. It seemed she'd had a few good years.

But Rivers continued reading, and anxiety whipped up inside her chest, thrashing like a kite caught in a gale.

January 1964

I found a silver flask in the flower bed by the driveway. The sun shimmering on it caught my eye. When I picked up the vile thing, opened it, and took a whiff, my heart seemed to crack into a hundred rigid shards, like the broken shells underfoot. My stomach emptied as I thought of what might come next.

I asked Frank about the flask, and he swore it wasn't his. He insisted some teenager must have thrown it out of a passing car or walking home from the beach in an effort not to get in trouble. I begged him to tell me the truth. I told him he could get help, and I would support him. I've heard of groups that meet to help each other overcome their issues. He cursed and told me I was crazy and that I should quit badgering him. If

I kept on, I'd be the one driving him to drink.

I don't know what to believe.

~~~

March 1964

The old Frank is back in full fury. I'm brokenhearted. He'd been well for so long. I guess I had become too comfortable, too at ease...too happy. Then one evening he just didn't come home. For three long days and nights, I prayed. I drove around with the girls. I called his friends and the clubs where he played. I called the police, for goodness' sake, thinking someone had killed him. I almost wished he'd been in a wreck or knocked in the head, that he was injured but would live.

If only Frank were just confused.

But I knew better. He was on another bender.

Then in the middle of the fourth night, he stumbled in, flipping on the lights, waking the girls, slurring his words, telling some big tales of where he'd been... Lies.

The misery has returned.

Sniffling, Rivers brushed tears from her cheeks. After five years of sobriety, Frank relapsed. The same amount of time Cooper had been in recovery. Would the grandson be able to maintain it any better than his grandfather? Another reason she could never risk her heart to someone who struggled with addiction—the evil always lurking in the shadows.

Painful memories tore through Rivers like an angry flash flood. The theatrical late entrances on school nights, Mom's voice, decibels louder than her normal volume, explaining how the office staff had attended some big event, then they'd all gone to Beale Street or the Peabody for drinks. She'd devise stories of huge traffic jams, or someone's car getting towed, or how she'd come upon a wreck where she just had to help the poor accident victims. Those were some of the customary lies, but then there were some downright nutty ones, too, that, even as a child, Rivers had thought farfetched. Like the time Mom claimed a gorilla had escaped the zoo and was on the loose, so she couldn't leave the bar. Another time there was a story involving an Elvis impersonator stalking her and how she'd had to take refuge at a "friend's" place.

With calm whispers, Dad would lead Mom back to the master bedroom of their little home and put her to bed. Once he had her quieted, he always came down the hall to find Rivers in her room. He would press a kiss on her forehead and repeat the mantra.

"God loves you, Rivers. He has a special plan just for you."

Looking back, Rivers had wanted to believe so badly that her mother was out saving accident victims or delivering stray puppies or doing any of the things in her crazy stories.

Not out getting smashed with another man.

The car accident had driven home the truth in a very public way.

The phone on the coffee table chimed with a text. Rivers set aside the journal and read the message. Gabby had sent the address earlier but now was asking if she should save a seat near the back of the church.

Rivers let her head fall forward. Maybe God had a special plan for her like Dad had promised, but right now, maybe that *special plan* wasn't what she wanted. Maybe she just wanted an easy and simple and uncomplicated life.

A life around sober people.

Chapter 21

On the back row of chairs inside the community church, Cooper struggled to keep his eyes open. Voices echoed around the walls of the old auditorium. The gang from Re-Claimed wore somber expressions, worry for Angelo pressing on their minds. Most addicts in recovery realized—if they were honest—they were straddling a razor's edge, only one drink or pill away from losing their sobriety. That's why the slogan *one day at a time* helped keep them sane.

"Wake up, or your crush will catch you drooling." Davis's elbow knifed into Cooper's arm.

"What?" His numb brain tried to make sense of the barb.

With an exaggerated move of his head, Davis pointed to the end of the row where Gabby stood, directing Star and Rivers their way. Star's face was pale, but her chin had a determined jut to it.

Rivers was the one who gave him a jolt. Her eyes wore dark circles, a weariness in their depths that tugged at his chest. Cooper blinked hard at the image. Gabby was a true miracle worker, but it seemed a little much for Star and Rivers to attend worship today.

Star sat with a wince on the end of the row, signaling for Rivers and Gabby to go past her. There were exactly four seats remaining. Gabby sat beside Star and set a large handbag in the chair beside her, leaving the chair right next to him for Rivers.

Her eyes met his for a moment before she sat. "Hi."

"If I'd known..." He stopped himself from saying he

154

would've picked her up. She'd made it very clear she didn't want his help the night before. "How did it go at the hospital?"

"Could've been worse." Clearly, Rivers was exhausted. She seemed to be forcing her eyelids open.

"Why is Star here?" He lowered his voice to a whisper.

She leaned closer but kept her gaze forward. "I think she wants to one-up me for some crazy reason. Like she's got something to prove."

He couldn't stop a smirk. He'd seen that before. "We'll have to figure out how to use that attitude to our advantage."

Her head pivoting toward him, Rivers cocked an eyebrow, but she didn't say anything. Didn't have to.

"I mean we as in the staff. I know that's not why you came to St. Simons, and you'll be leaving as soon as you..." How could he finish that sentence without sounding disappointed or hurt and without injuring her heart further? "...take care of your business."

Her lips clamped together, and the corners of her mouth turned down. Obviously, he'd chosen the wrong words. Again. But was there another less painful way to say *you're cleaning out the baggage of the dead?*

Music began, ending the conversation. Just in time to keep him from shoving his foot farther down his throat. He stood and joined the energetic praise songs, despite the battle-weariness weighing on him, and tried not to think about the woman next to him.

The minister began a sermon on Jonah, explaining how God called him to go preach to an enemy nation, but Jonah had run away, unwilling to accept God's mission. His attempted escape only landed him in a worse situation—the belly of a fish. Scrubbing a hand across his forehead, Cooper tried to focus on Brother Bruce's words.

"People, we are daily in a battle. Evil pushes and pulls against us. If Satan can't get us off track, he distracts us. Our intentions might be respectable in our busyness, especially in the world's view. We do a good deed. We take care of our family. We work hard at our job, we keep the laws of the land, and we go to church. We may even volunteer in the community. All good, but what is best?"

His volume and passion rose. "Jonah didn't mind preaching to his own people, but when God asked him to step out of that comfort zone and preach to his enemies in Nineveh, Jonah shook his head and ran. In pursuit of our good deeds, we may be failing those people God puts in our path, and in turn, failing to do what the Lord has commanded us. The lost are all around, Church. God doesn't ask if they are *your kind of folk*s, or if you're comfortable doing what He asks. There's not a qualifier when He says, 'Go.' He didn't ask you if His plan was okay with you, or if this is a good time for you."

Someone in the audience yelled, "Preach on." Another said, "That's right."

Rivers fidgeted. She dug into her purse until she plucked out a tissue and a piece of chewing gum.

What did she think about all this? Their church service was a little louder and livelier than some, and Brother Bruce was on fire today. Something must really have him stirred up.

"Like Jonah, we often run from the mission set before us. Who has every intention of telling others about Jesus Christ this week? As a Christian, shouldn't that be our intention?"

Several members answered "Amen."

"Luke 19:10 says, 'For the Son of Man came to seek and to save the lost.' Are we to do any less? Isn't that our mission, Church? We need to open our eyes. The field is ripe for harvest. Reach out a hand and offer that lifeline to eternity.

Guess what? Life is riddled with death. We don't know when our last day will come. We don't know the last day for the person sitting next to us. Do you believe God sent His Son to save you from your sins? Because He did. But He also sent His son to save that person you really don't want to deal with. That person who makes you uncomfortable, that person who pushes your buttons."

Rivers lifted the tissue and blotted her eyes. Was she crying? Cooper fought the urge to turn to see.

"What's more important to you? God's mission? Your good intentions? Your comfort? Your job or being on time to church? I mean, I want you here in the chairs, but what's the purpose of all this?" He swept his arms in a wide circle. "What is the purpose if we don't leave this room and share the light of the Gospel into the dark corners of the world where God has planted us?"

~~~

The words landed on her and pressed hard. When could she get out of here? The minister finally ended his message, which was slaughtering her heart, and now another man led the closing prayer. Rivers pressed the tissue under her eyes in an attempt to erase unwanted tears.

Before the echo of the final amen faded, she stood, hoping to scoot out, but Gabby was already helping Star to her feet, and Rivers didn't dare push past them.

"I better get this little chickadee in a bed." Gabby locked elbows with Star but turned back to Rivers. "We can hold art therapy tomorrow night with the ladies, if you want to try leading a session."

Conviction lay heavy on her heart. Wasn't she like Jonah, hoping to run rather than share the Gospel with people she considered the worst of sinners? Having grace for this sort of

157

weakness in others seemed to be a test she had to take over and over until she passed. And she was tired of repeating it. Maybe now was the time to truly learn some compassion for strugglers like Star.

"Okay. Does the lesson format matter? And what time?"

"After dinner, seven o'clock? You're welcome to eat with us, and you're free to be creative with the class."

"I'll see you at seven." Rivers shifted her gaze for a sideways glance at Cooper. His dark hair swept across his forehead in that careless, perfect way. He'd stayed back to talk to the minister and Shane, Jordan's step-uncle. From their expressions, the conversation wasn't a pleasant one. She'd love to get out of there before Shane started his pitch for selling her properties again. She had enough stress without that pressure.

Cooper glanced her way with those soulful eyes that shone like living onyx stones. His gaze began a twirling sensation in her stomach. She turned and focused on the exit.

Having grace and mercy for addicts didn't mean she had to be in a romantic relationship with one. Stella's letters and her own mother were proof of those risks.

~~~

And she was gone.

Cooper pulled his concentration back to the infuriating conversation at hand. Anger thundered through his arms to his fists as he stood with the minister and listened to Shane.

"So the petition states Re-Claimed is running a rehab in a residentially zoned area." Shane continued his explanation with a business-like air. As if this news wasn't ugly. "If it's found they're in violation of a zoning law, they could be facing a hefty fine per day."

"Since when did sober mean sinless?" Brother Bruce sighed.

A current of dread swept over Cooper. Another bomb dropping into his life. He couldn't believe what he was hearing. After five years in the same neighborhood with no incidents to speak of, someone had started a petition against Re-Claimed, wanting them to move. Good grief. "Why now?"

"Who knows?" Shane shrugged. "Someone new in the neighborhood, maybe. Or one of your residents' criminal history got out. Could be anything. With social media, rumors spread faster than fleas."

Brother Bruce's brows knit together. "Heard about this last night from a deacon. I scrapped the sermon I'd planned and let God do the talking. We can't change society without changing hearts, and Re-Claimed is doing that."

True, and Gabby had done her research. "Fair Housing laws should side with Re-Claimed. They are the functional equivalent of a family, and they can't be discriminated against."

"But the other side contends that you're providing professional services, which makes you a rehab facility. You could get tied up with legal bills either way."

Legal bills, fines, petitions. First the gallery and now Re-Claimed. Doubt and weariness assaulted Cooper's soul like the Atlantic's tides, threatening to sweep him out into the abyss. It seemed that everything in his life was being stripped away, and he didn't have much left to lose.

Chapter 22

After a nap on the couch, Rivers spent the afternoon and evening cleaning out another bedroom, sorting through all the little things people collect over a lifetime. She divided the items into piles.

Items that might be worth something, like a collection of hand-blown glass and crystal swans, she set aside. She'd have to get those appraised. Then there was a pile that charity might accept. After all, some people enjoyed wearing and decorating with vintage items. Another pile that might be of sentimental value to the family. Would Brooklyn and Pearl want anything? This was their mother's life. Why would they just leave it all? Picturing her almost-mother-in-law and her twin as little girls pulled Rivers back to the journal.

She paused her work, returned to the living room, and picked up the book. The draw to know more about this tragic family drama sucked her in like powerful, channeled currents of water pulling her away from safe shores. Lying on the blue-and-white Turkish rug, she propped herself on her elbows and dove back into the past.

March 1964

Pearl is so sick. I'm afraid for her life. Her appendix ruptured. I should have known better. I'm a terrible mother. I thought she was just upset about Frank. We all were sick over what he's become. This is all my fault for being such an idiot.

He finally sobered enough to come to the hospital. I shouldn't have let him, but Pearl was so glad to see him there.

I don't know what to do about him. How long will he last this time? I don't know what to do about my marriage.

~~~

April 1964

Pearl is recovering at home, but she's still weak. The infection was so bad. I grieve night and day about failing her. Brooklyn barely leaves her side. When one hurts, it seems the other feels the pain as well.

Frank is back, trying to help, but I am cautious with my reliance on him.

~~~

May 1964

Frank didn't come home, and I asked a neighbor to stay with the girls. They were asleep already, and I went looking for him at the club. I just had this feeling in my gut. And there he was—his arms wrapped around another woman, dancing, whispering in her ear. I can't erase the image, nor this final betrayal and devastation. I let him know I was there, then left to grieve alone.

Daddy paid his lawyer to begin divorce proceedings, and he has even agreed to see me again as long as I don't change my mind.

I won't change my mind.

~~~

July 1964

I'm pregnant. With all the insanity, I hadn't noticed the signs, but the doctor confirmed it today. I am afraid to tell anyone. Betty and Daddy will be disappointed. My friends will think I'm a fool, which I am, but I had forgotten how much so. I dare not tell Frank. He's so angry when he comes around, and I don't allow him to come inside. The girls shouldn't have to be exposed to such behavior. I know they miss the father they loved, but this is not the same man. I don't know how, but I'll care for this child, too.

~~~

September 1964

I had to call the police. Betty and Daddy insisted after Frank's harassment continued to escalate. I keep the door locked day and night. If he catches us outside, he is rough with me, grabbing my arms, shaking me and yelling. I won't change my mind about the divorce. I will protect my girls and this child growing in my womb. I have kept the baby hidden, wearing baggy clothing. Not even Betty knows. The divorce could be affected if anyone found out. I hope Frank never finds out.

Groaning, Rivers closed the journal and surveyed the cottage. How awful. Enough of this misery for now. No one in Jordan's family had ever mentioned another sibling, so whatever happened had to have been tragic. For all its charm, the walls of this cottage had seen much misery. One person's actions, one person's addiction, rippled out into the lives of so many others.

A breath of fresh air to clear her head would be nice. She should check in with Dad too. Rivers pushed to her feet, grabbed her cell, and made her way outside onto the back deck. Red lights flashed in the driveway next door. The muscles of her stomach compressed. What was wrong with Priscilla?

Rivers tiptoed barefoot across the yards, ignoring the broken shells stabbing her feet. Her neighbor sat on a gurney, arguing with the paramedic.

"I'll hire a driver to take me to the doctor tomorrow." Forehead contorting, Priscilla motioned to the house. "I can't just leave."

"Priscilla, can I help you?" Rivers ventured closer.

Her neighbor's expression softened. "Oh, sweetie, could you? My son called them. I was on the phone with him, and I guess I fainted. Now they want to take me to the hospital for tests."

"You should probably get checked out. I can go with you if you're nervous." Goodness. She really needed to keep a hospital bag packed here.

"Oh, heavens, I'm not nervous for me. I just can't leave poor Phoenix. He's probably having an anxiety attack. If you could look after him, my mind will rest, and I suppose I can go with them now."

"Phoenix?" Please, not the bizarre, rodent-looking, pet. "The possum?"

"You remembered." Priscilla's features relaxed.

"Okay." Rivers heard the word come out, though she hadn't meant to say it.

"There's a key on the rack by the door. Give these nice men your number, and I'll text you the instructions from the ambulance."

Once the ambulance drove away, Rivers ventured inside Priscilla's house. Perspiration beaded on her forehead. This was not what she had in mind at all when she offered to help. It seemed life kept throwing her curve balls.

Huddled in the corner of a large kennel, the animal's beady eyes stared up at her above a long snout. Its nose was pink, and its ears were more rounded than she remembered from their first meeting.

Sort of cute. Maybe. "Hello, Phoenix."

At its name, the animal pushed to its feet and took slow steps with strange fingerlike toes spread wide toward the kennel door.

Why had she called it, anyway? She wasn't getting the thing out until she heard from Priscilla.

Her phone began a series of chimes. And a string of instructions.

Phoenix has a litter box but likes to go outside. No leash needed. He

163

wanders the house but will need to be in the kennel when no one is home. He is a little lazy and sleeps a lot. He loves to eat and can be fed cat food along with fruit. His favorite is strawberries.

Rivers pocketed her phone and stared at her new charge. "Strawberries, huh? I hope Priscilla is stocked up because you'll be out of luck at my place. And moving this crate seems like a lot of work. Maybe I'll stay over here for a while."

Two hours later, the possum lay curled up and snoring beside Rivers on Priscilla's couch. They'd been out in the yard so he could do his business. No wonder no leash was needed, the creature moved slower than a three-legged turtle. They finally made it across to the cottage where she thought to grab the journal before returning across the yards.

She'd topped off the food bowl with cat food, but Phoenix seemed to give a sad pout, so she fed him a few strawberries she found in Priscilla's refrigerator. His little mouth was pink when he finished smacking the fruit. Rivers ran her fingers across the animal's fur. He was as soft as a kitten. Maybe the little fella was growing on her, but that long bald tail still freaked her out.

Although dreading what she'd learn, she turned her attention back to the journal.

October 1964

I'm in a dark place, and I feel I may never return. Betty is here to care for the girls, or all would be lost.

I can still smell the booze on Frank's breath. I can still see his rabid expression. I see the blood dripping from his arm where he broke our window and forced his way into the cottage. With angry fists, he beat me and threw me off the porch. I hear the girls screaming and relive their vain attempts to stop their father from hurting me. In his rage, he punched Brooklyn and knocked her out. I thought he'd killed her. The police arrived as Pearl ran out, carrying a butcher knife, ready to avenge her sister.

Like a nightmare in slow motion, I relive the carnage.

They say the baby boy I carried is in a better place, yet I mourn for him. They say the girls will recover, but will they truly ever recover their innocent hearts?

~~~

Breath catching in her lungs, Rivers brushed away a tear and petted Phoenix's fur.

No wonder Stella and Brooklyn had excised Cooper from their lives like a cancerous tumor. And Cooper's mother had followed suit. Pearl's bond to her twin was strong.

Chapter 23

"Have y'all talked about the petition?" Shane Turner stood in the doorway of Re-Claimed men's house. His calm expression seemed at odds with the statement he'd just made—the bomb that had been dropped on them yesterday after church.

"Kevin and Gabriella are looking into it, but they feel sure they've followed the law." Cooper drew a deep breath, trying to loosen the stranglehold of stress tightening his throat. Its grip seemed to be intensifying with each passing hour. Mondays, the gallery was closed, and he met with each client to see how they were progressing. He was only halfway through the list, so he really didn't have the time or emotional stamina for this discussion.

"But you know these two houses are on prime real estate. They could be sold and y'all could move into a really nice facility in Brunswick. There'd be plenty of extra cash left for helping even more of your people."

And Shane would be happy to broker that deal. Jordan's step-uncle had been good to him, but that didn't mean Shane wasn't a bottom-line kind of guy. "The houses were donated by families who'd lost someone to addiction specifically to provide a place for people to live who are trying to start over."

"You can't blame the neighbors for being scared they'll be robbed." His gaze became serious. "They worry their kids might get hurt."

His comment threatened to dredge up more guilt about Savannah, but this was too important to give in without a fight.

"What they may not realize is that there are already addicts living in their neighborhoods, working at their businesses, attending their churches and schools, and sharing their roads. The people living here are sober, productive people in recovery, which is good for the community."

"Not everyone will understand or believe that. I heard you lost one just this weekend."

Why the sudden negativity? Cooper's jaw tightened, and he kept any replies that came to mind to himself. A motto they often used here was KMS: Keep mouth shut.

Shane took the hint. "I'm here if you need me to get you a good deal."

"I'll tell Gabby and Kevin, but I have appointments." Already, Blake waited just outside the door.

"I'll check back." Shane took a step out but pivoted back once more. "You met Rivers?"

"Yep." He'd been waiting on this subject to come up.

"I'll handle the sale of the gallery for her and help you find a new place."

"Thanks for the offer." Cooper tried to present an appreciative expression that matched his words. Shane had helped, giving him a chance and allowing Re-Claimed to run the gallery, and they'd worked hard to keep it maintained. Kevin had also taken maintenance crews by the cottage at Shane's request for no charge. They'd cut the grass and performed various small repairs on the exterior, even painted it two years ago. The setup had been a win-win situation. Not that any of it mattered now since Rivers was going to get rid of both properties.

Once Shane left, Blake stood in the vacated spot. "Hey. They said I have to talk to you."

"You don't have to do anything, but if you want to work

167

to get better, come in."

Blinking hard, Blake lumbered to the couch and sank onto it. Deep furrows carved into his forehead, and his complexion held a pasty tint, especially compared to the dark circles surrounding his eyes. The doctors had prescribed medication to help the guy wean off the heroin, but getting clean would still be excruciating.

"I have the questionnaire you answered for us, and I think we can agree that your addiction is acute. You've taken a big step coming here, but given the severity, you might have a better recovery at an inpatient facility. I can find you a spot."

"Been there, done that, many times." Blake lifted one hand like a stop sign. "Not going back to a lockdown."

"Okay, then, it's good you're willing to give Re-Claimed a try. It worked for me. I was a tough case, too, but with God's help, I'm clean." Cooper leaned forward in his seat, giving Blake his full attention. "Where do you want to start?"

"Long story, but I can start at the beginning, I guess. I'll try to tell you without getting too deep in the weeds." Blake's eyes closed. "In school, back in New Orleans, I was good at baseball. Always had been, so that kept me in a popular group. But I never really felt comfortable talking to people. Felt awkward. I didn't know how to connect, you know?" He opened his eyes to check for a response.

Cooper nodded. "Man, I could write a book on it."

"The first time I took a drink, I felt free from all the uneasiness. I had so much confidence. And I just kept going. Anything and everything I could get my hands on, I tried it. But once I got a hold of some Oxy, that was my thing."

"Did you raid a medicine cabinet?"

His head bobbed. "My parents' was first, then my grandparents', aunts', cousins', and anyone else's I could.

Somehow, I got into college to play ball, but I still used. I sold to be able to keep myself supplied. There was a girl I met not long after Hurricane Katrina hit down there. Because the girl was special, I tried to quit, but it didn't work. I ended up getting arrested for distribution the very day that she told me she was pregnant. The cops had been watching me."

"What happened with the girl? The baby?"

"Never talked to her again. My family wouldn't bond me out, but finally a friend did. I was so jittery, I went right back to using a day later. Got caught riding dirty and was put back in jail until my trial nine months later."

"So you were in jail when the baby was born."

"When I got out, I asked some of Cammie's friends about her and the baby. They told me to leave Cammie alone. She had gone back to her family's place on the Mississippi coast, and they were taking care of her. I stayed clear of women after that." He shook his head. "No sense messing up some other kid's life. I was in and out of jails and rehabs, but a couple of years ago, I was clean awhile. Moved to the Mississippi coast, thought about connecting with my daughter, explaining things to Cammie. Tell her I was sorry. I was working at a seafood restaurant in Bay St. Louis, saving money to give them, but I thought I'd be okay having a beer now and then." He paused and swiped his fingers across his cheeks.

"You relapsed."

"Gradually, but along the way, I met Star. She taught in a gym where I worked out. I saw her boyfriend roughing her up after closing one night. I stepped in and kicked his tail, but it turned out he had some gangster friends. Long story short, we got out of town and headed east. We were working at the hotel here, but some rich guy got hot and heavy for Star. When she wasn't interested, he made up some bull about us. Got us fired.

We haven't had much luck since."

With Blake's height at well over six feet and his athletic build, he'd likely packed quite a punch to Star's rotten boyfriend. Cooper couldn't help but admire Blake's protective nature. "What are your reasons for making this try at sobriety?"

"I'd like for Star to be safe."

"What about you? How would you want things to turn out in your life?"

Sighing, Blake lifted one shoulder. "Don't know. Growing up, coaching seemed like an option. With my record, that can't happen. There isn't much out there for guys like me."

Not a lot of hope left in this man. "You'd be surprised. There are still people who want to give guys like you and me a chance."

"I'd just blow it. Star, though, she's not so far gone."

"But you're here, and today, you're sober, so there's still hope, Blake." The burden to speak life, especially in an addict's worst and weakest moment, weighed heavily on Cooper. "Do you believe in God?"

"You mean like working the steps? Higher power and all?"

"Yeah. You've used the steps before, and they will work when you keep with them." Cooper paused to choose his words carefully. "My Higher Power has a name. Jesus. I believe in a God who loves you so much that He sent His Son to die for all your mistakes so He could be with you for eternity. He is the God who has restored me to sanity while I walk with Him and submit my will to Him every single day—every single hour and minute. And sometimes those small increments feel excruciatingly long."

Blake let that sink in, and Cooper allowed the stretch of silence.

"Sounds okay, but I always seem to get stuck. What I want

and what I do are two different ballgames." Blake stood and pressed his fingers between his eyebrows. "I feel like I'm gonna be sick. Can I be excused?"

"We can talk more later." Cooper rose and followed him down the hall to the bathroom. "I'll tell Kev you're not feeling well."

He had no idea if he'd made any connection with Blake. Weariness blanketed Cooper's spirit, pressed down on his shoulders and heart. Storm after storm seemed to be rocking his faith, and without a lot of Jesus, he might just implode.

Chapter 24

The possum was growing on her. Rivers unloaded a bag of supplies at the gallery, but she missed her little sidekick already. He'd followed her around, sat when she sat, ate a whole lot when she ate, and slept when she slept, plus some. No wonder Priscilla worried about the little creature. He was sweet and seemed to crave companionship.

Growing up, Rivers never had the opportunity to keep a pet. At first, her mom and dad both stayed busy with work, and she'd been busy with dance lessons. Then her mom's accident happened. Now that she thought about it, her mother might actually do well with a therapy dog. Or possum.

Rivers took a deep breath. With the anxiety coursing through her midsection over teaching this class, she could use a therapy animal herself. At the studio entrance, Rivers knocked, then turned the knob to crack the door. "Hello. It's me."

Good, the room was empty. She'd have a minute to collect herself.

"We're coming." Gabriella called and waved from the sidewalk. The ladies trailed behind her, chatting loudly.

Star brought up the rear of the group, a sour expression pulling down her mouth. "This is stupid."

Anger flooded Rivers. Her job was stupid? Of all the rude, ungrateful people she'd met, Star just moved to the front of the line. Rivers held in a biting reply.

Definitely should've brought the possum.

Rivers set her bag inside the door and waited for the ladies to catch up. Weaving her fingers in front of her, she tried to pretend she wasn't a pulsing bundle of nerves and annoyance. Sweat broke out across her forehead, and her palms felt clammy. She needed to calm down. And ignore Star. Her go-to activity was prepared for tonight, and once she saw how the ladies participated, she could prepare from this starting point for next week. Or whenever another art therapy session was expected.

Once they'd filed in, Rivers began laying out and sorting the supplies she'd brought.

"You can have anything you want." Cooper had slipped up behind her, his presence throwing her even more off balance. Shaking his head, he shrugged and stared at the ground. "I mean the gallery is yours, but the supplies are purchased by Re-Claimed...or donated."

"Thanks." Rivers studied his uncomfortable stance. He probably meant he'd bought the supplies for art therapy himself. Therapists and teachers often spent their own money for their students, or their clients, in this case.

He still stood near, watching her—also unnerving.

She swallowed the growing lump in her throat and motioned toward the mix of items in front of her. "I hope you don't mind, but I thought this stuff from the cottage was perfect for art projects. I mean, if you see something you want, just grab it. In fact, I have a lot of things at the cottage I wanted to ask your opinion about. You could keep some or we could give to a charity."

"I don't need anything." His voice came out flat. "The Re-Claimed ladies run a thrift store. They'd be happy to take your donation."

"I still wanted to show you a few things, and I didn't get a

173

chance the other night."

"Okay. I can stay during your session tonight if you want me—"

"No." Once again, her tone came out sharper than she'd intended. And she hated the way it dampened his gaze. Her emotions seemed to be a churning mass of exasperation. "It's just, I'm already nervous, and I hear you can be a distraction to the ladies." Though butterflies flitted in her abdomen, teaching would probably be better than remaining in this awkward conversation. She glanced at Star who was glaring their way. Maybe teaching the class alone would not be better. A distraction could be good.

Why did Star hate her so much? Rivers ran through their time at the hospital. She'd only tried to help the girl. Why couldn't Star see that?

"I'll get out of your way, then."

"Thanks." She offered the best smile she could conjure through her agitation. "I mean it."

He left, and Gabby approached. "Everyone, this is our art therapist for tonight."

And she was on. Her heart raced in her chest. "Hi, ladies, I'm Rivers. I met some of you the other evening at dinner." Oh, great. Bring up the night Star was stabbed. "You can take a seat in front of an easel, and I'll explain our project."

They shuffled to a spot, their gazes weighing heavily on Rivers. Her face grew hot under their scrutiny. Kids were so much less intimidating.

Gabriella moved to stand in front of the closest canvas. "While they're getting settled, I'd love to hear a little about how you got started as an artist."

"Great question." And unexpected. Rivers took a deep breath. "From an early age, I wanted to reproduce what I saw.

174

Color excites me. I enjoy picking up a brush and trying to transmit my feelings from my heart and soul onto a canvas. That's one of the things I want you to consider. Painting, and art in general, is a personal experience. Allow your emotions freedom. Be prepared for disappointment in the results sometimes, but also let go of self-doubt."

One woman in the group had zoned out already, staring into space. Another applied lip balm and fiddled with her hair. Two girls in the back put their heads together and whispered.

Nice. Already they were bored. Rivers cleared her throat. "Anyway, I've always drawn and painted, and then I studied for a master's in art therapy. But enough about me." She lifted the canvas from the easel near Gabriella. "Tonight we're going to work on what I've dubbed our *Feeling Hearts*. Maybe there's a better name, but since I normally work with children, I keep terminology simple."

"We aren't children." Star scowled.

"I draw like one," the older redhead joked. "I can't make a stick in the mud."

"No worries. I won't judge." Rivers forced a smile and tried to make eye contact with the ladies who were actually paying attention. "On each easel, I've given you a canvas with a penciled outline of a heart. If any part of your heart is happy, show that with the colors you choose or even words you paint or write there. If you have anger or sadness, you can shade those parts of the heart. I've brought other multimedia pieces that can be glued to the picture if you like." She motioned toward the costume jewelry and fabric scraps from the cottage. "You won't have to share about the finished work unless you want to."

"Good. Because I've got some junk stored up in here," a blond chimed in, patting her chest.

"We all do." Rivers nodded. Finally, some participation.

"Humph." The grunt came from Star, who leveled a harsh look on Rivers.

Face simmering, she continued, "When we create art, we want to represent our journey."

"And what journey would you know, Barbie? You broke a nail once?" Something in Star's sarcasm struck a match in Rivers.

How dare she? River's vision went red. Every spark of anger and hurt she'd held in since she arrived erupted into flames and burned to spew out like molten lava. "How about the part of my journey when my mother came home trashed most of my life? That is, until the one night she didn't come home because she had driven away from an office party drunk and crashed her car, killing the man she was with—not my father—and ending up with permanent brain damage and causing us to get sued over the adulterous man's death. Don't worry, though, I didn't break a nail. Or how about the part of my journey where some addict shot my fiancé right in front of me? I didn't break a nail then, either." She slid aside the shoulder of her loose, short-sleeve top to reveal the bullet scars. "Even when he turned the gun on me. Except, unfortunately, I lived. Jordan didn't." She held up her hand. "But, hey, what would I know? I'm just a Barbie, right?"

The room fell silent. Mouths and eyes wide, the ladies stared.

What had she done? Heat rushed through Rivers and scorched her cheeks. It wasn't fair to these ladies to behave this way, no matter what Star said. "I'm sorry. I don't think I'm ready for this. The grief is still too—" She had to get out of here. Tears blurred her vision, and she made a dash toward the exit.

176

"It's okay, Rivers," Gabby called behind her.

But she opened the door, scooted through, and shut it behind her. Pivoting toward her car, she ran headlong into Cooper's chest.

Chapter 25

"What happened?" Cooper caught Rivers and rested his hands on her shoulders. He'd started to take off in the Jeep, but something in his spirit whispered for him to come back.

"I can't…" Her breath came in ragged puffs, and she burrowed her head against his chest. "I couldn't do it. I fell apart and blew up at them."

"What happened?"

"I was nervous. The ladies looked bored. Star made some snarky comments. I spouted off something about my mom, her wreck, and Jordan and me…getting shot."

"It's okay." Yearning wrapped his heart, and he slid his arms around her. If only he could heal her wounds. Moonlight fell around them, and the evening sounds of crickets chirping filled the salty air. He lifted her chin. "I'd trade anything to take your pain away."

She gazed up at him, blue eyes all weepy and beautiful.

Cooper swallowed hard. That gaze stirred longings he'd given up way before he'd gotten sober. Longings for someone to share his heart. Longings to love and be loved.

"You're always here when I need you." Her gaze fell to his lips. She couldn't be thinking of him in the same way he was thinking of her.

Though his pulse pounded, he was afraid to move, barely believing this was real. If she needed to use him as a temporary crutch and then discard him, he was willing. Unless doing so would cause her more pain.

She moved closer, and his mind went absent of all thoughts apart from her lips. Her mouth brushed his, soft and sweet and gentle, then explored with more passion. Though he tried to restrain himself, the call of her touch drew him. He kissed her back, lost in the moment and the emotion. He cupped her face, ran his fingers through her hair, soaking in the taste of her and the scent of lavender.

"What the—" Shane's voice broke into the moment. "Cooper, you of all people? Taking advantage of Jordan's fiancée?"

Rivers broke away, touching her fingers to her pink lips. "He didn't."

Shane approached from down the sidewalk. They hadn't even heard him drive up. His chin jutted and he scoffed. "Rivers, you don't believe he'd manipulate you to keep this place? That's what addicts do."

"That's not…" Cooper focused on Rivers, desperate for her to discard Shane's words. "I'll move from the studio tonight." He released her and waved a hand toward the gallery. "I'll clear out the artwork by the end of the week."

"No." Rivers caught one of his hands. "Take me away from here."

"Of course." He shot a look at Shane, torn between doing what Rivers asked and making the truth clear to Shane. But he led her to his Jeep and opened the door.

Shane stood, arms crossed, staring as Cooper drove them away.

"This was never about the property." He squeezed the wheel and stared straight ahead, pressing his lips together. What more could he say? There was no sense trying to convince Rivers of anything. She would believe what she wanted to believe. He drove out of town, across the causeway, past Brunswick, and then headed south, the full moon lighting the starry sky ahead of them.

When they reached the Sidney Lanier Bridge, Rivers gasped. "It's beautiful."

He slowed the Jeep. "Georgia's tallest cable-stayed suspension bridge." The architectural structure was a sight, the massive cables sweeping upward to form two giant pinnacles in the center.

"What body of water are we crossing?"

"The Brunswick River. We're heading toward Jekyll Island. I wasn't sure where or how far you wanted to go when you asked me to take you away."

"It reminds me of the Mississippi River Bridge back home. That's what I was doing that evening when"—her voice broke—"when Jordan was killed. He'd just given me that sketch pad."

The pad she'd been clutching that first day? No wonder she wouldn't let go of it. "I'm sorry. I can't imagine how horrific it was for you."

Silence reclaimed the ride, but again, there was nothing more he could say. They reached the public beach access, and he pulled into the lot and parked. "Want to walk?"

She answered with a nod and opened her door.

They crossed the lot and the boardwalk, past the dunes, to reach the water's edge. She plopped down, so he did the same. Not much of a walk.

A debate raged inside, whether to make conversation or shut up. He didn't trust himself to speak anything of worth with his turbulent emotions. Her kiss only confirmed what he'd feared.

He was falling in love with her.

"What are you thinking?" Her voice was soft.

Not about to tell her that. He turned to face her. "I wish I knew what you were looking for, Rivers. How I could give you closure, mend your heart, stitch up everything and tie a nice bow on it. I've come to care about you, but I can't figure out what to do for you."

"How could you? I can't understand what I'm feeling." She raised a hand and caressed his cheek. His breath caught, and he forced himself to hold still under her touch. "There's so much emotional history here, and it's fogging up the present. I'm drawn to you, but I can't figure out what's real. I don't want to hurt you. I shouldn't have…"

He placed his hand over hers. "I'm willing to take a chance, even if it means being hurt." And he was. If it broke him into a million pieces, he'd risk it all.

She leaned forward and pressed a soft kiss on his other cheek. "You're a good man, Cooper. A strong man. A forgiven man."

His eyes burned. For so long, he'd wanted to hear words like these from his family.

"I'm not."

"You are. You've turned your life around, which took faith and hard work, and now you have a heart for the lost."

If this was as close as he came, hearing the affirmation from Rivers would do.

"I messed up tonight." She groaned. "I was anxious, and I let Star get under my skin."

"You're shouldering too much alone. My family should be helping you. My parents. Aunt Brooklyn and Uncle Alex."

"It's no excuse for my behavior."

"Re-Claimed is a forgiving group." He laughed. "They have to be. When you're forgiven much, you forgive others much."

"Sounds familiar."

"My Luke seven paraphrase."

Her eyes shone in the moonlight. "I found old letters at the cottage from your grandfather to your grandmother. And her journal." She gave his hand a gentle squeeze. "He was an alcoholic. Your grandmother and the twins went through a lot of bad stuff. Maybe that's why they shut you out."

Cooper let the revelation sink in. Even if the past explained his family's reaction, it still hurt. "I had no idea. They never said anything." He'd tried to explain that he hadn't provided Savannah with the alcohol that day, but no one would listen. No one trusted him, which was his own fault. He'd lied too many times. He'd stolen prescription medicines from them, stolen cash from their purses and wallets, lied about where he was. Why should they ever trust him again? He didn't deserve it.

And he'd used that day.

"I want to give you the letters. The journal too. But if you don't mind, I'd like to finish reading it. I feel like I'm getting to know Stella."

Stella. His grandmother. He pictured her. Tall, graceful, smiling. Always thinking up great projects for the cousins in the summer. Whether it was going on a night walk to watch baby sea turtles hatch and make their way to the sea, or taking them to summer art classes, she kept life fun. Summers in St. Simons had been his escape from his hideous life at school.

Though he'd secretly believed his grandmother, like everyone else, favored Jordan, she'd tried to make Cooper feel special, encouraging him to pursue his art. She'd shown him love.

That was, until that last time he'd seen her.

Chapter 26

She'd actually kissed Cooper. Rivers stared out at the moonbeams floating on the waves, listening to their constant, haunting whisper. What kind of crazy realm had she fallen into? She'd even enjoyed the kiss—felt strong emotions surging through her. But it should never have happened. She shouldn't feel the way she felt. What would Jordan think?

God, I know Jordan's with you. I don't know what I'm doing. I need direction—some sign to guide me, or maybe a whole slew of signs. I'm so confused.

"I miss them." Cooper's voice came out shaky.

"Your family?"

"Yeah, even though I always felt like I was on the outside looking in."

He'd brought it up, but did she dare ask questions? Instead Rivers turned and studied his profile. The breeze ruffled his untamed, dark hair, and his eyes glistened.

"The last time I saw them was at the hospital."

"Want to talk about it? I've heard I'm a good listener." She tisked. "Barring my bad behavior tonight."

His feet shuffled in the sand, and his brows dipped. "I woke to bright lights, dazed and confused—my father and Sheriff Barnes standing beside my hospital bed. I tried to get up, thinking I still had to search for Savannah, but the pain in my chest laid me back down. The guy who pulled me out of the water had broken my ribs while giving me CPR. Of course, he saved my life."

"Thank the Lord he did." And she meant those words, though meeting Cooper had poked holes in her balloon of plans and a few of her presumptions.

He gave a small nod. "Once they heard I was awake, my mom and Aunt Brooklyn and my grandmother left the beach and came to the hospital. But instead of a visit to see how I was doing, it was a free-for-all of accusations. 'Why did you take Savannah out? What were you using? What did you give her? Where did you last see her? How could you betray us this way? You killed her as surely as if you'd put a gun to her head.'" His Adam's apple bobbed as he swallowed.

"Then my grandmother said she could never forgive me and left. My mom and Aunt Brooklyn followed. When my dad stayed, Mom leaned her head back in the door and said for Dad to choose, 'Cooper or our marriage.'" Cooper cleared his throat. "He said he loved me, and he was sorry, but he left."

"Oh, Cooper." She wove her fingers through his, craving to impart some form of comfort. She could picture the scene, the grief, the shock. She knew those feelings intimately. What would she have done if someone she'd known had accidentally—yet carelessly—caused Jordan's death? How horrible she'd feel if she had been the one to accidentally end a life. The shame and guilt and burden of that would be unbearable.

But He was pierced for our transgressions, He was crushed for our iniquities; the punishment that brought us peace was on Him, and by His wounds we are healed.

The verse swept through her soul, excavating memories of her sins, along with the realization that her guilt had caused her Savior's death. Nausea flooded her. Her sin, her shame had nailed Him to the cross.

Sure, she strove to do right, but she'd fallen short.

Tonight's explosion was a perfect example. And she'd judged. Oh, how she'd judged and held bitterness in her heart, especially toward her mother.

"You are forgiven." She spoke the words to herself as much as to Cooper, because God's love was that big and that good.

"I know I'm forgiven—in here." He touched his forehead. "But the knowledge gets muddy here." His hand went to his heart. "Right now I seem to be losing everything, even Re-Claimed. It feels like a punishment, but I know it's not. And, by the way, I would never manipulate you. Whether you trust me or not, I care about you."

How could his admission both set her on fire and turn her inside-out with fear?

"I care about you, too." Truth was truth. Even though she'd originally come to evict him from the gallery, now she wasn't so sure. But that eviction had nothing to do with the sober living house. "What do you mean *even Re-Claimed*?"

"There are some petitions going around to get us to move. We can fight it, but it's going to cost some serious cash. And frankly, it just hurts." He turned her way, conviction in his gaze. "I never wanted to be a part of one of these clubs, you know. I don't know why I have these brutal compulsions. I don't understand why my brain has to work the way it does when other people get to be normal."

Ouch. That didn't seem fair. "Honestly, I never thought of it that way. I realize I'm guilty of a lot of prejudice." She pulled her knees up to her chest. "Can I ask what it's like? Or is that too much?"

His gaze traveled upward toward the starlit sky. "It's like you're really hungry—starving, insatiably hungry—and all you can think about is finding food. Nothing else matters. And I

185

mean nothing. It consumes your every thought, and you'd trade anything to fill that gnawing." He sucked in a breath and shook his head. "You feel desperate, as if you can't survive until you get whatever chemical you're addicted to, even though the hunger will never truly be filled no matter how much you get.

"Once you find your fix, shame sets in. So much shame. For being weak, for breaking trust, for lying or stealing or whatever you did to get it. Depression and anxiety and guilt entwine, and you bounce from denial to helplessness. And that's just the emotional part. Physically, you feel horrible because you're killing your body."

"Sounds miserable."

"Pretty much."

"It's sad and wrong, but I've just thought of addicts as ruiners. Like how my mother ruined our family, leaving others to have to pay the stupid tax. I've never thought about the other side." Reaching over, she brushed her hand across his back. "I'm sorry for that."

"Thanks." He quirked an eyebrow and smiled. "I think."

"That didn't come out the way I meant it."

"It's okay to speak truth when you're confessing." He ran a hand through his hair then across his forehead. "Have you thought about attending Al-Anon, the meetings for families of alcoholics? The people I know who attend find it helpful. You don't want anyone's addiction to define you or steal your peace."

"My dad took me to Alateen meetings way back, but I wasn't ready then. I was mostly mortified. He attends an Al-Anon group, though." She pressed her heels deeper into the sand in front of her. "I think I should try again. Maybe even while I'm here."

"Perfect time to give it a shot, since you're stuck around the lot of us." He laughed quietly. "They actually hold some that coincide with the AA meetings our residents attend. They're down the hall from each other in the same church. Kev and Gabby go to them, unless there's a crisis like when Star and Blake were in the hospital."

"Oh! The hospital." She scrambled to her feet. "I need to walk the possum."

~~~

The stress definitely must've been getting to Rivers, or there was some strange lingo in Memphis he wasn't aware of. Either way, Cooper stood and brushed the sand from his shorts. "And where might you need to take that walk?"

"The cottage." She made a quick path toward the Jeep. "He's been alone awhile."

"Someone's at the cottage? Or the hospital?" He opened the door for her.

A little giggle slipped from her cute lips. "My neighbor, Priscilla, is in the hospital, and I'm pet sitting."

"Now it's coming together. Mrs. Kelly was always nursing some critter." He circled the Jeep and moved into the driver's seat. "A possum this time?"

She nodded. "His name is Phoenix. At first, he creeped me out, but he's really cute. I didn't realize they were marsupials. Like kangaroos, but different."

"Definitely different." Before he pulled out of the lot, he glanced over at Rivers. "What's wrong with Mrs. Kelly? And when did you get sucked into another predicament?"

"Time is kind of a blur since I got here, but just a day or so ago, an ambulance took her to the hospital. She's having some stents put into her arteries. She acted like she'd be home soon."

He shook his head. "I think *someone* might have a rescuer

187

syndrome. You seem to jump into a lot of messy situations."

Her eye roll was accompanied by a sarcastic smile. "Pot to kettle. Hello."

God knew he'd gotten himself into a number of predicaments trying to help people, so he couldn't help but laugh. "Guilty." He pulled out onto the main drive.

"We're more alike than I realized." Her voice was almost a whisper, and the ride back passed with only the sound of the wind against the windows.

Her words created a burn in his heart. If only they were alike. Rivers was everything good and light and wholesome, and she helped others from that pure place in her heart. While he'd been one of those "ruiners" as she'd called them, destroying not only himself, but others in his wake. The sooner he could summon the discipline to put the brakes on their emotional connection, the better.

God, give me the strength to do what's right for Rivers.

At the cottage, they both jumped out at the sight of a taxi in Mrs. Kelly's driveway.

"What in the world?" Rivers tore across the yards. "Priscilla?"

Cooper followed her, this woman who seemed to have no thought for herself. What if it wasn't her neighbor getting out? It could be a drunk at the wrong address or something worse.

But when they rounded the car, the driver held the door for Mrs. Kelly. Rivers offered her hand and helped the arthritis-ridden woman to a stand. Once they'd paid for the cab, it backed out.

"Why are you home this late? And alone?" Rivers wrapped her arm around Mrs. Kelly's waist.

"They released me this afternoon. I had a friend lined up to drive me home, but she had car trouble. It was a really easy procedure though."

"What about your family?" Rivers asked.

"My son's in Europe. He's a corporate pilot, so it's hard for him to change his schedule." She released a shaky breath. "Now he's all in a tizzy about making me move into one of those retirement living communities over in Hilton Head if I don't hire someone to help me at the house." Her voice wobbled with emotion. "He thinks I need someone in here every day. Either plan might drive me crazy."

"Why don't you stay with me tonight?" Rivers pleaded. "Phoenix will be fine, and there's plenty of room. I can get you settled in, then go get my car at the gallery. It won't take long."

"I don't know." Priscilla hedged, glancing between both houses.

"Please. I'd enjoy the company." Rivers wasn't letting this go.

Finally, Mrs. Kelly agreed. Cooper and Rivers got her and the possum settled, then headed back to the gallery to retrieve the Stink Bug.

When they arrived, the lights still shone from inside the studio. Cooper exited the Jeep. "That's odd. Gabby is particular. She'd never leave the place lit up."

"Maybe she's cleaning my mess. I'll run in and help."

"You don't have to."

"I insist. It won't take long, and I should apologize." She set off toward the entrance.

He always seemed to be following her. They reached the door and opened it to a cacophony of female voices.

"She's back!" someone chimed.

"Let's show her our work," another responded.

The women still sat at their easels. Gabby gave Rivers a hesitant look. "I hope you don't mind, but we finished the

189

project you gave us." She lifted her canvas, which was covered in paint, a colorful heart in the center. "I mean, we dove in deep."

Other ladies held their paintings up for Rivers to see.

A lump rose in her throat. "They're beautiful." She pressed her fist to her mouth for a moment as her gaze roamed the room. "I'm sorry I blew up at y'all."

"Now we know you're human." Gabby set aside her canvas, came to Rivers, and wrapped her arms around her. "It's too late tonight, but they want to tell you their stories when you're free."

"Of course. I'd stay now, but I have a houseguest." Rivers addressed the group. "I'm proud of you, and I'll come soon to talk with each of you one-on-one about your artwork, if you'd like."

After they said their goodbyes, Cooper walked Rivers to her car, where he caught her arm. Whispers of rain floated on the air, the green scent of it fresh and strong. "See, they forgave you."

Her lashes fluttered, then her gaze flickered toward him. "They did, didn't they? And they did well."

"Yep. You are inspirational." He couldn't stop his arms from sliding around her and pulling her into a hug. Under the canopy of clouds, he wanted nothing more than to taste her lips again, but he was determined not to be the manipulator Shane had accused him of being.

"This place, the art, the people, the sea, the struggle, and the faith—they're doing a work in me. I just wish I knew where it was leading." Her gaze zoned in on him, and her soft fingers brushed against his hair, undoing him. "Or what I'm supposed to do with you." A sad smile crinkled the corners of her blue eyes. "I better go check the possum."

Chapter 27

"Lord, thank you for waking me up this morning. And for creating this coffee." Davis slugged back the rest of the dark liquid in his mug.

With a half chuckle, the best he could summon, Cooper readied the gallery for opening with Blake in tow. Working without Angelo struck a harsh blow. No one had heard anything from or about him, and they couldn't spend more time searching. Ultimately, Angelo was responsible for his own choices. They'd move on. What alternative did they have?

Davis turned to face them once he'd hit the rest of the light switches. His gaze locked on Blake. "Dang, you look casket-ready, bro. You still that wrung out?"

A slight nod from Blake was all the answer he got. His skin had a weathered look, and his eyes drooped.

Cooper thumped Davis on the shoulder. "He doesn't need to be harpooned with the Grim Reaper jokes."

"My bad. Call me a Nincompoop and get it over with." Behind the counter, Davis grabbed a roll of paper towels and cleaner to begin the daily task of wiping down the glass doors and windows. "It'll get better, bud. Just hang on."

"Yeah, yeah, this too shall pass." Blake grunted. "I know the drill."

Blake's pain was obvious, and Cooper hated it for him. Unfortunately, there was little anyone could do. The guy claimed to be working the steps and had even written a letter to the mother of his child explaining what happened years ago.

"Stay hydrated. I brought a cooler with plenty of water and Gatorade. Help yourself." Cooper had seen the VW outside, and fighting the urge to go speak to Rivers—or rather, wrap his arms around her—was zapping his strength. That and the fact that he'd spent the night reliving their soul-rending kiss. Okay, it was unbearably smoldering, too. He'd probably disintegrate any minute and abandon his effort to keep his distance.

~~~

"The brown blob over half of my heart is my fear and anger."

In the bright studio lights, Rivers nodded and waited for Claudia to continue describing her gloomy painting. The older redhead had already been a heavy drinker when she'd witnessed a friend's death in a freak accident involving some lawn equipment. Her drinking accelerated afterward and included more and more substances. She'd lost her marriage, custody of her two children, and all visitation rights ten years ago.

"I hated myself for what I'd done, but I kept numbing because I didn't know how to go back. Then it took more and more. At some point, I couldn't stop without getting really sick." She chewed the edge of her fingernail. "I started skimming money from the company I worked for, stealing from my friends and strangers, shoplifting…and other stuff I'd rather not talk about." Her cheeks grew red, and a muscle ticked in her cheek. "Honestly, I'd say or do anything by that point. And I landed in jail." She pointed to the canvas. "The red circle around the brown is my shame."

Rivers gave her a sympathetic nod and tried not to focus on the red—the color of her nightmares. "What about the rest?"

"The blue outlining the heart is the peace of Re-Claimed and seeing the ocean nearby, and the purple background is for my King Jesus who is healing me. He gives me hope that, one day, I can reconcile with my kids."

Once they'd talked through Claudia's painting and feelings, the woman left. A wellspring of emotions cracked open inside of Rivers, reminding her of why she'd gone into art therapy and warming forgotten places in her heart.

Eagerly, she waited on the next resident. Yet, a prick of worry needled her. Her neighbor, Priscilla, had felt well enough to go home after breakfast, and she'd insisted Rivers go to the gallery to hear the ladies' stories once she'd learned about how the evening had transpired. But Rivers had promised to come back at lunch. Would the older woman be all right by herself all morning?

Cooper and Davis had kept busy up front "training" Blake, so she hadn't seen much of Cooper, which was fine by her. Trying to process the kiss had robbed her of a night's sleep.

She was glad she'd come to hear the stories this morning, despite how the embarrassment over her outburst still gnawed at her conscience. The ladies of Re-Claimed had poured their hearts into their pieces of art, and Rivers ached with each one as they laid bare their souls and shared the nature of their wounds. Their haunting stories bore testimony to both the pain of their pasts and the viciousness of addiction.

Their circumstances varied tremendously. This ferocious issue knew no boundaries. The enemy of the soul was a cunning one.

A light tap on the studio door alerted her to another resident. Rivers made her way over to open it and found Gabby waiting with Star. A few sprinkles of rain splatted into the dirt beside the walkway where Star stood.

Gabby's gaze bounced between Rivers and Star. "You two need a referee?"

"No." Star was quick to answer.

"We'll only talk as long as Star wants. No pressure." Rivers offered a genuine smile to the young woman. "I promise not to freak out."

One corner of Star's mouth lifted. "I've heard worse."

The chime of her cell phone announced an incoming call, and Rivers picked it up meaning to silence the ring. She noticed Priscilla's number lighting up her screen. "Excuse me, but my neighbor has been sick." She accepted the call. "Priscilla, is everything okay?"

"Oh, Rivers, I'm so frustrated." Priscilla sounded rattled. "My son is insisting I go into this retirement home in Hilton Head. I'm not ready for that. I'd never be able to take Phoenix, so I thought maybe a woman from the sober living house would want to have a job staying with me. I don't need a nurse or anything. If they could come for even a few hours a day, help me around the house, maybe he would leave me be. It'd be a win-win."

"Everything will be okay." Rivers tried to soothe her neighbor. "I'll ask around, and we'll find someone. Until then, tell your son I'm next door, and I'll check on you every day."

"Thank you, darling. I'm so fortunate to have a sweet neighbor who's willing to be helpful to this crippled lady and her weird pet."

Once they hung up, Gabby raised her brows as if waiting to be filled in. Rivers explained Priscilla's dilemma.

"I'll do it," Star blurted. Then she cut a glance at Gabby. "If that's allowed."

"Well, that hasn't been part of our routine, but I'm open to considering new ideas." Gabby tapped her fingers on her chin. "Seeing how you may not be up to the demands at the thrift store right now... I'd have to talk with this Priscilla and run it by Kev. We'd have to run a background check on you for that type of work, though."

"I understand." Star shifted her feet.

Rivers would stay out of the decision-making, but Star wouldn't be her first choice. "Would you like to talk about the art for a few minutes?" Waving her toward the easel, Rivers took a step away. The decision over Priscilla's care would take some cautious consideration.

"Sure."

"I'll leave you to it. Let me know when you're finished." Gabby eased out the door.

Rivers rolled a stool over next to the one Star had plopped down on. She hadn't taken the time to really look at this canvas. Black dominated the painting, the heart shape recognizable only by a faint white outline. Some tiny red streaks emanated from the edges. A few patches of brown muddied and crackled the inside. White also created a small square in the center with another tiny heart painted in red, as if it were locked in a box.

Rivers held in a gasp. Her chest squeezed as awareness washed through her. She'd seen something like this before in abused children.

"So how does this work? I talk first or you?" Star stared at the floor.

"Either. I can tell you put a lot of thought into this. And again, I'm sorry for the way I lost control last night. This trip has been hard, but that's no excuse."

Star's glassy brown eyes rose to meet hers. "I'm glad you said what you did. I shouldn't have railed you, but I don't like hearing a bunch of bull from people who have their nice families and nice lives tell me how to live. I thought you were

195

one of them."

Okay, that was close to an apology. "You never know what dwells in a person's past or their heart." She pointed to the shape on the canvas. "Want to tell me about yours?"

"If talking's supposed to help me"—she lifted one shoulder—"I guess I can."

"Sharing our stories can be freeing, and I bet you'll do better than I did."

A competitive gleam lit Star's eyes. "I'll give it my best shot." She swallowed hard and pointed. "Black is death. My dad died when my sister, Skye, and I were little girls. From an aneurysm, in his sleep, according to Mama, but I don't know if that's true. They were what you might call free spirits, traveling from place to place. We lived in a camper mostly.

"Anyway, Mama had what we called *the sadness* that would come and go. I guess she was bipolar or something. But she was a pretty woman and could easily find jobs and get her way. They usually let us play in a back room or in a booth at a café where she worked or even in the camper parked in the lot. In one town, Mama met this preacher at a diner where she was working. He was there with his wife and adult son, and he invited us to his church." Star shook her head. "I think she went because the son was nice looking. At first. They married a few weeks later." Her gaze focused on Rivers. "That's when we found out he was a monster."

Trying to keep her expression neutral, Rivers nodded, but inside, her breathing halted. So many children endured horrors that never should be imagined, and hearing their stories never got easier. "Only share what you feel comfortable with today. We can always talk again."

Star massaged her forehead with her fingers. "Mama tried." She inhaled a shaky breath. "I guess one night she just gave up.

Skye found her in the bedroom."

A pregnant silence followed, so Rivers ventured a guess. "She'd taken her own life?"

"Yeah." The single word came out with a scoff.

"I can't imagine how much that hurt you and your sister."

"Skye had a scholarship to college. She was leaving me, so I climbed out the window at sixteen and never looked back."

Rivers fought to keep her composure. "The walled off heart in the middle is how you're protecting yourself?" And the anger she'd thrown around was a way to do that.

"I guess that's why they pay you the big bucks." Star shot her a sarcastic look, but laughed. A real laugh that showed in her brown eyes.

"Not so much. I held a full-time and two part-time jobs until I met Jordan."

"Your fiancé?" Star studied her.

"Yeah."

"That stinks. I'm sorry about what happened." She threw one hand toward the ceiling. "Sometimes I don't get God, you know? Mama believed in Him, but I don't know."

The confession caught Rivers off guard. "My dad says God doesn't exempt the godly from hard realities. We live in a fallen world, but it's temporary. He also says we can speak our questions to God and listen for Him to answer."

"That could take me a while, because I've got a lot of them."

Rivers smiled at Star's honesty. "I can relate."

A clatter erupted into their conversation, and Cooper burst through the door connecting the gallery to the studio. "Did Blake come in here?"

"No." Rivers swallowed hard, fear caught in her throat.

Star sprung off the stool. "Is he missing?"

"He said he was going to the restroom, and we had customers up front." Frustration furrowed Cooper's brows, and he raked his fingers through his hair. "Davis is going to look for him outside."

Cautiously, Rivers stood and laced her arm across Star's shoulders. If they'd lost Blake, would they lose Star, too?

Chapter 28

"So this is the other place I inherited. My cleaning-out project." Rivers tried to keep her voice neutral while Gabby parked the Re-Claimed van in the cottage drive. "I'm glad we can load the stuff I've collected for the thrift store while we're here."

The ride over with Gabby and Star had been somber. Gabby had quickly decided to distract Star from Blake's disappearance with the job interview. Whether they let her work for Priscilla or not, they needed to keep Star busy.

A harsh wind pressed against them as they stepped onto the shell-lined drive. Heavy, dark clouds still held back the full rain that loomed above. In the distance, thunder rumbled.

"Let's load your donations before the bottom drops out." Gabby motioned upward and trudged onto the porch. "Then we can meet your neighbor."

Star glanced around the property. "Looks like a Coastal Living magazine cover."

"You like that one, too?" Rivers pivoted to study her.

"Why?" Star's chin jutted. "You don't think I've seen the same magazines as you?"

"I don't know what to think about you." Rivers smiled. "But I'm learning."

"Fair enough." Star gave a nonchalant shrug. "And I'm stronger than y'all think. I'm not falling apart about Blake. Yet."

"Good." Gabby wrapped an arm around her. "No sense worrying about what we can't control."

Though Star sounded tough, Rivers couldn't help but think about the canvas and the tiny box that walled off the heart in the center. "I hope you won't leave." Rivers spoke without thinking.

This time Star's head whipped around. "Why do you care?"

"I don't really know, but I do." And she meant it. Somewhere in this muddle, she'd grown attached to the people she'd met in St. Simons, even this young woman full of sharp contradictions.

Star shot her a curious look. "You must be a little touched in the head. An eager beaver for disappointment."

Rivers had to laugh at the honesty. "I must be." She turned to Gabby. "And I have an idea about how to fight back against that petition. We could host an art opening—kind of a gala— to raise awareness of how Re-Claimed is helping the community, not hurting. I've planned them before with a gallery in Memphis. I could have some of my work sent over, too."

"What petition?" Disgust laced Star's voice.

Oh, no. Rivers squeezed her eyes closed. Her foot was probably in her mouth and halfway to her stomach. She opened her eyes and slid her gaze to Gabby. "Sorry for bringing that up."

Gabby waved her off and focused on Star. "Just some neighbors who don't understand us."

"There's a thin line between *them and us*." Star scoffed. "Hypocritical, judgmental people can take their petition and shove—"

"Hey, let's stay positive." Gabby kept her tone upbeat. "My dad always says forgiveness is free, while trust is earned. I think the idea Rivers had for a gala is great. We have a wonderful and giving community, and the few frightened people may just need a human touch. Faces to put with Re-Claimed." She stepped back. "You know, I'm going to run next door for one second to let Mrs. Kelly know what we're doing. I'd like to find out exactly what she's looking for in an assistant."

Rivers unlocked the door and grappled for any other subject to change the conversation.

"I don't want anyone looking at my face." Star stalked inside, where she kicked off her flip-flops and then marched over to the donation bags. She scooped up two, then went back to her shoes and slipped them back on. "You'll have to find another freak for your circus."

Rivers pointed to Star's feet. "What's up with that?"

"Duh, I'm loading stuff in the van like y'all wanted."

"Your shoes?"

"This is a nice place. I've cleaned houses, and I learned not to track in dirt."

"You cleaned?"

"I've been a maid, a waitress, a telemarketer, a drycleaner, a greeter, a screen printer...I could go on for ages."

"But what do you want to do?"

Chewing her lip, Star shifted the load in her arms before answering. "I'm a certified fitness instructor. One good thing that came from my crazy ex-boyfriend. Anyway, I like teaching Pilates and spin and aerobics. I can even do private personal training."

"That's great. I could probably use some training." Rivers gathered several bags and followed Star to the van.

"You need to beef up a little, for sure."

A gale drove tiny raindrops and sand sideways, pelting them like needles. Rivers shivered. "I think this is enough for now. Let's run next door."

They barely made it inside Priscilla's before the bottom

dropped. After quick introductions, Star bent down to pet Phoenix. "What's your opossum's name? My sister had one she called Princess Chuckles—dumbest name ever."

Priscilla's eyes lit up. "You're not afraid of Phoenix?"

"There's not a critter that my sister didn't nurse back to health, so no. My mom always laughed and called her Elly Mae Clampett, whoever that was."

"We're going to get along fine." Priscilla smiled.

Lifting a grocery sack, Gabby nodded. "I think I've collected any prohibited items, so we'll give this job a trial run."

Star leveled a harsh gaze on Gabby. "What is that you've *collected?*"

"Cooking wine, vanilla extract, an airplane rum bottle, cold medicines with alcohol, and an old prescription."

Star's nose scrunched. "I'm not going to drink those."

Gabby pressed a fist to her hip. "Well, I've seen desperate people do it, so—"

"I've needed to do some cleaning out for a while, and I'd love for you to help this crippled lady." Priscilla took Star's hand. "And so would Phoenix. Would you?"

Star's gaze fell first to the gnarled hand holding hers then to the animal. "I'd like that."

With everything agreed and plans for Star to come back the next day, Rivers, Star, and Gabby ran to the van and drove back to the gallery. The rain slackened slightly as they let Rivers out by her car.

"I'll see you—" Rivers froze. A dark figure on the ground beneath a large moss-covered oak caught her eye. "Wait." She held up one hand, then jogged through the rain toward the lump, her heart surging to her throat as the outline came clearer.

A body. "Call 911!"

Warning bells reverberated in her head as she dropped to her knees beside the form, her gaze taking in Blake's features. Was he dead? She threw down her purse. Her fingers found his neck, searching for a pulse.

Nothing.

No pulse. Not breathing.

She shifted, straining for any movement under her fingers. Oh, God. Help.

CPR. She had to bring back her training. Squeezing his nose shut, she forced air into his lungs, then moved to his chest.

Press his chest. Give him breath.

She held Blake's face, tried to resuscitate him, and prayed.

Chapter 29

"Don't you dare leave me too!" Screaming, Star fell beside Blake's body.

Rivers continued counting compressions and breathing until Davis, Cooper, and Gabby ran up. Gabby held syringes.

"Slide back. I've got medicine that might help," Gabby ordered. "I've called 911. He needs Narcan."

Rivers shifted away, struggling to catch her breath as Gabby moved in.

Davis locked his arms around Star to keep the hysterical girl off Blake, whose lips were blue, his skin a ghostly white.

One at a time, Gabby inserted a needleless syringe into Blake's nostrils, releasing some sort of medicine, then she rubbed his sternum and called his name over and over. "Blake, come on. He's not responding." She started compressions.

An ambulance's wail mingled with Star's cries. Another blur of activity began. Rivers stood in the rain, arms wrapped around herself as the paramedics worked on Blake. Within minutes they had his unresponsive body strapped to a stretcher, then loaded him in the back of the vehicle.

"I'm taking Star and Davis in the van to follow the ambulance." Gabby shook her keys. "Cooper, call Kevin, and get me an overnight sub for my ladies."

Dazed and drenched, Rivers stared as they drove away. Her heart raced and thudded beneath her ribcage. Through sheets of rain, the red of Gabby's taillights mingled with the flashing ambulance beams. *The red of sorrow and death.* Blood. The crimson leaking from Jordan's chest.

"You did well, jumping in like that. It was all anyone could do. He's in God's hands now." Cooper's voice echoed through her consciousness.

Or was it Jordan's? Nothing seemed real. Not the mud where she stood or the rivulets of water slithering down her cheeks or the heartbreak she'd just witnessed.

The day at the river in Memphis with Jordan swirled through her mind. Just an ordinary day. And suddenly not.

And then Jordan was gone.

"Rivers? Can you hear me?" An arm wrapped her shoulders, warm and solid. It turned and directed her. "Come inside and dry off."

She followed the nudges, but what she really wanted was to curl into the fetal position and sleep.

Blinking, she tried to clear her head. What should be done? She couldn't fall apart when people needed her, but she couldn't seem to formulate a plan to help.

Instead of entering the studio or gallery, Cooper led her up a set of stairs and into the loft. The ceilings angled with the roof, low and with naked beams. He set her on a small, weathered gray couch, the only place to sit other than his bed—barely three feet away. How did he live here?

And how did he live with all the chaos and devastation that went on in his job?

Sure, she saw a lot of grief and tough situations as an art therapist, but she didn't live with those people all-day-every-day like Cooper did. Didn't have to watch the glaring, unmerciful tragedies and so much squandered potential.

After grabbing a blanket, he wrapped it around her shoulders. "I have a dry T-shirt or something you can throw on." He opened the chest in front of the couch that appeared to serve as both a coffee table and storage for his clothes.

He pulled out a blue shirt imprinted with a crab restaurant's logo and a pair of gym shorts and handed them to her. "Too big, but it's better than being wet. The bathroom's behind the door next to my bed. I'll leave you to change while I lock the gallery. We'll just close for the day."

As he stood, the line of his shoulders sagged, as if sadness weighed them down. His expression looked dark and afflicted. The scene with Blake had rocked him, too. And no wonder. Cooper knew the guy better than she did. He'd been working with him.

While part of her wanted to hold Cooper and offer affection and consolation, the rest of her wanted to find her own little box to lock away her heart. She couldn't allow herself to fall for Cooper and go through another nightmare like she'd just witnessed.

She'd lost one man she loved already. She couldn't go through that torment again.

~~~

He was failing miserably. Two clients in such a short period of time. Sighing, Cooper switched off the gallery lights and placed a sign on the locked door.

No one had heard what happened to Angelo. And who knew if Blake would make it. The guy hadn't looked good.

Rivers didn't look good either. Another trauma to burden her wasn't fair. As much as he'd fallen for her and longed to be with her, he needed to protect her fragile heart. Somehow he had to get her out of this chaotic world and back home. If only someone in her family could help her finish with the cottage. He sighed. Her father was probably tied up taking care of her mother.

Maybe his family. His palms slicked at the thought of

contacting them, but surely his mother and Aunt Brooklyn cared for Rivers, since she'd been engaged to Jordan. Was it worth reaching out to them? Would they even answer?

Rivers shouldn't bear her burden alone.

Dad would be the most likely to read a text from him.

With shaky hands, he pulled his phone from his pocket and searched for his father's number. At least, he hoped it was still the right number.

Rivers is in St. Simons cleaning out the cottage. It's hard on her. Could Mom possibly help? Or Aunt Brooklyn?

He struck out the name Rivers and changed it to *Jordan's fiancée.* Not only to avoid seeming too casual about her to his parents, but also to remind himself. Rivers may have kissed him in a weak moment, but she'd planned to marry Jordan. It was Jordan's death that drove her to St. Simons. It was Jordan who Rivers truly loved.

Cooper breathed a prayer and hit send.

He'd do well to keep reminding himself that he was not the man for Rivers. He wasn't worthy and never would be.

The phone sounded in his hand, and his breath caught. Just like that, Dad would answer? He checked the number.

Gabby. She'd have news on Blake. His stomach dropped like a stone from a cliff. Something inside warned him of bad news.

Chapter 30

"Knock, knock. Is it okay to come in, Rivers?" Cooper stood at the top of the steps outside his studio and cracked the door. "I can drive you back to the cottage if you want."

Rivers pulled the door the rest of the way open, her gaze clearer than when he'd left her. Seeing her in his clothes, her damp hair hanging in soft strands around her face, dealt him with the second sucker punch in a matter of minutes. Gabby's call hadn't been the news he'd prayed for.

"I can go to the hospital or fill in at the women's Re-Claimed house." She tucked one of the strands behind her ear and pulled her bottom lip between her teeth.

"There's no need." He tried to keep his voice from cracking.

"Why? I don't mind helping."

He placed his hands on her shoulders and choked back a sob. Blinking, he shook his head.

Realization washed over her expression, and her blue eyes filled with tears. "Blake didn't make it?"

"No. Gabby, Davis, and Star are on their way back."

"I tried." Tears cascaded down her cheeks. "I did what I could, but…"

He cupped her face and swiped the warm liquid with his thumbs. "He was already gone."

"But why did he leave? I don't understand." Her voice broke. "Star needed him. You guys were helping him."

He drew her to his chest and held her—maybe for the last

time. Somehow he had to get her out of here. "I don't think Blake meant to die. He just tried and failed to break addiction's deadly grip. The ER doctor thinks he unknowingly took a dose of Oxy or Xanax that was laced with fentanyl, but they'll do an autopsy."

"Oh, God, why?" The sound of her weeping and the quivering of her chest cut him through his core, breaking loose the tears he'd tried to lock inside. He wept along with her. It seemed Blake's death ripped open a hole in her universe. Maybe revealing to Rivers the true risk of loving an addict.

It was better she realize that now. Cooper pulled back. Brushing the hair from her face, he tipped her chin. "Let me take you home."

"No." She sniffed and swiped at her eyes. "If I can find where I threw my purse, I can get myself home. Your people need you."

His people.

~~~

Rivers quietly removed another box from the hall closet, careful not to wake Priscilla, who was sleeping in the bedroom down the hall. The older woman had decided to stay at the cottage for the night. Her decision was more likely an attempt to provide comfort than because of an actual need for assistance.

Rivers had continued cleaning out while Priscilla rested. Anything to distract herself.

Phoenix seemed comfortable wherever he could eat and sleep. Her neighbor had agreed to hold a place for Star as her assistant, and they'd prayed the young woman would stay sober to do so after such a shock.

At midnight, Rivers dropped to the couch with the journal. Did she have enough strength left to keep reading the sad stories?

She ran her fingers over the faded cover, then opened its pages. The journal entries were sparse as the girls grew up and later married, and Stella had stopped recording the dates. Many of the entries were less significant, but a few stood out.

It hurts that the girls want to live with Betty, but I understand they want to go to prep school and start fresh. My sister is a wonderful caregiver, and this place holds bad memories for them. Betty asked me to come back to Atlanta, too, but I hate to show my face around town and ruin Pearl's and Brooklyn's chances in society life. With me there, my scandalous marriage would be all anyone talked about. They've promised to at least stay with me on the island every summer.

~~~

Daddy purchased the gallery in town for me once he found out about my new hobby, and he even sent a truckload of paintings by Atlanta artists to get the business started. The gallery and painting give me fresh joy. I see God in each flower and sunset and sparkling wave. He is healing me of my loneliness and grief.

~~~

Brooklyn and Pearl both had their babies, only two months apart. Pearl's boy came early and was sick for so long. Finally he's doing better, poor little thing, but I still worry for his health. The flurry of activity has been overwhelming, but a joy. I found a helper at the gallery and went back to Atlanta for three months. Times have changed, and the past seems forgotten in my circles. I love being a grandmother, and perhaps I'll do better in that position than I did as a wife and mother.

~~~

Brooklyn gave birth to the most adorable baby girl. Savannah is a delight. I see the sadness in Pearl's eyes, though she does her best to cover it. She's been unable to have more children, but she claims she will spoil Savannah as if she were her own.

The Art of Rivers

~~~

Jay reminds me more and more of Frank every time he visits. Not just in the way his dark eyes carry hurt, but in the way he spends hours alone with his video games if I don't plan outings and lessons for the kids. He's withdrawn and angry at the world, and I don't understand why.

Jordy, of course, excels in everything he touches and somehow wins admiration everywhere I take him, so he's never a worry. On the other hand, Savannah's beauty and carefree spirit keep me on my toes. I never know what mischief that child will create, so I'm hoping the art classes and swimming lessons might keep her safe for at least a few moments.

~~~

I found a bag of green, smelly leaves in Jay's backpack. The odor was impossible to miss. I don't know why he thought I wouldn't notice. Pearl was beside herself when I told her, but she admitted it wasn't the first time. She said they'd taken him to counseling hoping to help him with whatever underlying issue was driving him to do such a thing.

My heart breaks thinking of the road ahead of us all if Jay is like Frank. Please don't let it be so, God. He's Pearl's only child. The only child she was able to conceive because of my neglect of her—the scar tissue from her appendix surgery.

~~~

Jay is in a treatment facility this summer, so he couldn't come with Jordy and Savannah. We miss him. Jordy said he's tried to reach out and help Jay, but he doesn't know what to do. None of us do. Pearl has asked for help from anyone who will listen. She's searched for friends, mentors, youth ministers, churches, hobbies, counselors, whatever she can think of that might help Jay. I pray for him every day and night.

~~~

Jordy will attend college at Mississippi State in the fall to study architecture on a full scholarship. I'm so proud of him. Jay was admitted to Florida State. I just hope he will be well enough to attend.

~~~

Savannah has found a set of friends here and stays out running on the beach with them until midnight. That girl never meets a stranger, and boys flock to her. I hope she has better sense than I did when it comes to men.

~~~

Jordy and Jay didn't come yet this summer. They are both so busy now. They've finished their four-year degrees but will go on to pursue graduate degrees. I haven't seen Jay much in the past four years, but when he comes, I can tell he's still in trouble.

~~~

Savannah came on alone, but the boys promised to each spend a weekend here with her. I smelled alcohol on her breath last night when she finally came in from the beach. She giggled and claimed someone had spilled a beer on her. I warned her about the dangers of drinking, but my words seemed to fall on deaf sixteen-year-old ears. I don't know if I should tell her about Frank. I don't know if I should tell Brooklyn about my suspicions.

~~~

Savannah's gone. Jay is in jail. The girls are devastated. All is lost.

~~~

The last pitiful entry had been written shortly before Stella's death. Jordan said she'd died two weeks after Savannah. Stella's heart had stopped during her sleep. She had lost hope.

Rivers closed the journal and shut her eyes. "God, no matter what happens, please don't let me lose hope."

Chapter 31

Cooper stood with Kevin in the doorway of Gabby's room. Gabby'd given up her bed and had sat in a chair watching over Star all night. The girl hadn't spoken since the news of Blake's death.

Gabby sat on the edge of the bed, rubbing Star's back. Steam rose from the breakfast on the nightstand, the aroma of coffee and bacon filling the air. "Is there anyone you want to talk with?"

The sheets crinkled, and Star tucked them farther over her head. "Rivers."

"What?" Cooper shot a questioning look Gabby's way.

"I said, I'll talk to Rivers." Star spoke louder. "But can the rest of you leave me alone? Please."

They cleared the room and shut the door. As they walked into the common area, Cooper pinched the bridge of his nose. Star's request was the last thing he'd expected. "Not Rivers."

"God's working, Coop." Gabby nudged him. "Let go, and let God."

"But Rivers has been through enough. Too much. I'm trying to figure out how to get her out of this place as quickly as possible."

"You didn't bring her here, and you don't get to send her back." Gabby held up four fingers. "You're falling into the trap: Managing, Manipulating, Mothering, and Martyrdom."

Cooper rolled his eyes. The Al-anon phrase she was quoting was all too familiar, but that wasn't what he was doing

213

by trying to protect Rivers.

Or was it?

Gabby wagged one finger now. "You can call her and tell her Star's request or I can, but the decision is hers to make."

"Duly noted." Of course, Gabby was always right.

A firm hand squeezed Cooper's shoulder. "Haven't you learned not to argue with my sister?" Kevin raised his brows, his brown eyes nailing him with a serious look. "You really care about this girl, don't you?"

"I care." Cooper tried to sound nonchalant.

"Oh, that's the understatement of the year." Gabby scoffed. "I saw y'all lip-locked outside the gallery, so pretending to be all casual with me is about as successful as"— she made her dramatic gestures—"I don't know—trying to organize a parade of cats."

"And now you're using a Davis quote on me?" Cooper shot her a mocking leer. "Maybe you've got a crush?" Could he divert her attention by teasing her?

"Oh, no, Mr. Smarty Pants. I don't play that. Don't even try to mess with me." She was mad now. "Cocooning yourself from joy isn't what we teach here, and you know that better than anyone. You can keep sailing your shame boat out to sea and let guilt rob you of your joy if you want, but you and I both know that isn't our Savior's Gospel." She pinned him with a glare.

"I'll call her." Maybe he could word the request in a way that would give Rivers an easy out. Because he doubted Gabby would soften her tact. Especially now that he'd ticked her off.

Thirty minutes later, and despite his efforts to covertly persuade her not to come, Rivers marched through the front door of the Re-Claimed women's house. The phrase *face set like flint* came to mind. He knew better than to get in her way.

"Hey." He pointed to the beach bag slung over her arm. "Going someplace after this?" Not that it was any of his business.

"No. How bad is she?" While he told the little he knew, she dug around and pulled out an old book. "This is for you. I finished reading Stella's—your grandmother's—journal." Gloom etched her features, tugged on her mouth. "You can choose whether you want to open it or not, but I'll warn you, it's sad."

His hand wavered before accepting the book. He felt like he was grabbing a snake before seeing if it were venomous or not. Maybe there were things about his grandmother's life he didn't need to know.

"I brought my sketch pad and pencils." She nodded toward the bag. "I'm not sure why, but I felt like I should."

"Keep following the Spirit's lead, then." He offered her a sympathetic smile as he remembered that first day in the boat and the way she guarded that thing above her own life. Neither of them had realized the heartache those tides would sweep in.

~ ~ ~

"I'm here if you want to talk, Star." Rivers settled into the chair next to the bed. "If not, I'm just here." She could say she was praying. She could say how well acquainted she was with the grief of losing someone she loved, but Star knew those things. In the early days after Jordan's death, visitors had meant well, and their reaching out was appreciated, but nothing they said took away the pain and loss. She'd had to grieve. Her father had known to just be there.

Star needed to be allowed to grieve.

"Thank you." Her voice from under the covers was mumbled.

Three hours later, Rivers had outlined, from her best

215

recollection and from a social media search, a sketch of Blake. She'd found one picture where he looked happy, his face turned toward Star in an obvious selfie.

"What are you drawing?" Star slid up to a sitting position and tried to corral her mussed hair into a ponytail.

Oh, Lord, maybe I should show her the ocean pictures instead.

No. This is what her hands and mind had conjured. "If it's okay. I wanted to…" She sighed and turned the pad. "I was working on this for you. If you want it."

"Oh." Star pressed her fingers over her lips.

"I'm sorry. I shouldn't have—"

"It's beautiful." Her voice was raw and honest. "We could frame it and put it on a stand at a memorial." Her lashes blinked, heavy with tears.

"Here." Rivers grabbed a tissue from a box beside a tray of uneaten food on the nightstand and handed it to her. "I'm glad you like it."

"Could you help me plan one?" She wiped her eyes and nose. "A memorial, I mean."

Plan another funeral? Help me, God.

"If it's not too hard on you." Star waited for an answer.

Though walls seemed to crash down inside Rivers, unleashing the wreckage she'd worked so hard to cover, she nodded and forced herself to calm down. "I will."

Chapter 32

"How did you get through it? Because I don't think I can." Star's teary gaze drilled into Rivers, begging for answers she didn't have.

"But for God, I wouldn't have." Rivers squeezed Star's hand. "We need each other too."

Waves lapped not far from their feet as they waited for the other mourners to arrive. The sun sank lower on the horizon, and a late afternoon breeze lifted the scent of the salty ocean air.

Rivers had been blessed to have her father by her side during Jordan's funeral, praying and encouraging, holding her up, along with Jordan's parents. And Cooper's. Star didn't have the benefit of a parent being there. They'd phoned Star's sister, but they'd gotten no answer or returned call, so Star had no family to lean on. Rivers had determined to see the girl through the memorial, no matter how many painful memories the experience dredged up. And God knew it had. She'd had to hear terms like autopsy and coroner's report again.

Blake's body would be returned to his parents in Louisiana, and since they'd been estranged from their son for years, they had no idea who Star was. They'd not been inclined to include her in any funeral they'd hold there. Besides, New Orleans was a good ten hours southwest.

Rivers had spent the last few days planning with Star while they sat with Priscilla. The women had bonded quickly, which had been a blessing in so many ways. Maybe with that bond in

217

place, Star wouldn't give up her sobriety.

Star had said Blake loved being near water, so they'd made arrangements to hold the memorial at the beach across the street from the cottage. Rivers had finished the drawing of Blake gazing at Star. They'd framed it and placed the picture on an easel in the sand.

The men of Re-Claimed had set up a small podium and chairs on the shore facing the Atlantic, then went home to change. Star had asked Davis to speak. Perhaps she'd seen the same spiritual spark in Davis that Rivers had noticed. Perhaps he gave her hope for sobriety.

Two vans pulled up, and Star's lip quivered. "They're here."

"God is here, too." Rivers wrapped an arm around her. "We can do this."

The mourners made their way down the beach, each stopping to shake Star's hand or give her a hug. Gabby and Kevin both offered a long-stem rose.

Cooper brought up the end of the line with Priscilla's arm in his. She hobbled along slowly until they reached the group. Priscilla held Star's neck for a long moment then kissed her cheek.

Cooper nodded at them both with tired eyes, and then helped the older woman to a chair.

Once everyone was seated, Kevin said a prayer. Gabby led the small group in singing Amazing Grace. Her strong, deep voice belted above the waves gently cresting on the shore in front of them, and the rest of the Re-Claimed residents sang along through tears and sniffles.

They might not have known Blake long, but the tragic death still stung. Rivers had talked with several of the ladies over the past few days about their sorrow. It tunneled deep into their psyche, intensifying their unspoken fears. Would they be next? Would they be lost to this fierce enemy?

Davis came forward and offered Star a sympathetic smile. He held a notepad and another notebook, both of which he laid on the podium. "Hi, friends. Like you all, I wish this were just a fun day at the beach watching the sunset, but it's not. So I want to say what I believe God has given me to help make sense of this loss, the best sense we can find on this side of heaven.

"My grandpappy used to quote a phrase when I was a kid that never meant anything to me back then. He'd say, 'Davis, every tub has to sit on its own bottom.'" One side of his mouth lifted. "One day when I was in Afghanistan on patrol, the meaning suddenly became clear. I'd been pretty good at blaming other people for the junk in my life rather than taking responsibility and sitting on my own bottom."

He held up the notebook. "Most of you know every resident of Re-Claimed is given a flimsy notebook like this and encouraged to work the steps. You know number eight, about making a list of all the people we've harmed and being willing to make amends. Blake had begun a list, and with Star's permission, I'll read a short portion.

"'To God, my parents, my friends, my brother, my daughter, the mother of my child, and to Star,

"'I'm sorry for all I've put you through. The lies. My absence. Letting you down. Not being the son, brother, father, or friend I should have. For allowing you to be hurt or causing pain.

"'I hate what this slavery has done to my life, but I hate even worse the hurt I've caused.'"

Davis tapped the opened page. "Blake was trying to take responsibility for his life and his choices. I respect that. If we confess our sins, the Bible says, God is faithful and forgives. And, in my mostly humble opinion, I believe God accepts Blake's confession. But Blake also wrote some words I think some of us can relate to."

Davis looked down at the notebook again. "'Drugs have stolen everything inside me. I feel empty and lost. I want to make a new start, but the voices in my head say otherwise. I don't know if I can fight them.'"

Davis squeezed the edges of the podium and shifted his feet in the sand. "Many of us have heard those dark voices whispering lies, and I'm standing here today begging and praying you'll understand there *is* Someone who can destroy that darkness wanting to devour you. There is a Lighthouse in the middle of your stormy waters. Don't keep standing at a distance, holding back from the Savior. When you feel that deep thirst or hunger, Jesus is what you are hungry and thirsty for. Turn that craving over to Him. Show God your problem, then show your problem your God. Say to the darkness, what'cha gonna do about my big God?" He pointed toward the sky.

"Every human, at some point, has been a prisoner of the enemy and sin. That's why God sent His Son to save us, to free us. You accept the Son, and you are free indeed." He looked at Star. "Blake told me he believed this. From what you've told me about him, he was a protective sort of man. He did his best to keep you safe. That's such an honorable trait. And I think he'd love nothing more than to see you"—he let his gaze roam the other mourners—"and to see every one of us beat those dark voices." He looked at Star again. "In God's power, I pray that you do. That we all do."

He scanned the crowd, and then his focus landed on Rivers. "I pray through the Holy Spirit right now that every single one of you see His light overcome the darkness you battle. You can survive your worst nightmare with God's help." His voice rose in power and volume. "There is life after death, *here and now.*"

His words landed on Rivers and their meaning soaked into her soul. Maybe she would leave this place of both pain and healing, but this place wouldn't ever leave her.

Chapter 33

Cooper lingered after the memorial.

The sun disappeared in the west, leaving a touch of gold against a deep purple sky. They'd removed the chairs and podium. He'd walked Priscilla home, and now the residents loaded into the vans. Rivers stood with Star, saying goodbye for the evening.

This situation had to have been tough on Rivers. Had to have brought up memories of death and loss. But she'd been there for Star, and she'd amazed him once again with her care and grace. No wonder Jordan had loved her.

They were a good match. Jordan and Rivers should be together. There was no Cooper and Rivers.

He needed to remind himself of that fact over and over—like the slogans they repeated in AA—until it became ingrained in his mind. Because even though Jordan was gone, there had to be another great guy like him somewhere in Memphis for Rivers. Memphis, the city where she belonged. Not St. Simons.

The vans rolled away, and Rivers walked toward him, her sandaled feet sinking in the dry sand. "Hey." Her gaze met his, somehow communicating the volumes of the day's sadness without words. When she was close enough, she fell into his chest and embraced him.

He should hold her at arm's length in so many ways, but his heart wasn't listening or obeying. All slogans flew out of the window, and he melted into her. With nothing but a hug, she burrowed deeper into his soul than any human ever had.

Long moments passed before she pulled back and wiped her eyes. He missed the contact immediately.

"Thank you," she whispered. Her blue gaze locked with his.

"This has been hard." He cupped her cheek, her skin soft beneath his fingers. "You've been a trouper."

"Last night, I spoke with Gabby, and I'm not selling the gallery. I'm not leaving Shane in charge of things anymore though. I'll call him tomorrow. Gabby and Kevin will oversee the properties, but nothing else has to change."

Properties? What did that mean? His heart raced. "Why? What changed your mind?"

"What y'all are doing—what you're doing—is important. Doing life with the people of Re-Claimed, it's God's work. A life-changing, life-saving ministry." A cool breeze lapped around them, and she licked her lips before continuing. The small action drew his attention to a dangerous location, so he wrenched his gaze back up. "I'll leave the cottage in their charge, too. Keep the place like one of those online vacation rentals, and Gabby's ladies will clean it between residents. Extra income for us all."

Her lips, her heart, her words drew him like an irresistible force. Maybe it was the strain of the day, maybe it was the intensity of his emotions, but he lowered his mouth to hers. His fingers slid to the back of her head, relishing the silkiness of her hair. Attempting to exhibit a morsel of control, he kissed her softly, gently.

She returned his efforts with fervor. Her fingertips pressed into the muscles of his back, her lips roving, probing, seeming to crave to know him more.

He had to stop this madness he'd started. Breathless, he pulled back. "Rivers, I'm falling in love with you—"

"I—"

"Wait." He touched his index finger to her lips. "I know you have to go back to Memphis. I know we can't be together for at least a dozen really good reasons. My past. My family. Your parents need you. Your job in Memphis. My job here."

His heart raced with what he was about to suggest. "But could we just press pause on all those reasons and enjoy your last days in St. Simons? Together? I'll help you clean out the cottage. We can work on the gala you had in mind. Then, when it's time, I'll let you go."

Her blue gaze searched his face, worry carving a crease between her brows.

Letting her go would be harder than he wanted to think about, but he couldn't allow his feelings to hold her back. He shook his head. "You don't have to fret about me. I have a good support system. Better than good. Gabby, Kevin, and Davis know my feelings for you without me having to say a word." He let his forehead rest against hers. "I've never loved a woman this way. Though it'll be bittersweet, I want to be an adult and just love you one day at a time, while I can."

He let his finger leave her mouth to caress her cheek. "Sorry. You can talk now."

She drew his palm to her lips. "I think I'd like that." Her lashes lifted with her gaze, revealing pent-up tears. "But I'd enjoy a few more of these." Standing on her toes, she planted soft kisses on his forehead, his cheeks, his lips. "If that's allowed in your plan?"

Plan? His eyes closed, and his mind went blank. All he knew was her touch.

"Cooper? Can you hear me?" Her voice held a laugh. "Maybe we should just sit in the sand and look at the stars." She released him and plopped to the ground.

He sat beside her and took her hand in his. His brain buzzed with happiness. She'd said yes. Did she love him the way he loved her? He didn't know. It didn't matter. He'd enjoy the rest of the time he had with Rivers.

Then he'd let her go.

Chapter 34

The week with Cooper passed too quickly. Rivers clung to him beside the Jeep, unwilling to let go yet. Stars peeked out between the mossy branches of the trees, and the Atlantic breezes had turned cool as fall arrived in St. Simons.

She touched his cheekbones, brushed his nose, his chin, letting her fingers memorize his every feature. His breath quickened, but he didn't move, just allowed her to continue her study of him. His dark hair, dark lashes…those eyes that held her captive. And oh, those lips. She'd miss their kisses when she went home.

Only one more week until the gala, and they'd be saying goodbye.

If nothing else, they'd both learned that they could love again.

She laid her head against his shoulder. Her heart wanted more of him, and her chest ached at the thought of leaving. She knew he was hurting, too, but he'd kept a smile on his face—kept their interactions positive.

They'd gotten the details of the gala nailed down. Other than the furniture and artwork, they'd finished cleaning out the cottage. Bitterness coated her tongue as she thought about the patio storage room filled with Cooper's paintings, hidden away like outcasts after the accident. His talent, even from an early age, was something his mother should have been proud of. Why would she have wished that Cooper could be like Jordan? They were two very different men with their own special God-given talents.

If only his family could see that Cooper had changed. If only they could forgive him. Maybe their relationship could never be the same, but they could heal. Not so she could be with him, but so he wasn't as guilt-ridden, and so he and his family could all move on in a new way.

"What's going on in here?" Cooper brushed kisses across her forehead, then tipped her chin.

"I wish your family could know the man I'm holding."

"I understand why they can't." His gaze dropped for a moment, then met hers. "I broke trust too many times. Let them down. Lied."

"When I used to ask my dad how he still loved my mother after all she'd done, he had this quote he'd always recite. 'Not forgiving someone is like drinking poison and expecting the other person to die.'" Her throat tightened. "I've been searching my own heart the past weeks and finding bitterness I'd stored up about Mom and the drunk driving accident."

"And has that changed?" His dark eyes looked hopeful.

"I think I've given up the poison for a healing stream. I think my relationship with Mom will be better when I get home." Though her eyes stung, she smiled.

He pulled her close and held tight, his hands caressing her back. "God knows how much I love you, Rivers. I'm so proud of you and all the hard stuff you've worked through. How you've grown close to Star and worked with the ladies by leading art therapy for Gabby."

Her eyes shut as she melted into him. He'd told her he loved her a few times now, never waiting or expecting a response back. And she hadn't given him one. Couldn't say the words yet. Maybe she'd never be able to. Maybe because she felt she was betraying Jordan. Maybe those three words

227

committed too much of her heart to another man she'd soon lose.

"We should say goodnight," he whispered, voice husky.

"We should." Rivers brushed his lips with light kisses.

When she stopped, he released a long breath. "You're not making it easy on me."

Guilt pricked her.

"It's okay." He rubbed his nose against hers. "I'm teasing." Taking a step back, he held her at arm's length. "Let's take an afternoon off and do something. Get outdoors. Climb the lighthouse by the pier, rent bikes, walk through Christ Church... I don't know. What would you like to do?"

So much. She'd barely toured the area, and there was a lot she wanted to experience here—with Cooper—but their time was fleeting. One question nagged her, though. "Why haven't you taken me for another ride in your boat since that first day?"

His smile faltered. "I can. We can." His Adam's apple bobbed with a hard swallow. "I just worry that something would go wrong."

Like with Savannah. As she suspected, he still carried that weight. "Can you let that go? It would be good if we could work through your lingering fears and guilt."

He laughed and pulled her back against his chest. "Okay, Miss Therapist, but you're wearing a life vest."

"As soon as we can get an afternoon away, it's a date."

~~~

"Talk some sense into me, Gabby." Rivers leaned against the white van in Priscilla's driveway. An early morning chill still hung in the air.

Once Star had exited the vehicle and made her way into Priscilla's house, Rivers had caught Gabby and spilled the details of the past week dating Cooper. Her mouth still tingled at the memory of his lips on hers, the genuine smile that lit his dark eyes each time they said goodnight.

Gabby shook her head and offered a compassionate smile. "Cooper is a good guy. There's always a chance of relapse, but then again, no one is guaranteed anything in this life." She shrugged and waved a hand around in her dramatic fashion. "I only wish if y'all care about each other, you could find a way to be together for all the days you have. In life. Not just the rest of your time here."

"My dad needs me in Memphis to help with Mom. And Cooper's got his work here that he doesn't want to leave. Then there's his family and the whole Jordan connection. Our relationship just can't work long-term." She imagined the hurt their dating would cause to Jordan's family, and the guilt that would put on her and Cooper. Too much pressure for a relationship to survive.

"I have one more question for you. You don't have to answer. Just ponder." Gabby's brown eyes shone golden in the morning sun. "Are you sure you aren't letting fear steal your happiness?"

The words rang truer than Rivers wanted to admit. What if she let herself love Cooper, and then she lost him? Especially if she lost him to addiction? She'd looked up the relapse statistics, and they weren't encouraging. What if Cooper slipped? The sheer terror of stepping onto that roller coaster was enough to make her keep some distance with her heart. She knew too well the desperate days and sleepless nights her father had endured with her mother. She wouldn't want to live her life wondering if or when that would happen.

"I forgot." Gabby snapped her fingers. "I've had a great response to the gala invitations we sent to the community. I've got to head to the thrift store, but I'll get the numbers to you."

"That'll help to give a headcount to the caterer. Cooper's collecting gift cards to add to the door prizes and has rounded up speakers from your successful graduates." Rivers checked the lists she'd created on her phone the night before in a vain effort to get her mind off Cooper's kisses. "Oh, did you handle the music?"

"I have a guy." Gabby smiled and raised one eyebrow. "It's taken care of."

"Wonderful. I'll bring Star back to Re-Claimed tonight in time for dinner. See you then." Everything was coming together.

Gabby drove away, reminding Rivers that she'd do the same soon. For good.

A lump formed in her throat. Saying goodbye wouldn't be easy. At least when she returned to Memphis, she'd leave her new friends in good shape. They'd have the gallery, the funds, and she prayed, the goodwill of the community, despite the petition circulating.

Inside the cottage, she scanned the walls. Some of the paintings could be sold at the gala. She'd double check that Pearl or Brooklyn didn't want them. After that she'd have to figure out the value, but her Memphis connections could help with that.

The yellow key to the storage unit caught her attention. She hadn't had the chance to go there yet. Who knew what that place held. Maybe Shane.

Calling Shane was already on her to-do list anyway. She'd ask about the storage unit before she let him know he wouldn't be making any hefty real estate commissions.

No time like the present. She pressed Shane's contact.

Three rings later, he answered, breathless. "Shane, here." A loud clatter banged in the background.

"This is Rivers. Is this a bad time?"

"Just lifting some weights."

"I can call back."

"It's fine. What do you need, Rivers?" His tone seemed edgy.

Okay. "I'm almost finished in the cottage, and I thought I'd check out the storage unit. Do you know what's in there?"

The banging stopped. "There's nothing. No need to waste your time."

"Why was Stella renting it?"

"She rented it for the gallery's art overflow, then the family thought they might store the contents of the cottage, but no one ever came."

"So they paid rent on an empty unit for five years?"

"Look. I just did what they asked." Annoyance laced his voice.

"Right." Now that he was already perturbed with her, she was about to make it worse. Might as well blurt it all out. "I'm not selling the cottage or the gallery. I'm turning over the management to Gabriella and Kevin."

The line went silent for a long moment. "I've got to go. Another call." The connection ended.

~ ~ ~

Rivers punched the four numbers written on the back of the keyring into the keypad at the Reliable Storage driveway. The gates swung open to allow her entrance. Just because Shane said nothing was in the unit didn't mean she shouldn't check for herself. A quick computer search had given her the address, and after a few wrong turns, she'd found it. Not far from Shane's office.

She parked near the overhang where people were supposed to unload. If the unit was empty, she wouldn't be blocking the entrance for long.

She'd spoken to someone from the office on the phone to find out where the climate-controlled spaces were located, but when she arrived, the clerks were on a break, according to the note taped to the glass doors. It would've been nice to have someone lead her directly to the right spot, given her trouble with navigation. The building was larger than she'd realized, too, rising up three floors. Fine, then. She'd locate the unit herself.

Inside, the overhead lights did little to brighten the dark structure. Rivers roamed the maze of halls, checking the numbers against the one on her key. Their organizational system made no sense to her at all.

She hadn't found four-thirty-two on the first level, so she climbed a steep set of concrete stairs to the second floor. Creaking and rattling sounds echoed in the empty halls. Chills slid across her shoulders as she wound around the web of corridors. Her own footsteps seemed to boom in her ears.

Why was she getting freaked out? This was just a storage facility, and though it was dark inside this windowless building, the sun still shone outside. Being shot had really ramped up her paranoia. Her fingers went to that familiar indention on her shoulder. The place where the bullet had carved away flesh.

The numbers grew closer to the one she was searching for, and she slowed her steps. Four-thirty-nine, four-thirty-eight. Almost there.

Rattling and pounding reverberated from around the corner, and maybe footsteps, too. Heart racing, Rivers glanced back toward the hall that led to the staircase. Being alone in this building with a stranger suddenly seemed like a bad idea.

She jogged back the way she'd come. Yes, she was crazy, but she had to get out of there. Where was the staircase? Her palms began to sweat as she turned down the next hall. Was she having a panic attack?

Finally, the red exit sign came into view. Sprinting, she took the stairs and blasted out of the building. She didn't stop running until she jumped into her car. Once inside, she hit the locks and sucked in a deep breath. Hopefully the unit was empty, because she wasn't coming back alone. The place was too creepy, and she was still too paranoid.

She cranked the car and headed back toward the cottage to pick up Star at Priscilla's.

Chapter 35

"Get Davis to lock up, Cooper." Kevin practically burst through the front door of the gallery. "I need you to come with me."

"What's wrong?" Cooper's heart jumped to his throat. Not something else.

"Dad wants to talk to us."

"Okay." What now? Cooper found Davis in the studio washing out the coffee pot. "Kev needs me. Can you take care of things? Lock up?"

"Everything okay?" Davis's brows furrowed.

"He didn't say."

"I got this."

Cooper checked his back pocket for his wallet, grabbed his keys, and headed outside with Kevin. Down the sidewalk, Sheriff Barnes stood near his patrol vehicle. Kevin's dad was a tough lawman, but fair. Still, his stern appearance sent a wave of anxiety through Cooper.

When they reached the car, Cooper stopped and crossed his arms. "What's going on? One of the guys in trouble?"

"We found Angelo." The sheriff's words were clipped.

There was something he wasn't saying.

"Is he alive?" *Lord, let him be alive.* He didn't want to lose another man, and he cared for Angelo, had invested in Angelo. He'd believed Angelo was on a good path.

"He's down at the station." Sheriff Barnes nodded.

Relief swept through Cooper. At least Angelo wasn't lying

on the coroner's table.

Sheriff Barnes opened the back door of the SUV, and his mouth took a downward turn. "Would you mind riding to the station? I'd like to ask you some questions."

In the back of the vehicle? Was he going to handcuff him next? Cooper's brain buzzed with questions, but he kept his mouth shut and took a seat. He trusted Kevin and his family. They'd been good to him.

Kevin got in the front passenger side, so maybe being in the backseat was more about space. Cooper prayed that was the case. The memory of the last time he'd been in the back of a police car flashed through his mind. Leaving the hospital in handcuffs. The grief. The depression.

Like now, no one said much on the way to the station. The sounds of the radio conversations and the road filled the ride.

When they reached the parking lot, Cooper waited until Sheriff Barnes opened his door, then followed him into booking, Kevin at his side.

Sheriff Barnes directed them to a small room with a small desk. Chair on either side. No window. Middle of the building. This was a room where they questioned suspects. "Have a seat." He motioned to the chair in front of the desk. "Kevin, you wait outside."

They might have just been asking him questions, but this felt way too real. His heart thudded, and he was careful to keep his clammy hands out in the open.

Kevin left, and a female deputy entered with Sheriff Barnes. The woman took the seat on the other side of the desk, and Sheriff Barnes remained standing. Cooper sank into the chair and waited.

"I'm Deputy Walden." The young woman shuffled through a few papers, then settled on one and picked up a pen.

"You're not under arrest, but I'll still read you the Miranda rights."

"I know them. I waive them." Cooper's heart thudded against his ribs. "I don't need an attorney."

"If you'll just sign this waiver then." She scooted a paper and pen toward him.

Once he'd signed, she continued, "When is the last time you took your boat out?"

Cooper tried to pinpoint the day he'd gone out. With Blake's death and with Rivers being in town, he'd neglected his practice of patrolling the sandbars. Oh Lord, he hoped no one had been lost to the sea. "It's been two weeks."

"Where's the key to your boat?"

Cooper fished in his pocket and pulled out his keys. He turned through them. The key to the loft, the gallery, his Jeep, the Re-Claimed men's house, but no boat keys. He went through them again, more slowly, just to be sure. This didn't make sense. He had an extra, but he'd always kept one on this ring. "I normally have one here. I don't know where it is."

She wrote something on her notepad. "And how do you enter the gate at the marina where your boat is kept?"

"With a code."

"When was the last time you saw Angelo?" The woman's gaze drilled into Cooper.

"The day he skipped out of Re-Claimed. He worked at the gallery."

"No contact since?" This time the question came from Sheriff Barnes.

"None." Cooper was dying to ask what in the world was going on, but maybe they had to get the preliminary questions out of the way first.

"Can you make a detailed statement of your whereabouts

and who you were with since the day Angelo left?"

"I'll do my best." Though it would be awkward to admit how much of that time had been spent with Rivers. He hated that she might be dragged into whatever was going on.

"Okay, when you finish, we'll talk." Sheriff Barnes handed Cooper a sheet of paper and a pen. He and the deputy left the room.

Through the open door, Cooper slid a look toward Kevin, but his friend's expression gave nothing away. If he was here for moral support, he wasn't helping much. Cooper's insides roiled.

Something serious had gone down with Angelo.

~~~

"Hey, ladies." Gabby met Rivers and Star on the sidewalk in front of Re-Claimed. "I've got subs at the houses for a little while. Daddy needs to talk with Rivers and me down at his office." She directed her attention to Star. "You good with that?"

"Sure. See y'all later." Weary-eyed but offering a nod, Star turned toward the house. The girl had been giving sobriety a serious effort, even while grieving.

Apprehension rippled through Rivers. There was something strange about Gabby's tone. "My car or yours?"

"You drive. I'll direct." Once they reached the VW, Gabby folded her long legs and sat on the passenger side.

Rivers cranked the car and followed the directions Gabby gave. "What's going on?"

"Something with Angelo. Daddy wants to verify Cooper's alibi."

"Alibi?" Good grief. She hadn't expected trouble to come this fast.

"I don't know the details, so let's not worry." Gabby

237

seemed to be making extra effort to keep her tone upbeat. "Turn here."

Rivers complied, and they continued on their course. Questions snaked through her mind, but she kept them to herself.

Had she trusted too quickly? Was Cooper the man she'd believed? Was she a complete idiot?

They'd know soon enough. She took a deep breath and blew the air out with a silent prayer. *Show me the truth, God.*

At the parking lot, the yellow key ring lying in the cup holder reminded Rivers of her earlier escapade. "I meant to ask if you'd come with me to see what's in a storage unit Cooper's grandmother had. I would ask Cooper, but I didn't know if there'd be painful memories for him there. And I know it sounds silly, but when I went over there this afternoon, I was totally creeped out by the place." Not unlike the way she felt right now.

"Of course." Gabby raised her brows. "Is it in a sketchy location or something? Give me the key, and I'll get Daddy to go."

"The key's in the console. The area seemed all right. Probably just me being a baby." She hoped.

"That's understandable." Gabby pocketed the ring and then sniffed a couple of times with her nose scrunched. "First let's take care of the current situation. And then maybe get some deodorizer for this Bug. How can you stand the sour smell?"

"Years of practice." Rivers tried to keep her voice and her posture steady as they walked across the lot, despite the nervousness crawling over her like she'd stepped in an angry pile of fire ants.

Gabby opened the glass door and led her in, speaking to

people she knew along the way. They reached an office doorway. A tall, beefy man in a sheriff's uniform stood with Cooper and a female officer. The man's face had that stern, don't-mess-with-me aura, like a high school principal on steroids. Cooper's expression held a twisted mix of emotion when he met her gaze. His eyes offered an unspoken apology, but his lips stayed pressed shut.

The sheriff turned to Cooper. "Would you step into the hall and shut the door? I'd like to talk to Gabriella and Ms. Sullivan."

Cooper complied. Rivers followed Gabby and the sheriff and the female officer into an office.

A wave of dread washed over Rivers, weighing down her steps into the dull room. The door clicked shut behind them.

"Ms. Sullivan, thank you for coming down. I'm Sheriff Barnes and this is Deputy Walden." He turned to shake her hand with the firmest grip Rivers had ever endured. If she weren't so intimidated, she'd have squealed or at least complained she needed her hands for her work. The woman's grip wasn't much lighter.

"Call me Rivers." She made a pathetic attempt at a smile.

"I hear you've helped over at Kevin and Gabriella's project. It's much appreciated." He pulled one of the empty chairs from beside the wall. "Have a seat."

Wow, she felt like she was in a time-out. And she had no idea why. Her heart raced. What in the world had she gotten mixed up in?

"Would either of you like some coffee or water?" Deputy Walden asked.

"No, ma'am," Rivers squeaked out.

"No, thanks." Gabby took another vacant chair and scooted it up beside her.

"I'm sure you're wondering why I've asked you down here." Sheriff Barnes sat behind a desk.

Understatement of the year. No. Too many things had gone haywire in the last twelve months for today to make the top of the heap. She could get through this, whatever this was. She'd been through worse. *Lord, help me.*

"Would you write the times, dates, and locations you've been in James Cooper Knight's presence since the disappearance of Angelo Thomas?" He pushed blank paper toward both of them. "I have a calendar if you need to look at one. I've marked the date Mr. Thomas last resided at the Re-Claimed."

This was serious. Rivers stared at the paper and picked up the pencil. A knot lassoed her midsection, pulling tight as her brain went blank. Was Angelo even alive? "Can I ask why?"

"I can't disclose the details yet."

Gabby grunted. "What's going on, Daddy? If Angelo got into some mess, it didn't involve Cooper. We keep him too busy to get into trouble."

"We're covering all the bases before we move forward." His voice became soft. "Honey, your statements could help Cooper."

"Fine." Gabby huffed. "They better. I need him." Then she gave her dad a humble look. "Thank you, sir."

Maybe the man wasn't so scary. Rivers summoned her courage. "I think I'll need that calendar, please." She wanted to get this right. If Cooper was in the middle of some scheme, she'd be furious, both with him and herself. If he wasn't, then she sure didn't want her memory to be the cause of more trouble.

She just wished she knew which it was.

~~~

Cooper checked his phone again. It seemed Rivers had been in Sheriff Barnes's office for hours, but only thirty minutes had passed.

"This is crazy." Kevin shuffled his feet like a caged animal in the chair beside him. "I need answers."

"Answers would be nice, but like most situations in life, we're not in control."

"Good reminder, bro." Kevin chuckled. "Let go, and let God."

"That." Cooper nodded. The AA slogan fit. Because like always, he'd have to trust that God knew what He was doing. He prayed that Rivers was trusting Him, too. She didn't deserve to go through more drama. And again, it was his fault.

The door to the office swung open, and Sheriff Barnes stepped out. "Come in. I'll explain what I can, because some of it will be on the news at ten o'clock."

"Thank you." Kevin breathed out an exasperated huff.

They rose and joined Rivers and Gabby and the deputy in the room. Rivers met his eyes, but he couldn't decipher what might be running through her mind. What must she think of him?

"Have a seat if you want," the sheriff offered two chairs that were pushed against the wall.

"I'm fine." He couldn't sit another second. His nerves were way too ragged.

"Me, too." Kevin must have reached his capacity as well.

"Okay, here's what I'm allowed to tell you." Sheriff Barnes faced all four of them. "Angelo took Cooper's boat late this afternoon. Not sure if this was the first time he'd taken it, but when he did, he clipped another larger boat."

Great. Cooper held in a groan. He hadn't thought to look for Angelo on his boat. And his insurance would not be happy about paying out on some yacht.

"The other boat called for the police because of the accident, but also because of Angelo's erratic behavior." He leveled a gaze on Cooper. "And because your boat began taking on water. It ended up sinking."

No. Cooper shook his head as his stomach plunged. What next? "I only had liability insurance."

Gabby took to her feet, shaking a finger at him. "Well, you can quit your guilt patrol. You are forgiven, Coop."

"My boat rides weren't always about that." He'd like to believe he might someday be able to let go of his culpability in Savannah's death. But the blame seemed to be ingrained in him as much as it had been ingrained in the minds of his family. "I like nature—"

"Where is Angelo now?" Kevin interrupted his lame explanations.

"Booking." The deputy spoke up. "Mr. Knight, we'll need you to agree to not leave the county during the investigation. Would you agree to undergo a polygraph tomorrow?"

"Yes, but this sounds like more than a boating accident."

"Angelo was in possession of a bag containing four kilos of uncut heroin when he got off your vessel and onto the other boat."

A collective gasp traveled the room. Gabby's mouth fell open. For once, she was speechless. And Cooper understood her astonishment. Angelo was a small-time heroin user, only selling to pay for his own drugs. That amount was way out of line for the guy.

Cooper shook his head. "Kilos?"

Sheriff Barnes nodded, then stood and opened his office door. "He won't be coming back to Re-Claimed. Not for a number of years, at least. He's talking a bunch of jumbled nothing right now. Seems he'd sampled the product." His tone was gruff. "Thank you all for coming down. We'll be in touch to set up your polygraph."

Rivers stood. She and Gabby neared the doorway.

Kevin pressed his fingers to his temple. "What did he get himself into?"

"What did he get our good name into?" Gabby huffed.

Turning his gaze to Rivers, Cooper searched her expression. Would she think he'd been involved? Whether she did or not, it didn't matter. One week after agreeing to be together, if only temporarily, she'd been thrown into the midst of a criminal investigation.

He was selfish to ask her to devote any piece of her heart to someone like him. That ended now.

He didn't know why Angelo had used his boat, but he'd rather step down than shine a bad light on the mission. "I'm resigning, effective immediately. I'll rent a hotel room. Rivers and Gabby can find someone to take over the gallery."

Chapter 36

Stunned and brain-scrambled, Rivers followed Gabby out to the parking lot. This was definitely a roller-coaster moment, and she hadn't expected the fierce drop so soon. Kevin and Cooper, a few steps behind on the sidewalk, spoke in hushed tones.

Midstride, Gabby stopped and turned. She pointed at Cooper. "You are not resigning. I know you're not guilty, and it'll seem like you are if you quit now."

"She's right," Kevin agreed. "The polygraph will back up your statement, and you could voluntarily submit to a drug test."

Cooper raised his gaze from the ground to Rivers. He seemed to be waiting for her verdict.

She swallowed hard, floundering to figure out what she actually believed to be true. Was she foolish or blind? The man she saw before her wasn't a drug user anymore nor was he a drug dealer.

Have I been deceived somehow, God?

Only last night, she'd said she wished Cooper's family could know the man she knew. Now a gentle nudge in her heart told her to trust her own words.

Rivers took a step toward him. "I don't believe you're involved with whatever Angelo was doing. You shouldn't give up your work. It's too important."

He didn't speak, but his eyes widened, as if he couldn't imagine her still being on his side.

"Why don't you give Cooper a ride home in the Stinky Bug?" Gabby tapped Rivers on the back. "Kev and I will stay until Daddy can drive us. We'll see if we can come up with a plan."

Cooper shook his head, his focus still on Rivers. "You don't have to. Honestly, if I were you, I'd catch the next flight to Memphis and get away from my trail of misery."

"You're not me." Rivers retrieved the keys from her bag and motioned with her head toward her car. "Come on."

The hum of the motor and Cooper's directions claimed the ride back. They both seemed embroiled in their own thoughts. Rivers churned ideas over and over in her mind. How could they make this situation better? There had to be a way to disconnect Angelo's illegal acts from being tied to Cooper or Re-Claimed.

"Angelo passed his last drug test. And it's not one he could fake." Cooper broke the quiet. "Sure, he'd admitted he was still struggling some, but nothing that would add up to this. I mean, the kind of cash it would take to come up with that much heroin—no way Angelo had it. He was a small-time carrier, only did it to be able to afford his own stash. And in less than two weeks, he'd have finished his probation."

"Maybe the temptation was too much. If someone offered him a lot of money or a lot of…"

"Heroin. You can say the word. I won't jump out of the car to look for some." He banged his hand against the dash. "But dang-it, why take my boat? I see why you think of us as *ruiners*."

She wished she hadn't been so honest about her inmost thoughts. "You aren't that."

"Anymore, you mean. Because I was. Like Angelo, I took people's trust and buried it in the Atlantic. Only I was worse. I

245

took my cousin under."

At a stop sign, Rivers glanced at Cooper. His face contorted with pain. This situation had swept him into a black pit, and she wasn't sure how to drag him out or even throw him a life ring.

"Don't give up hope." She pressed the gas, recognizing the area, at last, and turned toward Re-Claimed rather than the gallery. There was no way she'd let him thrash in this mire alone in that tiny studio. Maybe Davis could help.

Unless he'd been involved.

No. She trusted her instincts about both Davis and Cooper. She'd not been around Angelo as much to have feelings one way or another about him. She pulled to a stop in front of the Re-Claimed houses.

"Why are we here?" Cooper stared out the windshield.

"I may've turned off those annoying alarms you set on my phone, but I still need dinner. I thought maybe they'd have some leftovers." She offered him a smile and touched his arm. "Let's get some food, find Davis, and sit outside to eat and talk."

He lowered his head, his eyes pressed shut. "What if I don't want to?"

"I didn't ask." She opened her door. "Let's go."

~~~

"If you'd said Angelo'd wrapped himself in tin foil and claimed to be a Martian, I'd have been less shocked." Davis kneaded his forehead and stomped the concrete. "I mean, I'm bumfuzzled and mad as a wet cat. I'd rip him a new one if he were here. How could he do this to us? To God? I thought I knew the man."

Cooper understood Davis's bewilderment and anger. But what really confused him right now was the support Rivers was showing him. How could she still believe in him? Couldn't she see he wasn't worth it?

Yet, here she sat on the front porch step of Re-Claimed, eating her dinner of chicken nuggets and trying to figure out how to prove his innocence. Other than Gabby and Kevin, no one had ever believed in him or stood up for him. Honestly, he often didn't believe in himself. He should've seen this coming, seen some clue that Angelo was floundering.

"What about surveillance cameras? Maybe one would show Angelo leaving. If he left with someone else, they might be recognizable." Rivers pointed toward the security company sign on the front lawn. "There's one at the gallery, too, right? The video might help figure out at least part of what happened."

"Yeah, if they haven't been recorded over. The loop is only so long." Cooper sighed. "I've never had the need to check into it before, but Kevin might know how long they last."

The sheriff's car pulled up, and Gabby and Kevin stepped out before it pulled away again. The siblings made a somber trail down the sidewalk.

"This is so frustrating." Gabby waved both arms in the air. "God, send us some miracles, please, in the name of Jesus."

"Amen," Davis answered. "Rivers had an idea. Can y'all find out if there's anything of interest on the surveillance cameras at the houses and the gallery?"

"Good thinking." Kevin nodded. "They might have one out at the marina, too. I'll call Dad and the security company. See what we can get going." He squared off in front of Cooper. "We're going to figure this out. You're not going down with your ship."

Another car pulled up front. Shane's red Audi.

Rivers grunted. "Not him. Not now."

"What?" Cooper stared at her. "Has he been bothering you?"

"He wanted me to sell everything, and I've told him I'm not going to." She raised one shoulder. "I don't feel like dealing with him."

"I'll deal with him if he causes anyone a lick of trouble tonight." Gabby straightened her spine, and her hands fisted.

"Shane better watch out." Davis chuckled. "That's one scary woman right there."

Shane made his way down the sidewalk in a quick stride. "Oh, man, I just heard. I can't believe your boat is gone. I'm so sorry. I know what it meant to you—the patrols."

"Yeah." Cooper held in a groan. If only that were the worst of it. Word sure traveled fast in this little community.

"Look, I'm sorry I was a jerk to you and Rivers the other night. I was just caught off guard, and I'm trying to put together this big deal." Shane pulled a keyring from his pocket and held it toward Cooper. "Take my boat out. I never have time to get on the water. In fact, I'm planning to sell it. You can let me know how she's running."

"I'm fine." Cooper shook his head, ignoring the offering. "You're boat's more of a mini-yacht, anyway."

"Come on. Take her for a run." Shane smiled, hopeful. "You can let me know if you notice anything that needs fixing."

Stepping in front of Cooper, Gabby swiped the keys, then turned back to face him. "Let's do it, Coop. Let's all take tomorrow afternoon off and hit the waves."

"I don't know." This seemed like the worst possible time to take off on a joy ride. Unless Gabby wanted him off-site for a while. But wouldn't it look bad for him to be enjoying himself while Re-Claimed was under suspicion?

Rivers put a hand on his shoulder. "You did say we should do something fun."

"All of you?" Shane's brows knitted, and his smile disappeared. "My boat's not that big."

"Not all the residents." Gabby's fist went to her hip. "Me, Kev, Cooper, and Rivers. We need some time away from here."

"What am I, chopped liver?" Davis snorted.

"Someone has to run the gallery." Gabby shot him a sarcastic look.

Arms crossed, Davis pretended to pout. "Well, if you're going to be that way, I could really use a good foot massage when y'all get back."

Cooper held his tongue. Gabby would get her way, but the timing seemed all wrong.

~~~

"Is this right?" Rivers looked down at the life vest she'd put on. So bulky feeling, but at least Cooper wore one, as well, since he'd insisted she had to.

"Here, let me snug it a little." He pulled at the straps, barely glancing at her face. His brows had yet to unfurrow. "Are you sure you want to go out? This was Gabby's idea, and now she and Kevin are bailing on us."

"It'll be good for us to catch some rays and relax." She tried to sound perky. "Just for a little while. I'm sure she wanted to come, but they couldn't find anyone to fill in." Probably because of the announcement about Angelo's arrest on the ten o'clock news.

"Just a quick ride, and then let's take the Jeep over to Tybee Island or something."

"Sounds good." Taking his cheeks, she forced him to look at her. It was obvious Cooper was nervous, but he needed to

249

do this. "Breathe. I'll be fine."

"You better." He gave her a half-hearted smile. "This is a nice boat."

"Wonder why he's selling? Seems like he could squeeze in a ride here and there. Take clients out." She let go of Cooper's face and glanced around. The vessel was much larger than Cooper's. It even had a roof over what he'd called the cockpit.

"Shane's always been a wheeler-dealer." Cooper untied the ropes that held them to the dock. "Better sit down now."

Rivers plopped into the chair next to the captain's seat. "Jordan didn't talk about him much."

"You probably know that Jordan's grandparents on his dad's side were divorced, but he may not have mentioned that his grandfather married a much younger woman with a son— Shane. Jordan's dad had never been close with his stepbrother, but I guess since Shane lived here, they asked him to handle their business after my grandmother died."

Cooper took his place and cranked the motor. Before long, they'd cleared the marina and canal.

The heavy Atlantic breeze stirred the waves and ruffled the branches of the palm trees on the nearby beach. Rivers ran her fingers across the top of her head. Her hair would probably end up in large goofy spikes by the end of this ride.

Though the shore was still in sight, the farther they traveled, the more the vastness of the ocean made her feel small. The image of being lost to this deep expanse sent a chill scampering across her shoulders. How scary it must have been for Savannah and Cooper that terrible day.

"There's the lighthouse." Cooper pointed through the windshield. "We could check it out later. It's a museum now."

"I'd like that."

He slid a glance at her. "You would?"

"You're not getting rid of me yet."

"If you're sure." His gaze focused forward again.

A whiff of something like oil and burnt tires hit her nose. "Do you smell that? Like something burning?"

Cooper's head whipped toward the back of the boat. "Oh, God, help us." He cut the engine and swiped his fingers through his hair. "Rivers, you're going to have to jump overboard."

Her gaze followed his to see billowing black smoke rising toward the sky.

"Now, Rivers!" He scrambled up, pulled her to her feet, and pushed her to the nearest side. "Jump!"

"What about you?" Her heart battered her chest at the sight of the water and waves.

"I'll follow. Go!"

She plunged over the railing into the chilly waves of the Atlantic.

Chapter 37

Thrashing more than swimming in the deep, dark water, Rivers aimed toward the shore. The surf splattering her face spurred panic. Wild ideas flashed through her mind—terrifying movies she'd watched where sharks circled before attacking. Her chest tightened, and she swam harder.

A good bit of water lay between them and the bank, so she needed to stop freaking out. Maybe Cooper knew how to keep them safe. She glanced over her shoulder for a glimpse of his face.

Where was he?

Nothing. She stopped swimming and flipped onto her back for a better view.

Still on the boat behind the captain's chair, he stood holding a fire extinguisher. He couldn't seem to get it to work. Why hadn't he jumped in with her?

Flames burst from the motor, towering several feet, orange against the blue sky.

Rivers could barely breathe, but she forced her voice out. "Cooper, jump!"

He turned toward her with a torn expression.

"Please!"

He moved to the front edge of the boat. "I'm—"

An explosion rent the air, throwing debris high before plummeting shrapnel into the water. Her heart catapulted to her throat.

"Cooper? Cooper!" *Oh, God, where is he?* She kicked back

toward the wreckage floating on the surface. *Let him be okay.*

A cloud of black smoke ballooned from the remnants of the boat, incongruent with the white clouds above. As she swam closer, she turned in circles trying to locate him in the chaos.

God, help us.

A wave splatted against her, and she blinked against the salt water burning her eyes. A spot of orange materialized near the flaming vessel. Her heart leapt, and she swam hard toward it.

As she neared, her heart thrashed in her chest. Cooper. He wasn't moving. His skin was a ghostly white. His life vest had kept his face above water, but clearly the blast had walloped him.

"Cooper, can you hear me?" She cradled his head in her hands. "Wake up, please."

A trickle of red ran down his temple. Her breath stuttered. His face seemed so lifeless. White spots clouded her vision. Images of Jordan crowded her mind, the blood seeping from his chest.

No! He can't be gone. "Cooper, you have to stay with me." Was he breathing? She placed her hand near his mouth and nose, hoping to feel air coming and going, keeping him alive. Maybe she felt something. So hard to tell.

She wiped a strand of damp hair from his eyes. "I need you. Please don't leave. I don't care what anyone thinks about us."

What should she do? She had to keep heading to shore, pulling him with her. Gripping the back of his vest, she kicked, keeping the lighthouse in sight as a guide. With wobbly arms and fatiguing legs, she continued a steady pace. The currents seemed to fight her every move. Desperation swamped her hope as the waves pulled them back toward the fire.

253

"Oh, God, I need help."

Behind her, a motor rumbled, and her heart skipped. She flipped onto her back, still holding Cooper.

"Miss, are you okay?" An older man called from the side of a fishing boat.

"Help him!"

"That thing might blow again." The man piloting the vessel motioned toward the fire.

The boat angled sideways, and the first man leaned over the side. "Please hurry, miss." He eyed the flames still consuming Shane's boat.

"Him first. Careful. He's hurt."

"We'll get him. Cut the motor, Clyde, and come back here." He tore off his shirt and shoes, then slipped into the water.

His partner leaned over the back of the boat. Together they eased Cooper on board.

Once they helped her in, she scrambled to Cooper's side. "Oh, Lord, save him."

"Call 911 again, Pete. Have them meet us at the pier near the lighthouse." Clyde went back to the captain's chair while his friend spoke on the phone.

The ride to shore took forever, though they jarred hard over the waves at an alarming speed.

A moan slipped from Cooper, then a ragged, shallow breath. His lips took on a bluish tinge.

"Cooper, can you hear me?"

Again, no answer. He was alive, but something was very wrong.

~~~

Why hadn't she told Cooper she loved him when she had the chance?

The Art of Rivers

After an intense ambulance ride to the hospital and a night spent pacing the waiting room, Rivers stood at Cooper's bedside. Tubes and needles hung from his hands, his mouth, his chest. With ribs broken and one lung collapsed, the ER doctors had intubated him to help him breathe. A bruise darkened the skin near his left eye, and a cut had been glued together on his forehead.

They wouldn't give her much information since she wasn't related to him. Should she call his family? Would Mr. and Mrs. Knight even want to know? Gabby hadn't been certain of what to do either when she'd stopped by.

Rivers touched Cooper's fingertips, not wanting to risk dislodging his IV or the monitor wrapped around his index finger.

"God, you won't take Cooper from me, too, will you?" A sob escaped from deep within her chest, and she raised her eyes upward, tears streaming. "I love him. Please let him be okay. I have to tell him."

"Rivers?" a familiar voice spoke behind her, and she turned.

"Daddy?"

Her father stood just inside the small room. Another man spoke with the doctor. The man had salt and pepper dark hair, and when he turned toward Rivers, her breath caught. Cooper's dad was here, too.

"Mr. Knight?"

"Rivers." Cooper's father nodded, his expression grim and his attention focused on his son.

Dad strode to reach her, concern creasing his brows, his hair a little more gray than she remembered. "Were you hurt? I heard a boat exploded."

"I'm fine. What are you doing here?" Her gaze bounced

between her father and Cooper's.

"Jim called and said you needed help finishing up at the cottage." Daddy nodded toward Mr. Knight. "So we decided to bring your paintings and check on you. I picked him up in Atlanta on the way yesterday afternoon. We would've come sooner, but getting a sub at school for the week took a few days."

"How did you find me *here*? And where's Mom?"

"When we arrived at the cottage, your neighbor explained you were at the hospital. The young woman helping her said your mother could stay with them." He touched her shoulder. "Are you sure you're okay?"

"I'm fine, but…" Her voice broke, and she fell into his arms. "Oh, Daddy, pray for Cooper."

Chapter 38

"Is my son going to be okay?" Mr. Knight turned his attention to the doctor.

Rivers let go of her father and tried to focus on what she was hearing. Broken ribs, punctured lung, burns on right arm, concussion… Nothing she hadn't already known.

"But he'll live, right?" Rivers needed to know more. "He's going to recover?"

"Barring infection or pneumonia, he should make a full recovery. We had him sedated, but he should come out of it soon. Between the broken ribs and the burns, he'll be in some pain, but we'll manage it."

A rustle and tapping sounded from the bed, and Rivers rushed back to Cooper's side.

His eyes fluttered open, and he put his hand to his mouth and nose.

Rivers gently caught his fingers and held on. "Don't try to talk. There's a tube helping you breathe. You'll be okay. I'm here."

He focused on her and blinked. He signaled with his other hand as if he were writing.

"He needs a pen." Rivers turned to the men.

Her father strode to the cabinet of drawers in the room and grabbed a pen and paper, then offered them to Cooper. The man knew his way around hospitals as well as most doctors.

With a shaky hand, Cooper scribbled four words. "No pain

meds. Addict."

Tears stung Rivers eyes. The first worry Cooper had was not for his health but his sobriety.

"What did he write?" Mr. Knight spoke behind her.

She turned to face him. "He doesn't want pain meds. He's been in recovery for five years."

"He'll still need something." The doctor made a note on his electronic pad then directed his comments to Cooper. "We'll work with you on managing the pain without using opioids."

"I should've come back sooner, son." Mr. Knight joined Rivers at the bedside. "Years sooner. I'm sorry."

A tear rolled down Cooper's cheek, and he held out his hand to his father, who clasped it gently with both of his.

The beauty of the moment caught in her throat. She soaked it in and made a picture in her mind that she'd always treasure. Perhaps, now Cooper would have one advocate, one person in his family on his side. If only it hadn't taken another tragedy to repair their relationship.

Rivers was still confused, though. Who'd called them? "How did y'all get here so fast?"

Mr. Knight cleared his throat before answering, obviously overcome. "Cooper texted me a week ago that you needed help. I sat on it a couple of days—like an idiot—trying to figure out what to do, then I contacted your father. We agreed to take off work and come spend the next week. We made hotel reservations and were on our way yesterday, arriving late last night. We didn't know about the accident until this morning."

"Honey, have you been here all night?" Her father placed a hand on her shoulder. "One of us can sit with Cooper."

"I'll stay," Mr. Knight offered.

"I'm not going anywhere." She bent and brushed a kiss on

Cooper's forehead, stroking his dark hair. "I love you, James Cooper Knight."

~~~

"Thank you, God." Cooper coughed, which hurt, but he could finally speak. He'd had enough of this hospital bed and was hoping the doctor would release him when the man made afternoon rounds.

"Don't get in a hurry." Rivers gave his fingers a light squeeze and smiled as if she could read his mind.

"Love you," he croaked. The other words he couldn't wait to speak. If something had happened to her out in that ocean, he'd be in a straitjacket for the rest of his life.

Her cobalt eyes met his as she bent close and brushed a kiss to his lips. "I know, and I love you too."

"You love me?" His heart melted in his chest. In a million years, he'd never expected those words from Rivers.

"I do. I wish I'd told you sooner." She swallowed hard. "I thought I'd lost you."

"Um, am I interrupting a moment?" Mr. Knight knocked and took a step through the doorway. "I can wait outside, but I brought Rivers a cup of coffee and breakfast from a friendly lady named—maybe named Gabby?"

Cooper blinked to make sure he wasn't dreaming. Like he had every time he'd woken with Rivers or his father at his side. He never dared to imagine his father would come back or that Rivers would say she loved him. It was probably just the trauma that made her say the words, but still. He didn't deserve the care of either, yet here they were—one of them always with him.

"Thank you." Rivers smiled and wrapped one arm around his father's back. "That smells wonderful."

Yes, this was surreal. If he was dreaming, he sure didn't

want it to end.

Well maybe the IV part, the drug cravings, and the severe discomfort in most every inch of his body. Even with the small amounts of meds they'd administered, he felt his urges simmering, but he tried to focus on prayer and all he'd learned working the steps the past five years. The repetition of the mantras and slogans and Bible verses that came to his mind sustained him in the moments he needed them most.

"How are plans for the art show?" his father asked once Rivers had settled into a chair with the food.

She swallowed before speaking. "Wonderful. Everyone has really stepped up despite..." She glanced Cooper's way before finishing. "You know, the bad press."

His father nodded, his gaze falling to the floor. "Did they find out why the boat exploded? You both could've been killed."

Shane had to be pretty upset about the boat, and the Angelo situation still hung over Cooper's head, too. Another scandal for the family. *Why now, Lord?* Right when things could be improving. At least with his father. Cooper's chest tightened, earning a sharp pain, but he held in the groan.

Rivers spoke between quick bites. "When Gabby came by last night, she said her father and the department were being tight-lipped about everything. At least, they should let us know what went wrong with Shane's boat. That was so scary."

Either she was starving, in a hurry, or both, because the way Rivers shoveled eggs into her mouth, he wasn't sure she could breathe through bites.

Cooper reached for the pen and paper he'd kept beside him and wrote. Slow down. Don't try to do too much. He couldn't resist drawing a little rose beneath it. Breathe. He handed the note to his father, who read it, smiled, and passed the paper to

Rivers.

"I am breathing." She wiped her lips and smirked. "And I'll smell the roses at the gala in four days, mister."

He hated that Rivers had gotten stuck doing double duty. She stayed here twelve hours at night, then scuttled out to take care of everything he should be doing. At least her father was in town to help.

"I want to come." His voice sounded strange in his own ears. "If it won't make things worse."

"Oh, you're coming." Rivers set the food aside, stood, and then threw her arms up in the air, doing some little twist that had his heart racing. "You and I are going to dance, even if I have to push you around in a wheelchair."

He'd be there, because that night would be one of the last they would have together before she left for Memphis.

Chapter 39

"But you two are so close, and somehow, the relationship works. It makes sense of all the tragedy." Cooper's father straightened his bow tie in the mirror. "Eventually Pearl and Brooklyn will get over it." He shrugged and raised one brow. "Maybe. Some day."

Not likely. Cooper kept his mouth shut on that topic, though. "Rivers may love me, but nothing has changed. She'll still be leaving for Memphis. Her parents need her. She has a career there." Cooper leaned into the straight-backed hotel chair. Dad had insisted they stay together after the doctor signed the release. Since the loft barely had room for one, they'd stayed in his father's suite at the King and Prince Resort. Still nothing but the best for this family. The hotel had probably been a good idea, though. Getting dressed in the rented tux had already zapped his strength. He'd appreciated his father's help and care. Because nothing would keep him away from Rivers tonight.

"So, why not move to Tennessee? I'm sure Memphis has plenty of…"

"Addicts?" Cooper raised his brows, but smiled. They were still navigating this new relationship.

"Jobs." His father held out both hands in surrender. "People who need help. I've heard you're good at what you do."

A dark heaviness slammed against Cooper's mood. "Wouldn't know it from this past month. One client overdosed and another landed in jail."

"But their sobriety isn't up to you. Each person has free will. You can't take responsibility for other people's choices. That's stinking thinking. You need to detach a little."

Though it hurt, Cooper had to laugh. "Have you been going to Al-anon?"

"Maybe."

His father gave him a tender look. One that smoothed some of the raw edges of Cooper's heart. Though, believing he could be loved again unleashed a new set of fears and terrifying vulnerability. He'd surely screw it up somehow.

"You ready?" Dad stood and grabbed his keys.

Clashing emotions churned within Cooper. Ready to see Rivers, yes. Ready for the rest of the world? Or the press? Or the Sheriff's Department personnel? Or Shane? None of the above.

With cautious movements, Cooper stood and made his way to the door. Every move stung the burns on his arm, and every breath reminded him he had broken ribs.

"Ready as I'll ever be."

"You've battled worse and won. You've got this." The love in his father's expression gave him hope.

He prayed Dad was right, because tonight would be an all-out war with his emotions.

~~~

"What do you think?" Rivers marched into the studio and offered her father a weak smile.

"You look stunning, sweetie. Blue's still your color." Her father beamed and planted a kiss on top of her head. "I'm so proud of you. I want to hear all about it when you get back to the cottage tonight. Wake me up if I drift off on the couch. And don't forget to have some fun."

263

"I'll try." Rivers wished they'd stay for the gala, but Dad was afraid things were too overwhelming for her mother already.

"Pretty color." Mom ran her fingers over the dress.

"Thanks, Mama."

Her mother's gaze slid up. "Did you get hurt?"

The satin formal Gabby had picked up for Rivers at the thrift store fit well enough, but with the wide v-line neck, the scars on her shoulder were laid bare for all to see. The disfigured skin reminded Rivers of the awful crime that had stolen Jordan's life. Still, somehow, St. Simons and the people she'd met had offered a healing balm for her wounds. All God's doing, of course.

"I was hurt, but it's getting better."

"Sorry." The corners of her mother's mouth pressed down.

"It's okay." Rivers wrapped her mother in a hug. She'd missed her parents so much. They'd been sweet to make a special trip to encourage her.

"What else is wrong?" Daddy cocked his head and leaned against the counter, looking as if he were in no hurry to get Mom back to the cottage.

Moisture burned her lids, but Rivers refused to let herself cry.

Star had spent twenty minutes applying the eye shadow and mascara for her, so Rivers didn't dare mess it up with her faltering emotions. How was she supposed to enjoy herself knowing she'd be leaving in less than forty-eight hours? She'd be saying goodbye to everyone soon. To Gabby and Star. Priscilla and Phoenix. Davis.

Cooper.

She sniffed and gathered her composure. "I'll miss

everyone here."

"Then stay. It's not like you have a social life in Memphis."

Rivers let her mouth fall open. What was Daddy saying?

"Honey, you work too much and spend what little free time you have with your mom and me. You're in your twenties, live *your* life. No matter the horrible reason, you have the funds to move here."

"I couldn't leave you and Mom. Y'all need me."

Dad nudged her around to face him and placed both hands on her shoulders. "Your mom and I are not your responsibility. We're grownups. We can figure out our own lives." He shook his head, tears filling his eyes. "I should've told you that a long time ago. I leaned on you way too much, and it was wrong. Can you forgive me?"

"Daddy, I wanted to help." The makeup would be slathering down her cheeks any second now because her composure just sprouted wings and flew out the window. "I love y'all so much."

"We love you, too, but we'll manage. I promise." He squeezed her shoulders and smiled.

Part of her wanted to believe his words were true. That she had the permission to choose where she wanted to live and spend her time. Another part questioned what it would mean if she were free to be with Cooper. The idea was unfathomable and exciting and utterly petrifying.

What would it be like to truly open up her whole heart and commit again? To start over?

"What about my work, my clients, my paintings of the river?"

Lines crinkling the corners of his eyes, he shook his head. "I'm sorry if this hurts your feelings, honey, but someone else can handle your position and treat your clients. God's not depending on you to take care of the world or do His job." One side of his mouth quirked. "And good grief, paint something else for a change. Some ocean pictures would be nice."

A smile tugged at her lips while her insides churned. Could she really let everything go? Did she have the courage?

Chapter 40

Swaths of moonlight filtered through the mossy oaks. Cooper and his father managed to find a parking place between the gallery and Re-Claimed, but the traffic had been heavy. Maybe that meant tonight would be a success.

Or there'd be a lot of nosy people looking for a freak show.

No. He wouldn't listen to that dark voice. Gabby and Kevin had been praying and working hard. Rivers had thrown herself into the planning.

"Looks like a big turnout." The sound of Dad's voice still caught Cooper off guard. "The people of St. Simons have always been big supporters of art and charities. Don't worry."

"You're right. They've been good to Re-Claimed." And that was the truth. Whenever Gabby or Kevin had mentioned a need, God had laid it on someone's heart to provide.

Small white lights hung from the tree limbs on either side of the path to the gallery. Kevin stood outside greeting guests and shaking hands. He looked a lot like a politician with his glad-handing, but these events were like that, from what Cooper could remember from when he'd had to tag along with his parents to fundraisers.

Near the door, his anxiety kicked up. He tried not to let the muscles in his chest tighten. He'd learned how badly that hurt. His ribs already ached enough.

"Hey, hey. The Knight men are here." Kevin grinned and shook their hands when their turn arrived. "Glad you could make it."

"Glad I'm alive." Cooper smiled back.

"Amen." Kevin pointed inside the door. "Dad's here with a special announcement."

"Okay." Probably coming with the handcuffs and a warrant to arrest him. After the heroin was found on his own boat, he ends up on another boat that explodes. The situation was suspicious, even to Cooper.

"Go on in. I'll be there in a few."

With no excuse to wait any longer, Cooper led his father through the door.

"This looks great." His father perused the walls between the dawdling couples dressed in their finest. He paused near a large abstract, taking in the work.

What would Dad think of this piece? Cooper held his breath until his already aching chest demanded to be filled.

"It's yours." His gaze turned and locked on Cooper. "I'm impressed."

Though difficult to believe or let sink in, the words soothed some of the crushed places in Cooper's heart.

"Thanks," he managed to squeak out.

"You've got quite a talent. More than one, actually." He rested a hand on Cooper's shoulder. "I'm proud of you."

Cooper's soul soured with shame. In the steps, they learned to make amends, unless doing so would cause more harm. He'd written his family members early in his recovery, received zero responses, so he'd not bothered them again. Standing there with his father's warm approval, not trying harder to reconnect seemed like a mistake. Now that his father was here, maybe he could try again.

"I'm sorry for the years I ruined. For the pain I caused. I could list all the things—small and large—I'm sorry for, and they could fill a book. Lying, stealing, not cooperating, the horrible disrespectful words I said, for turning away from God." He swallowed hard. "For taking Savannah out on the boat when she was drunk and I was using. For not being the son you wanted me to be—"

"Can you forgive me?" His father's eyes glazed with moisture.

"For what?" The question made no sense.

"For the times I was too busy with work or television or a million other distractions to really listen to you. For the times I should have spoken encouragement instead of criticism or advice. For the moments I let slip away doing things that seemed so important at the time, but were actually frivolous and worldly. For not seeing sooner that you needed help. For not being the father you needed me to be."

"Dad, no. What I chose to do wasn't your fault."

"I know that, but I made choices, too. I regret them. Deeply. Do you forgive me?"

"Of course, but—"

"You're forgiven, too."

Cooper's face warmed—his whole body, really—years of brokenness dissolving in this earnest moment with his father. Not unlike the way his heavenly Father had been healing his soul, being forgiven by his earthly father gave his heart fresh joy.

"Hey, handsome. I've been waiting for you." Rivers whispered next to his ear, and his heart cartwheeled inside his chest.

He turned to face her, and if he'd been warm the moment before, he was blistering now. He might need to be intubated again because his lungs seemed to have stopped working. Shimmering blue fabric wrapped her thin form and made the color of her eyes shine brighter. And she was smiling at him, calling him handsome. Someone needed to throw cold water in his face to wake him up. The whole night already seemed too good to be true.

"Remember to save your strength for when the music starts." She twirled and wiggled in a little dance. "You've only been out of the hospital four days."

Speechless, Cooper blew out a long breath. His lungs worked all right, but he'd lost command of his eyes. They were locked on this sweet woman he was hopelessly in love with.

She brushed a kiss on his cheek. "We're about to begin with the greeting and introductions, but I'll be back for my dance." She worked her way through the crowd to join Gabby near the front counter.

Gabby lifted a microphone. "Good evening, friends. Thank you for coming out."

The hum of the crowd died down, and she continued, "Through tragedy, God gave my brother and me a vision. A vision to provide a place of healing. A place to reclaim God's children whom Satan sought to steal, kill, and destroy through the chains of addiction. We have been so blessed by you, our community, who support our vision. You've given your money, resources, job opportunities, and time to help rescue those souls enslaved by the enemy. Thank you for that." She smiled and scanned the room. Her smile captured people in a good way. Somehow she was like a beacon of hope, and her light spilled out on all she met—the light of the Lord flowing out from inside her.

"Before we start the festivities, we'll have a few of the Re-Claimed alumni share their success stories. But first, my father would like to make an announcement."

Making his way from the corner of the room, Sheriff Barnes strode over to join Gabby. He took the microphone, his shoulders straight, his face the epitome of I'm-not-giving-anything-away-until-the-right-moment. One of the many reasons he made a great law enforcement officer.

"I'm happy to celebrate the work being done here. I'm proud of my son and daughter for dedicating their lives to serve citizens of our community." He shot a look at Gabby, then to Kevin, who'd finally come inside. "Addiction isn't the plight of any one demographic." His serious gaze traveled the room. "Drugs are devastating our children, parents, sisters, brothers, cousins, and neighbors. I've seen them steal the lives of medical professionals, teachers, law enforcement officers—any career you could name, along with teenagers and the homeless.

"There aren't enough jails or funds to house all these members of our communities indefinitely. We have to find ways to rehabilitate." He lifted one hand. "Sure, there will be a failure here and there, like what you've read in the news lately, but there will be success stories like the testimonies you're about to hear. In relation to that news story, I have an announcement that will address concerns you might have about this place and the work being accomplished."

Whispers circulated the gallery.

"Six arrests were made this afternoon here and in Brunswick, in connection with heroin trafficking and conspiracy. One resident who'd recently left Re-Claimed, along with a local real estate agent and a dock worker, were among those from St. Simons. In Brunswick, a local pharmacist, a port authority employee, and a career criminal. More arrests may follow, but no other connection to the sober living facility was found during our investigation." Sheriff Barnes glanced Cooper's way, and his lips quirked to an almost smile.

Relief poured over Cooper. Tension he'd been blocking

from his mind unleashed its grip on his muscles and nerves. He barely heard the rest of the speakers in his euphoria over the blessings flowing through his life tonight.

The music began, and Rivers sashayed around a group of people, a bounce in her step and her eyes shining, pinning his heart in his throat. She was so beautiful. Inside and out.

"Hey, the silent auction is taking off." Her hands met in a prayer. "God, grant us funds and goodwill to meet the needs of the gallery and Re-Claimed. Amen."

"Amen."

Davis and Gabby popped up from behind.

A frown folded Davis's forehead. "Don't push me, Gabby. I'm not in the mood. No one else is dancing, and I will not be the first penguin to jump."

Cooper felt for the guy. Though he deflected with humor, Davis had taken Angelo's betrayal hard.

"Let's all go dance together." Rivers gave Davis a sympathetic smile. "I love this song."

"Taylor Swift?" Davis quirked one brow. "Didn't know you were a Swiftie."

"A good song is a good song." Gabby laughed. "Personally, I think he's scared to dance with me because of our height difference."

Gabby did have him by a number of inches.

Standing up taller, Davis jutted out his chin. "I'm not short, I'm fun-sized."

"Then prove it, big man." Gabby held out her hand. "Let's show them how it's done."

After an exaggerated huff, Davis accepted.

"Yay!" Rivers clapped. "I know Cooper's hurting, and Davis may not be into dancing, so thanks."

"Well, Swiftie, nobody said I don't like to dance." Davis

smirked. "Prepare to be impressed, cause if I'm going out there, I'm about to throw down."

Cooper offered his arm to Rivers. "I wouldn't miss a moment of this night for all the pain in the world. Let's go."

~ ~ ~

The slow tune signaled an end to the band's last set, and Rivers drew closer to Cooper. The silent auction had been finalized, items and contributions collected. Caterers cleared away the food. The night would end soon, and immense questions still muddled her thinking. Could she give up her life in Memphis and start over here? With Cooper? What would that look like?

One thing she knew—she didn't want to say goodbye yet. She gave him a flirty smile. "Why are you still so far away?"

His dark eyes unsure, he lifted his arms to encircle her waist, and she rested her hands on his shoulders. The position felt so right, somehow. Though God knew she'd loved Jordan, she loved Cooper, too.

"I feel selfish, keeping you standing on the dance floor." She studied his face for any sign of fatigue. "You just got out of the hospital."

"You couldn't get rid of me if you tried." He smiled, and his lips captured her attention. She couldn't wait for the event to end so she could taste them again.

His gaze fell to her shoulder. "Are you sure you weren't hurt?"

How she hated that scar. "Apparently I'm titanium or something. Only the people around me get badly injured."

"That's not your fault. We live in a broken world." He lifted his fingers to touch the indentation the bullet had left, the pressure soft against the sensitive skin. "I know I'll never be the man Jordan was, but I do love you, Rivers. You have

273

my heart, and I'd give my life to shield you from more pain. I don't know what that means for us. I'm willing—"

"I could move to St. Simons." The words popped out before she'd thought them through.

Cooper met her gaze. "What? I was going to say I could move to Memphis, if you wanted."

She'd blurted out her offer before she could overthink the decision, never thinking he might make an offer of his own. "You'd do that?"

"Yes." Eyes shining, his words came out husky. "You'd come here? For me?"

Nodding, she lifted her hands to cup his face. "So now we have a couple of options."

"I don't deserve you." His eyes closed, his dark lashes wet.

Her heart squeezed for his obvious lingering shame. "Don't you dare say that ever again." Forget what the few remaining stragglers at the gala thought.

Gently, she claimed his lips, sliding her fingers through his hair. She should stop, but he was kissing her back now. His hands gripped her waist and drew her closer, and she melted into his embrace.

"I told you," a woman's voice came from nearby. "It is Rivers and him. Jay."

Oh, no. She knew that voice. Opening her eyes, Rivers pulled away.

Five feet from her looking angry, haggard, and appalled—horrified, even—stood Brooklyn, Pearl, and Jordan's father.

Their fierce gazes landed squarely on Rivers, and Brooklyn stepped closer. "How could you do this to us?"

Chapter 41

The joy Cooper had felt evaporated. Seeing his mother's face for the first time since the accident gouged a giant hole in his heart. The shock and disappointment, aimed at him again, sank his insides with dread. Through sober eyes, he could see that his mother and her twin sister had both been aged by grief.

He should have known this was coming. This was reality. He should have put on the brakes with Rivers when she first arrived.

But like always, he was a source of contention for everyone he cared about.

"I'm sorry, but I'm also not sorry." Rivers took a cautious step closer to Brooklyn.

What was she saying? Cooper studied Rivers, then glanced at his aunt.

Aunt Brooklyn's brows knit at the strange statement.

"Cooper has been sober for five years. He's a changed man." Rivers glanced at him, her gaze warm and brave. "And I didn't come here expecting to find him, much less fall in love with him."

Brooklyn's jaw dropped, as did Mom's and Uncle Alex's.

Rivers was defending him? Levees crumbling, the warm currents of his emotions spilled to flow where they would. He'd never loved anyone more.

Sheriff Barnes walked over and stood behind the family, scrutinizing the interchange. The lawman's heightened radar for conflict surely detected the tension.

"I will always love Jordan." Rivers voice held strong though tears coated her eyes. "He can't be replaced in my heart. But I found love again in a good man who, with God's help, has fought terrible battles with addiction and came out on the other side. Alone here, Cooper discovered a new purpose. He shares the good news that people can break their chains and recover. He counsels the downcast and offers hope."

Aunt Brooklyn held up a hand for Rivers to stop. "Jay killed my daughter. He gave her alcohol and took her out in a boat. I can't—"

"Ma'am, I hate to interrupt." Sheriff Barnes stepped between Rivers and Aunt Brooklyn focusing on the older woman. "I gave a report to your husband and your mother five years ago that exonerated Cooper. The evidence proved that your daughter had received the alcohol from another minor in town, not from Cooper."

Silence descended on the room before Mom's head spun toward her sister. "What? Brooklyn, is this true?"

Brooklyn's mouth opened and closed, gaping and grasping to make sense of what Sherriff Barnes had said. "I... I didn't know." She turned her gaze toward her husband. "Did you tell me? I don't remember."

Uncle Alex shook his head, his eyes beseeching. "I didn't want to upset you more. You were incoherent with grief over losing Savannah."

Cooper's father stepped closer, his face contorted. His knuckles whitened as his fists balled. "You mean I've lost five years with my son I'll never get back? Everything could have been different with a few spoken words."

"No." Cooper's adrenalin soared. "I never should've taken the boat out that day. I didn't give Savannah alcohol, but I had been using. I deserved to be blamed. Please, don't fight." The last thing he wanted was to further break up his family.

Rivers held her palms upward, and her gaze bounced among them all. "I've worked through a lot of emotions here in St. Simons. We all make mistakes. Some sins are much more obvious, while others are the hidden bitterness leaching through our hearts and words and actions. There's a cleansing freedom in forgiving. Not that it doesn't take time and work and even a restart when we relapse into that bitterness."

Mom inched closer, her eyes watery. "Jay... I mean Cooper. I'm sorry." She gave him a sad smile. "I forgot you prefer Cooper."

Could she really open her heart to him again? "Call me whatever you want. I love hearing your voice again."

She tentatively stepped forward and embraced him.

Cooper tried unsuccessfully to cover a wince.

"Sorry." She let go and cupped his cheeks. "Your father said you'd been hurt. Are you all right?"

"I'm fine." Joy flowed over him, like a cool spring in the desert. He'd thought this day would never come. "The hug was well worth a little pain. A true miracle."

"I've been so stubborn." His mother shook her head. "So wrong."

"No. Don't do that to yourself. When y'all left me here after the accident, I hit my rock bottom. With nothing left, I reached up to God. If you'd stayed, that might not have happened." Cooper smiled through tears. "In all things, God works for the good of those who love Him."

~~~

The reunion had been touching, but Rivers couldn't ignore the fatigue showing by the droop of Cooper's eyelids. "Why don't y'all take Cooper back to the hotel, and I'll come by when I finish here."

"Good plan." Mr. Knight retrieved his keys from his pocket.

The loving expressions on Cooper's and his parents' faces lifted the sails of her heart. There would be more rocky emotions to tread with Brooklyn, but the fact that Cooper had his parents in his corner gave her courage.

Once those three left, Rivers and Jordan's parents faced each other like stone statues. What could she say to make things better? To make them understand?

The room had emptied of guests, and only a few residents were still cleaning up, but Sheriff Barnes still stood between them, fidgeting and scratching his arms as if he had fleas. Not the normal stance for this tough lawman. "I hate to be the bearer of more bad news at a moment like this. I wanted to wait until tomorrow and not spoil the event tonight."

What now? A torrent of anxiety poured over Rivers and drew perspiration to her upper lip. Thank goodness, Cooper was gone. What new bomb would drop on this poor family?

"Get it over with, Sheriff." Jordan's father's face seemed to have aged in the few minutes he'd been here.

"It's your stepbrother. Shane Turner." The sheriff's brows crunched together in the center of his forehead. "He was arrested today for drug trafficking and conspiracy." He shot a glance to Rivers. "We retrieved security footage at the marina and around the gallery and Re-Claimed. He was with Angelo and gave him the bag of heroin. After finding that evidence, I checked out your storage unit with my K-9. We figured that was where he was keeping drugs and other stolen items. Maybe even art intended for the gallery, he sold for himself instead."

"Shane was a drug dealer?" Mr. Barlow's eyes widened.

Taking in a deep breath and letting it out with a sigh, Sheriff Barnes nodded. "There's more. Your stepbrother was in deep with the wrong people. Owed money. We're participating in a joint investigation with the Memphis police to find out whether he was involved in the murder of your son and the attempted murder of Rivers. Also, there's evidence he might have been behind his boat explosion."

The words slammed into Rivers, but her mind had trouble absorbing their meaning. "But why?" Nothing made sense. Why would he want them dead?

"He had a buyer for the properties that would mean he'd get two hefty commissions, maybe a kickback to help him pay off debts. We're still trying to put all the pieces together."

"I'll kill him." Mr. Barlow's complexion distorted to a dark shade of purple.

"Sir, we'll get justice—"

"Justice? I want my son back." His chest heaved in a sob, and he covered his eyes with his hand.

"I'm sorry, sir. I understand." The sheriff nodded and took a step back.

Brooklyn wrapped her husband in her arms. "Let's go, darling. Let's get you home."

Shell-shocked, Rivers watched the Barlows leave. No words came to console. No bright Scriptural wisdom popped into her mind. If this was true, they'd been wronged. She'd been wronged. Jordan killed. Cooper had almost been killed by one man's greed and stupidity. And a family member. There would be more publicity. A trial.

"You'll get through this." Gabby's voice wrapped around Rivers, followed by her strong arms with a hug. "You've got Cooper, your parents, me and Kev. God. We'll work it out. Together."

"I'm going to need you to make good on that commitment." Rivers embraced her sweet friend and held her tight to keep from sinking. "Because did I tell you I might be moving here for good?"

Gabby's head whipped back, eyes popping wide. "Get out! Are you serious?"

"Cooper and I are going to give our relationship a fighting chance."

"Oh, sister, I'm going to wage war for y'all in the heavenly realms with prayer."

Rivers managed a smile. "That's exactly what we'll need."

Chapter 42

Six months later

"Isn't this early for you on a Saturday morning?" Cooper followed Rivers down the boardwalk toward the beach. The sun had barely risen, and the sky still held a slew of pinks and yellows. He should enjoy the sight. Instead, his stomach balled in a knot. He and Rivers had been working together at the gallery and Re-Claimed for six months. To him, their relationship had been going well. Too well. Something was bound to go wrong.

She'd been acting weird when she'd asked him two days ago to put this sunrise walk on his calendar. "What's up?"

Lips pressed tight, Rivers shrugged. "Just a walk and a talk."

The knot squeezed tighter. A talk usually meant goodbye, didn't it? He studied her perfectly combed blond hair. It had grown longer these past months. Now golden strands lay against a silky aqua shirt that brought out the color of her eyes. He'd never seen her wear that blouse in the six months she'd been working with him in St. Simons. And he definitely noticed what she wore. He noticed everything about this beautiful woman.

She'd probably realized dating him was a big mistake and had her car packed, ready to head back to Memphis.

She continued down the beach to a quilt that had been laid on the sand, a long wicker basket holding it in place. "This is a good spot. Come stand here with me."

"Isn't that someone's stuff? Maybe we should go down the shore a bit."

"Nope." Digging in her heels, she turned to face him and held out her hands. "Step closer and look at me."

Cooper steeled himself as he neared and took her hands. What was this adorable but directionally impaired woman up to?

"I know we've only been in a relationship for six months. There was that other month, too, when we were riding the seesaw about each other after you first found me on a sandbar out there."

Yep. She was about to cut him loose. "You don't have to explain. I—"

She touched her finger to his lips. "Just wait. And maybe take one step to the left and maybe angle your body a half inch?"

"Okaaay." This was getting bizarre, but he shuffled over, which placed the sun shining in both their faces.

"Life has black moments, those dark, heartbreaking days we wish we could blot out and forget. But life is also full of sunny yellows and green days, blue skies and pink flower days, we wish we could hold onto forever."

He gave a slow nod, more confused than ever.

"To be honest, I've been hoping and praying for a shiny, gold and diamond kind of day lately."

Here it comes. She'd hoped for something more.

A hesitant smile lifted her lips, and she kneeled down on one knee. She plucked something from her pocket but closed it in her fist. "You see, I'm not sure you believe how much I love you. Because I love you big—in a gold-and-diamond kind of way. I'd like to share the dark sorrows and the bright joys with you. I'd like to create the art of life with you. And I didn't think you'd get around to asking any time soon, so I borrowed this from your mom."

Opening her hand to reveal his mother's engagement ring, Rivers lifted her brows and gave him a shy look. "If you'd like to marry me, you could take this and slip it on my finger until we pick out our own bands." She tilted her head. "If you'd rather not marry me, you could take the ring back to your mother, as that would be kind of awkward for me."

Could this be happening? Her hopeful expression left Cooper's heart in a puddle, and he hit his knees, holding her hands in his. Maybe he was hallucinating due to brain damage or something. "You seriously want to marry me?"

"Serious as a heart at——"

"Don't jinx us."

"God's in control." Her gaze locked on him. "We aren't jinxed, and you haven't answered. Or asked. Whichever."

Heart surging into overdrive, he held the ring near the end of her slender finger and took a shaky breath. "I'd be honored if you would marry me, Rivers."

"I can't wait to marry you." Her eyes shone as he slipped the ring over her knuckle. Then she took his face in her hands and pressed her lips to his.

When she released him, he caught his breath and gave her a mischievous smile. "Let's catch a flight to Vegas, if you can't wait."

A flirty giggle floated from her lips. "I would, but your mother made me promise we'd give her at least a month to plan a small wedding." Rivers kissed him again, this time on the cheek. "Now turn your head toward that dune with the sea oats and smile before Gabby and Davis spontaneously combust. She insisted I let her take pictures because people do these sort of things now and post them for all to see."

He chuckled. "I'd like to avoid any more explosions." He pivoted to spot his friends crouched behind the dune disguised under straw hats and sunglasses and armed with a camera. Cooper laughed, heart brimming with joy. "Definitely a shiny gold-and-diamond kind of day. Best day ever."

"So far." Rivers caught his chin and delivered another round of sweet kisses.

"So far." He breathed a sigh. "Thank you, God."

~~~

Exactly a month later, Rivers raised a glass of sparkling cider to toast with Cooper. "Just for today, I will love you with all I am." She smiled, relishing her new husband, his smoldering dark eyes locked on her. "Tomorrow, I will wake up and start all over again, loving you with all that I am."

"Just for today, I will love you and fall to my knees to thank God for you. I will strive to do the same every day that I live on this earth."

Their glasses clinked, and they took sips of the bubbly cider while the photographer snapped several pictures. They set the crystal flutes on the table when another guest came to speak to Cooper. They'd eat and drink in their suite later, but there were a few hundred guests to greet in a short amount of time.

"You look stunning, darling." Pearl kissed Rivers on the cheek and then touched a strand of her hair. "I'm thrilled to have you as a daughter."

"I'm happy to be a part of the family, too. Your veil was perfect with Mama's dress."

"I was happy you wore something of mine. Brooklyn loved the portrait of Jordan you sent her. She and Alex wanted to be here, but it's still too emotional for them."

"I understand." The grief would never fully go away over

Jordan's loss, or Savannah's, but maybe someday she and Cooper could have a less strained relationship with his aunt and uncle.

Rivers surveyed the crowded ballroom of the King and Prince. "How did you manage all this?"

"I've been praying and dreaming of this day since Cooper was born. There was a time I thought it would never happen." Tears filled Pearl's brown eyes. "You're an answer to hundreds, no, thousands upon thousands, of prayers." She shrugged and one side of her mouth quirked. "And it helps that Brooklyn and I dabble in politics. We've racked up a lot of connections."

"Nice. We might be partners in fundraising for the right causes."

"Exactly." Pearl gave her a satisfied smile. "I was thinking the same thing. Great minds and all."

"Look at my beautiful girl." Dad winked as he approached, Mama clinging to his arm.

Rivers kissed him and then her mother. "What do you think about the dress, Mama?" She'd always wanted to wear her mother's wedding gown, embellished with ivory lace and pearls. And with such a short engagement, she'd been glad it fit with only a few adjustments.

"Very pretty." Her mother's eyes lit with her smile. "Love you."

"I love you, too."

"Hey, hey, hey. The music's about to start." Sauntering up, Davis waggled his brows and made a goofy face. "Doing my job as best man here. You have to take that first dance as husband and wife, and I read the perfect scripture for Cooper this morning in my daily devotional. You want to hear it?"

Cooper shook his head. "You don't. Trust me."

"Okay, I'll tell you." Davis sniggered. "When you pass

through the rivers, they will not sweep over you."

"Okay." Rivers gave him a slow nod.

"Don't you get it? Rivers? Like a double meaning with your name and all." Davis held both hands out, expectant.

She raised her eyebrows at him. "Not really." The band started, and Rivers grabbed Cooper's arm. "That's our cue. Let's get this party started."

"Thank the Lord, for more reasons than one." Cooper cut his eyes toward Davis, then led her to the dance floor. "Interesting choice. Is this 'Jesus Freak?'"

"Yeah. I love this song. Don't you?"

"I'm always willing to let my freak flag fly." He swung her around, then into his arms. "I can't wait to dance with you to any song for the rest of my life."

"I'm going to hold you to that." She giggled. "Or I'll sweep over you, like a raging river."

"You already have, and I love it."

Don't miss the next book by
Janet W. Ferguson.

Star Rising
A Coastal Hearts Novel

Have you read other Coastal Hearts stories by Janet W. Ferguson?

Have you read the Southern Hearts Series by Janet W. Ferguson?

Did you enjoy this book? I hope so!
Would you take a quick minute to leave a review online?
It doesn't have to be long. Just a sentence or two telling what you liked about the book.

I love to hear from readers! You can connect with me on Facebook, Twitter, Pinterest, the contact page on my website, or subscribe to my newsletter "Under the Southern Sun" for exclusive book news and giveaways.

https://www.facebook.com/Janet.Ferguson.author
http://www.janetfergusonauthor.com/under-the-southern-sun
https://www.pinterest.com/janetwferguson/
https://twitter.com/JanetwFerguson

About the Author

Faith, Humor, Romance
Southern Style

Janet W. Ferguson grew up in Mississippi and received a degree in Banking and Finance from the University of Mississippi. She has served as a children's minister and a church youth volunteer. An avid reader, she worked as a librarian at a large public high school. She writes humorous inspirational fiction for people with real lives and real problems. Janet and her husband have two grown children, one really smart dog, and a cat that allows them to share the space.

Publisher's Note: This book is a work of fiction. Names, characters, any resemblance to persons, living or dead, or events is purely coincidental. The characters and incidents are the product of the author's imagination and used fictitiously. Locales and public names are sometimes used for atmospheric purposes.

Saint Simons Island, Georgia, is a real town, but other than the name, the events in the location are fictional. None of the events are based on actual people. The charming city made the perfect backdrop for my novel.

Made in the USA
Columbia, SC
01 September 2022

66429209R00178